THE GREAT PRETENDER

THE GREAT PRETENDER

JIM LESTER

Cover design by Helena Mariposa and Antonio Arguello of Mariposa E-book Transformation

Cover created by Antonio Arguello of Mariposa E-book Transformation

Edited by Helena Mariposa of Mariposa E-book (& Editing) Transformation.

*"Look out kid,
they keep it all hid . . ."*

— Bob Dylan

CHAPTER 1

1957

My father was afraid of Joseph McDonald.

I couldn't blame my dad. Mr. McDonald was built like the boxer Joe Palooka in the comics and he was yelling and screaming at both of us like a crazy man.

"You keep that little monkey off my property, you hear?" Mr. McDonald shook his finger in my dad's face.

My father nodded and tried not to look scared but he didn't quite make it.

"That's why I built that wall!" Mr. McDonald's face glowed red like an atomic explosion. "I built that wall so my family could have some privacy. I didn't build that wall for unsupervised juvenile delinquents to come hurdling into my backyard on their way to God knows where. I'm warning you. Keep the little monkey out!"

Needless to say I was the little monkey.

My dad didn't say a word. He just kept nodding like his head wasn't screwed on tight enough.

The three of us stood at the imaginary line that divided our yard from Mr. McDonald's property. Our houses were part of a new neighborhood that my mother said was Arkansas' first version of the suburbs. The houses were all similar, all small, all freshly painted and each house had a little side yard that connected your yard to your neighbor's lawn.

Our clothesline was located in the side yard. The grass was all trampled down where my mother stood to hang out the wet clothes, and I could hear the shirts and sheets flapping in the wind right behind us, punctuating each angry sentence from Mr. McDonald.

Over the summer, Mr. McDonald had built a shoulder-high stone wall that sealed off his backyard from the rest of the neighborhood.

About an hour ago, my best friend, Tommy Lee Rush, and I had ignored the warning of the wall, vaulted over it and cut through the McDonald's yard. Bad idea.

Real bad idea.

Puffy, gray clouds drifted across the sky and the mid-October sun slowly sank behind the ridge in the distance. My white T-shirt and blue jeans weren't doing anything to protect me from the coolness of the coming evening. Or the wrath of Mr. McDonald.

Not that I was afraid of Mr. McDonald. Not really. I mean who slugs a kid . . . right in front of his father?

"If we don't cut through your backyard," I said, since my dad seemed to have temporarily lost the ability to speak, "Tommy Lee and I have to go all the way down to the big ditch and back up the hill to get to the school. That's way out of the way. We were only in your yard for two seconds. We didn't hurt anything."

Joseph McDonald's eyes opened wide, sending his eyebrows to the top of his forehead. He shoved up the sleeves of his green sweater, revealing his hairy arms. Then he took a step toward me.

My father had positioned me between him and Mr. McDonald, standing behind me with his hands on my shoulders. Suddenly my dad squeezed my shoulder hard—his meaning couldn't have been more clear. "Shut up! Right this second."

I ignored the squeeze. "How could seconds hurt? Huh?"

My father tightened his grip on my shoulder and real pain shot through my neck. Fear had turned my dad into the muscle man Charles Atlas. "Please excuse Archie, Joe," my dad said in that syrupy voice he used when he talked business on the phone.

Mr. McDonald frowned.

"May I call you Joe?" My father said.

"No."

"Well, then . . . uh . . . Mr. McDonald, ever since Archie turned twelve several months ago," my father plowed on. "His pants have gone north of his socks and his mouth has gotten a little too big for his own good. You understand."

I could tell from the look in Mr. McDonald's eyes that he didn't understand at all. I thought he understood beating my dad and me both to a pulp.

"Growing boys, you know." My father's voice trailed off. To use his business vocabulary, this was turning into a no sale.

Growing seemed to be my middle name lately. My father still hadn't gotten over the fact that I was already taller than he was. This year I was the tallest kid at Edison Elementary. Taller even than Amy Lou Rawlins, who had been the tallest kid in our school since we started first grade together.

Even my teeth were big. My mom said I'd have to wear braces on them the way my second best friend, Sandra Harrison, did. I wish they had braces that would fix my cowlick or make the gazillion freckles on my face disappear. They both made me look like some goofy farm boy.

"You know how it is." My father's pleading voice went up a couple of octaves.

"No," Mr. McDonald snapped in his clipped Yankee accent. "I don't know how it is. I never got that chance."

It was the fall of 1957 and my hometown of Little Rock had become the biggest news story in the world. Cross my heart. The whole world.

Last month the governor of our state, Orval Faubus, used his National Guard soldiers to keep a handful of colored kids from going to Little Rock Central High, where Tommy Lee's big brother, Mike, played football and basketball.

President Eisenhower got mad and sent the army to Little Rock to make sure the Negro kids could go to Central. Troops in full battle gear with helmets and rifles invaded our town as if we were North Korea. The story appeared in all the papers and even on TV.

My dad didn't think colored people and white people should do anything together. He always said that's why we have separate drinking fountains and bathrooms and Negroes don't eat in the restaurants we'd go to like Frankie's and the Shack. Dad would say the races should stay apart. He'd get pretty worked up about the whole thing. That's why he could never find out about My Big Secret.

Since Mr. McDonald was a Yankee I guess he thought we ought to have gone to school with the Negroes the way the kids up North did. Tommy Lee says he'd die before he'd sit next to a colored kid in school. I couldn't make up my mind on that one.

At the moment, I was more interested in what a boiling mad Mr. McDonald might do to my dad and me.

So I pressed on. "Sir," I said in my best kids-must-be-polite-to-adults-no-matter-what voice. "I'm awful sorry you feel that way, but me and Tommy Lee—"

My father's grip threatened to snap my collarbone.

"Don't you understand English, kid? Stay off my property!" Mr. McDonald's mouth curled into a wicked snarl.

I was face to face with the scariest looking human being on the planet Earth. Or any other planet. The Devil at the gates of hell couldn't have looked any scarier than our next-door neighbor at that moment.

Even though my mother told me Mr. McDonald was past forty years old, which I guess was pretty old; he was what my friend Sandra called a "flatbelly." As opposed to my father who was a definite "roundbelly." According to Sandra, all grown-ups were either flatbellies or roundbellies.

"You need to respect other people's privacy," Mr. McDonald growled. He had a big bushy mustache and wide shoulders and his whole face was covered with tiny nicks. My mother said they were pits—acme pits or something.

Without a doubt the scariest thing about Joseph McDonald though was The Scar. The first time you saw the man The Scar was all you could look at. You couldn't take your eyes off of the thing even if you tried. The Scar was gross—thick and pink, starting where his hairline ended and winding its way down the right side of his face, across his right cheek, ending up on the side of his throat. The Scar reminded me of a little pink river flowing between hundreds of tiny craters.

Nobody knew where or how Joseph McDonald got

The Scar. Tommy Lee said he heard Mr. McDonald got it while serving a term in prison. Sandra said she heard he got The Scar on a bear hunt when a giant grizzly attacked him. Either one sounded about right to me.

"Well, now Mr. McDonald," my father said in his most icky polite voice. "We certainly respect your privacy."

Mr. McDonald flicked his tongue over his lips like a snake.

My father pushed back the jacket of his suit and reached into his shirt pocket for his red pack of Pall Malls. He offered the pack to Mr. McDonald who shook his head no. Then my dad shook a cigarette out of the pack, stuck the cig in his mouth, and lit up with the Zippo lighter my mother had given him for his birthday.

My father, Warren Lane, had thick dark eyebrows, which was hard to explain since he didn't have any hair at all on his legs or his chest or most of his head for that matter.

Hair is a hard thing to understand. Some men don't have any on their head but have hair all over their chest and legs. Tommy Lee's dad had hair all over his back and, according to Tommy Lee, all over his rear end. I hoped I wouldn't wind up with hair all over my rear end. Especially if I don't end up with any hair on my head like my dad. I mean what a waste of hair.

"Let's cut to the chase, Lane," Mr. McDonald growled. "I'm not running a freak show in my house for all the neighborhood snot noses to gawk at. You understand me?"

So that's what he thought me and Tommy Lee were doing in his backyard. He thought we wanted to sneak a peek at his son. "You mean the kid in the can?"

It just fell out of my mouth.

Mr. McDonald's already red face went into super atomic burn, and he began clenching and unclenching his fists. He took an angry step toward me. This is the end, I thought. The last good-bye. The final buzzer. Adios, Archie. It's been nice knowin' ya.

My father squeezed my shoulder until tears gathered in my eyes.

"Listen, you little wiseass." Mr. McDonald glared at me. "Let me remind you of something, huh? We all have our little secrets, don't we? You know what I mean?"

There was something in the way he looked at me, staring into my eyes like he wanted to peer inside my head that let me know that my own personal Hiroshima was about to explode.

"I dunno." I went for the all-purpose kid answer for any occasion.

Mr. McDonald stuffed his hands in the pockets of his tan slacks and rocked back on the balls of his feet. "Oh, I think you do, son. I think you know all about keeping secrets. How about when your folks are gone and you crank up that hi-fi over in your house until it's blaring all that rock 'n' roll garbage so loud that the pictures on my walls next door shake. How about that for a little secret?"

My father took a step back, off balance. "Archie? Do you do that? When your mother and I are gone? You listen to that screaming Negro singer—Little Ronald?"

"Little Richard, Dad, and I don't play the records that loud. Honest." I glared at Mr. McDonald.

"Warren," my mother called to us from behind the screen of our back door. My dad and I turned around.

Mom wore her apron with all the ruffly things on the collar. "It's Mr. Rath from your office. He says it's important. He's waiting on the phone."

Relief washed over my father's face as he turned back to face Mr. McDonald. "You'll have to excuse me," he said. "Business calling. But I will promise you one thing. Archie will never play those awful records again. You have my word on that."

Good-bye rock 'n' roll.

My father stomped out his cigarette butt on the lawn with the heel of his shoe, gave my shoulder a last squeeze, and headed for the house.

Talk about an awkward moment. Me and Mr. McDonald stood there facing each other in the quiet of the late fall afternoon with the breeze flapping the laundry on the clothesline behind us.

"Speaking of secrets, son," Mr. McDonald said. "How about what you and your creepy little buddy do on Sunday afternoons when nobody else is around? That's a heck of a secret if you ask me."

He knew!

Joseph McDonald, the meanest, scariest man on the planet knew My Big Secret. The thing that my parents could never ever know about no matter what. The biggest Secret of them all. My heart started trying to hop out of my chest and flop around on the lawn. How could Mr. McDonald possibly know?

Didn't matter.

I had lost the ability to speak, which had to be a first. All I could do was nod like some mouth-breathing zombie. No more smart mouth. If Joseph McDonald told my parents about My Big Secret my childhood would end. I would be banished to my room until I was fat and bald and forty.

"So do we understand each other?" Mr. McDonald said. "You don't cut across my property and I don't tell your old man about your secret. We got a deal?"

I nodded. And mumbled something that sounded sorta like "okay."

"Then get outta here."

He didn't have to tell me twice. I spun around and marched back across the side yard that led to our house.

When I reached the screen door, I turned around and looked across the yard at the figure of Joseph McDonald, who was still standing next to the clothesline, his hands planted on his hips, the late afternoon shadows falling all around him. He stared right back at me, delivering an unmistakable warning.

CHAPTER 2

Dinner sat on the chrome dinette table in the breakfast nook when I got back from being chewed out by Joseph McDonald. Left over roast beef, frozen eggplant casserole, cold green beans, and slabs of Wonder Bread patiently awaited our arrival.

The dinner could have waited until pigs flew or the Cubs won the pennant as far as I was concerned.

The Wonder Bread, which they claimed would build strong bodies eight ways, was the only thing on the table even close to being edible. I swear.

That was because my mother, Terri, was a seriously lousy cook. Mom hated cooking and never put much effort into the evening meal. Or any meal for that matter. She said cooking bored her. My mom would rather read a Thomas Costain novel or go see a Humphrey Bogart movie or listen to a Razorback football game on the radio than learn to cook anything worth eating.

Truth be told, I'm the only kid at Edison Elementary who actually liked the food in the school cafeteria. Whatever glunk they'd serve at school, it was always a major improvement over what I ate at home.

Despite not putting much effort into her cooking, my mother was strangely touchy about the results. My father and I consequently learned to abide by an unspoken rule. We never criticized what my mother cooked.

No matter how gross it might be.

I sat down at the table and waited for my dad to get off the phone with his boss. It didn't take long. As soon as my father slid into his chair and tossed his napkin in his lap, my mother had to remind him about Mr. McDonald. It took all I had not to shoot her an angry look.

"How did it go with Mr. McDonald?" my mother asked cheerfully as she passed the bread to my father, who helped himself to three slices.

I took a bite of eggplant casserole. It tasted like glue.

"It went okay," my father lied. "McDonald's a typical Yankee, thinks he knows everything. But I told him right off the bat I didn't appreciate his yelling at Archie and Tommy Lee. Archie promised not to scale the man's ridiculous wall and cut through the McDonald's backyard anymore. It's all taken care of. We won't have any more trouble with McDonald."

My father shoved a forkful of eggplant into his mouth and shot me a look that said I'd be smart not to cross him. End of conversation.

I slathered butter on a slab of bread, added a spoonful of grape jelly from the jar with Disney characters on it, and rolled the bread into a cylinder. I took a sip from my glass of milk, which my mom must have poured around noon. It was the same temperature as a hot summer day.

"He's such a strange man," my mother said, fiddling with the lacy collar of her dress. "He's the only neighbor we haven't gotten to know since we moved here."

"I reckon every barrel has a bad apple," my father said as if he was passing on the wisdom of the ages.

I stuffed the bread roll in my mouth and settled down for the evening meal, which usually meant a two-way conversation between my mom and dad. Children should be seen and not heard. More wisdom of the ages.

My mom asked my dad about something at work, and I started drifting off into my own little world of basketball, the Hardy Boys, and baseball cards.

But I had to be careful.

Last year I took a bunch of tests at this doctor's office, and one afternoon I snuck a peek at the scores on my dad's desk. I wasn't supposed to see the results but I did. The test report said, "Archibald has an overactive imagination and tendency toward hyperactivity." Whatever that was.

I thought it meant I daydreamed too much and shot my mouth off when I should have kept my trap shut.

Sounded about right.

Archibald was my real name. Archibald Yell Lane. A name I was less than thrilled with. I was named after a former governor of Arkansas named Archibald Yell, a distant relative of my father. Who wanted to be named Archibald?

My dad started telling a long story about a laundry truck that crashed into a telephone pole. My mom just listened. She was a good listener.

She was also a beautiful woman. She had long, dark hair that curled around her shoulders and a pretty face. I once overheard Tommy Lee's father refer to my mother as a "looker," which I thought meant she's fun to look at. Mom's thirty-three years old and Tommy Lee's dad looked at her every chance he got.

I thought Tommy Lee's mom looked like a

groundhog, but I'd never tell him that.

"Martha told me that both of the McDonalds are Scottish and moved here from Boston," Mom said. Martha Harrison, Sandra's mom, was our own walking, talking version of the Camel News Caravan. She always seemed to know what everybody in the neighborhood was doing or thinking about doing. "Martha says that's why poor Mrs. McDonald drinks so much."

"I think it's the Irish that drink too much," my father said. "The Scots save money and the men wear skirts."

"No, no. That's not why she drinks," Mom smiled. "Martha says Mrs. McDonald drinks because she's homesick for Boston or maybe because, you know . . ." Mom looked at me and frowned. "Well you know. That awful thing with their child."

"I spent some time in Boston during the war." My dad said, hacking at his roast beef with little results. "Boston was colder than Siberia and the people weren't very friendly." My dad was not the world's best listener.

Mom smiled. "I ran into poor Mrs. McDonald one afternoon over at the Piggly Wiggly. I tried to be friendly since we're next-door neighbors and all, but she seemed standoffish and distant. Not to mention she smelled like a brewery."

"I bet dollars to donuts that McDonald fellow drinks during the day too." Dad made drinking during the day sound like a crime on a par with mass murder. "What does he do for a living anyway?"

Work was a big deal to my dad. He worked all the time. He also had a constant shadow around his jaw like vice president Nixon and, like the vice president, Dad always wore a suit. My mom said wearing a suit was important to my dad because if he wore a suit people would know he didn't work with his hands the way Uncle Clyde and Grandpa Lane did in the lumber mill down in south Arkansas.

Dad started life down in Crawfordsville, a little stop in the road in Lafayette County. His dad, Grandpa Lane, still worked in the sawmill down there. The whole family was really poor, and everybody slept in one room in the back of their little shotgun house. Now Dad's an assistant manager of the Royal Laundry and Cleaners in the capital city, and all the folks back down in Crawfordsville think he's hit the big time.

Here's the thing about my dad. Money is important to him but not as important as respect. His family didn't get a lot of respect while he was growing up. People laughed at the whole family because they were poor and wore old worn out clothes and didn't speak good English. My dad won't let that happen to us. That's why he works all the time.

What my dad really loves to do is hunt and fish. When he was a kid he and Uncle Clyde roamed all over Lafayette County, shooting rabbits and squirrels or fishing in the tributaries of the Red River. Dad's always loved to hunt and fish. Only he never does anymore. That's pretty sad if you think about it.

"Martha told me Mr. McDonald is some kind of commercial photographer." My mother apparently wasn't going to let the subject of the McDonalds go. Dad had already let the subject drop which was fine with me.

"Doesn't sound like an honest job to me," my dad said. "Snapping pictures? How much work can that be?" A tiny smile crept around the corners of his mouth. "He must do all right at it though. He made enough dough to buy that car." Despite the smile, Dad's voice dripped with envy. I couldn't blame him.

"That car" was a jet black 1956 Thunderbird with a hardtop and little porthole windows. The whole top came off to make a convertible. Mr. McDonald washed his car all the time, and the Thunderbird always looked shiny and new. Every morning, from my bedroom window, I could see the T-Bird parked in the McDonald's carport. It was a nice way to start the day.

"Why did the Boston McDonalds come down here to Little Rock anyway?" My dad took one last stab at the roast.

My mother's fork stopped halfway to her mouth as she shot my father a frosty warning glance. "Because of the research center over at the medical school, I imagine." She lowered her voice.

My father mumbled something that sounded like "humpt."

"Martha says Mr. McDonald is a decorated Marine." No one was better at changing the subject than Terri Lane.

"If you say so," my father growled, growing tired of hearing about Mr. McDonald.

I couldn't stay quiet any longer. I had to let them know what kind of a big creep they were dealing with here. "Tommy Lee says Mr. McDonald was a bank robber or a smuggler and went to prison, but he beat up so many of the other prisoners that they let him out."

"Do you believe everything Tommy Lee says?" My father had a point.

"Martha said Mr. McDonald was once a big football star. An All-American some years ago."

"Do you think he ever played against the

Razorbacks?" In a state with no professional sports, playing football for the University of Arkansas Razorbacks was the secret dream of every kid from the Mississippi Delta to the Ozark Mountains, myself included.

"I don't think so," Mom said. "I would remember if he had." She would too. Mom knew everything about football. Basketball too. Her dad, Grandpa Vickers, had been a high school coach. Their family talked football and hoops all the time, and Mom was our family's expert on sports, although I was starting to give her a run for the title.

My dad hated sports. He asked if there was coffee with dessert.

While Mom poured his coffee and served all three of us a dish of chocolate ice cream out of the carton, Dad changed the subject.

"Terri," my father said, clearing his throat the way he always did when he needed to talk about something unpleasant. "McDonald says Archie plays those little records extremely loud when you and I are gone."

At least it wasn't My Big Secret.

"You mean the McDonalds can hear the music all the way across the yard? All the way over in their house?"

"That's what the man said. No wonder. All that wailing and screaming. It's disgraceful. I can't believe the boy spends his allowance on that jungle noise—that Presley boy from Memphis and that other Jerry Lewis. Last summer Reverend Kramer said it sounded like the Devil's own music."

"I'm sure Archie and the other kids will grow out of it," my mother said, winking at me when my dad looked down at his coffee. "Like the Davy Crockett fad.

All the kids are crazy about it one day then they move on to something else the next day. Who has a coonskin cap today?"

"I hope you're right," my father said, scowling at me.

"I agree with you that playing the records too loud is serious business." My mother glanced out the window at the McDonald's house, measuring the distance with her eyes. "All that noise might disturb that poor creature . . . the McDonald's child. Bless his heart."

"You mean the kid in the can?" I said.

"Oh, honey, don't call him that. He can't help . . . what happened to him." My mother scrunched up her face. I could tell she was about to cry. "It's so sad. It's something all parents fear. I imagine that's why Mr. McDonald doesn't want you and Tommy Lee cutting through his yard. He knows that the neighborhood kids call his son the kid in the can, and I'm sure it makes him angry to think some of you might dare each other to run through his backyard and sneak a peek at his poor son. Can you blame him for being so angry? To have such a terrible thing happen to his son—such a tragedy—and then to have the neighborhood kids making fun of the boy."

"What is it?" I scraped the bottom of my ice cream dish with my spoon and licked the spoon front and back. "What's wrong with the McDonald's kid? Is he being punished or something? Why do they keep him in that big can?"

CHAPTER THREE

My mother blew on her coffee even though the cup had had plenty of time to cool. Then she scrunched up her nose. The nose was the giveaway. When my mother crinkled her nose that way I knew she was about to tell me something I would need to know when I got to be a grown up.

I had figured out there was a set amount of stuff you were supposed to know before you could be a grown up but nobody could stand to hear it all at once. So they fed it to you slowly. Starting when you're about ten, they gave it to you bit by bit. Then, by the time you got to be a grownup, you knew it all and you could go from there on your own.

"Archie, the McDonald's son has polio."

Polio. My mother said the word. Out loud. Nobody ever said the word. If you said the word, you might get it. That's what I heard on the playground. Sandra told me polio made little kids' legs shrivel up and then they had to walk on crutches.

Here was some grown up stuff I wanted to know about. "That's terrible," I said. I wasn't sure what else to say. "How . . . how . . . did it happen?"

"The doctors think polio is some kind of virus," my mother said. "It attacks the muscles and leaves the children paralyzed. They can't walk and it never goes away. Their parents try to massage their little limbs or put their legs in steel braces or put the ones with paralyzed breathing muscles, like the McDonald boy, in iron lungs. That's what the can is called, Archie. It's called an iron lung. It breathes for the boy."

"Why don't the McDonalds put the poor creature in the hospital?" my father growled. I don't think he wanted anyone feeling sorry for Mr. McDonald.

"Martha told me home care is less expensive," my mother said. "And hospitals are so impersonal. A boy needs his parents."

"Is that guy in the DeSoto who comes over to the McDonald's house a lot a doctor?" My bedroom window was like a big TV set always tuned into the comings and goings over at the McDonald's house.

"Don't spy on the neighbors." My father's tone indicated he had had enough discussion of polio and the McDonalds. He pushed his chair away from the table, got up, and kissed my mother on the cheek. "Enjoyed the supper, Hon," he said. "I'm going to catch up on the news in the *Democrat*," he added, referring to the evening paper. The *Democrat* and *Field and Stream* were the only things my dad ever read.

My mother and I watched Dad disappear through the door that connected the kitchen and the living room.

"Come on, Bobby Layne, let's get this kitchen cleaned up." My mother liked to refer to me by the names of various sports stars. I think her father, the coach, did the same with her. I thought it was fun if she didn't do it in front of other people. It was a lot better than calling me something gross and mushy like Honey Bunny. Actually I kinda liked it.

I always cleared the dirty dishes off the table and

handed them to my mother at the sink. She wore yellow rubber gloves and plunged the dishes into steamy suds, washed them with the brush, and put them on the rubber rack. Then she rinsed the dishes and I dried them with a kitchen towel. The same routine every night. We were a great team.

"North Carolina!" Mom called over her shoulder as I gathered up the plates and silverware from the table.

"Easy. The Tar Heels. Give me a hard one." The Nickname Game. My mother knew the nickname of every college team in the world. The game made doing the dishes a lot of fun.

"Georgia Tech?"

"Wasps? No, wait. Bees? No. I got it. Yellow Jackets. Good one. You almost had me."

"Stanford?"

"Warriors? Braves? Indians? Yeah. Indians. Got it. Right?"

"Right," Mom laughed. "You're getting harder and harder to fool. You'll be the expert before too long." She pulled a sudsy plate out of the sink and scrubbed off the crud with the brush. I stood next to her for a while and neither one of us said anything.

"Can I get polio?" I asked as I started my drying routine. I attacked the plate with the dishtowel like I wanted to erase the little blue ducks that lined the border. "Is that the real reason I'm not supposed to jump over the wall and cut through the McDonald's backyard? Because his son has polio and I'll get it if I get too close. And then I'll get put in a big can for the rest of my life. That's it, isn't it?"

"No way, Bob Waterfield. You're as safe as you could possibly be." My mother draped her rubbery, sudsy hand around my shoulder and pulled me close to her. I could smell her perfume through the heavy scent of Liquid Joy. "He's not contagious. That's why the doctors let him stay at home. I promise. Besides, you took the Salk vaccine at school. Remember? When everybody went to the cafeteria and got a shot. Year before last? I'm sure you remember." Good-natured sarcasm hovered at the edge of my mother's voice.

I remembered all right. That day our whole class had marched to the school cafeteria and had stood in line waiting to go into a makeshift booth behind a short curtain. You couldn't see what happened to the kids in the front of the line once they disappeared behind the curtain. We all stood there not knowing what was going to happen, shuffling our feet like we had to pee or something.

Our teacher, old Miss Norbert, hovered by the door to make sure nobody could escape and a couple of nurses in crisp white uniforms directed the whole operation. One of the nurses talked to each kid right before they disappeared behind the curtain.

You could see a nurse's white stockinged legs behind the curtain along with the doctor's legs. The doc was sitting down, doing something to each kid. Another nurse took over and directed each boy or girl to the other side of the cafeteria when they left the back of the booth. Our class had become a human assembly line.

Everything seemed okay until Johnny Nelson staggered out of the booth in tears. Johnny Nelson was big and tough. This was his third try at the fourth grade. When Miss Norbert asked him a question in class and he didn't know the answer he stared at the teacher until she looked away and called on somebody else. Johnny

Nelson feared nothing.

But when he came out of the booth he was bawling his head off. Giant tears streamed down his cheeks like rain on a windowpane. Johnny shrieked and wailed. The nurse tried to comfort him. No luck. What did they do to you behind that curtain?

Then Ronnie Thompson made it two steps out of the booth and whoosh, his whole breakfast hit the cafeteria floor.

I heard Tommy Lee's voice from the back of the line. "I ain't goin' in there! No way! You can't make me go in there! This is America!"

Miss Norbert jerked Tommy Lee out of the line and dragged him over to the corner, where she bent down and shook her finger in his face and yelled at him.

I was two kids away from going behind the curtain myself. The girl in front of me was Doris White. She was skinny and her skin always looked dirty and she smelled like a wet dog. The nurse led Doris behind the curtain and the doctor inside the booth did something to her. And Doris passed out cold.

Her head hit the cafeteria floor, thudding like a cantaloupe.

When she came to, the nurse fanned Doris with a copy of *Collier's* magazine and one of the teachers got her a drink of water. Doris was shaking and sobbing and her dirty skin was all pasty looking and Miss Norbert led her off to the Health Room and it was my turn to go into the booth.

The nurse said, "This won't hurt."

No matter what they did to you that's what they always said. Even if they were about to whap you up the side of the head with a two-by-four they'd say,

"This won't hurt." I swear.

They're all liars. Kids were pouring out of the Booth of Pain, yelling and crying and puking and passing out and she was telling me this wasn't going to hurt? Who's gonna believe that?

It didn't hurt.

It was just a shot. Just like the booster shots we got every summer.

"Such a brave boy," the nurse who guided me out of the booth said. "See that wasn't so bad, was it?"

"No, ma'am, I guess not." I walked toward the other end of the cafeteria where all the kids who had gotten their shot were gathered for juice and animal crackers. Grown-ups thought juice and animal crackers could pretty much make up for anything.

I looked at Tommy Lee who stood three kids away from going behind the curtain. He looked scared. He lifted his hands with the palms up and shrugged as if to say, "How was it?"

I started to give him the okay sign—the thumb and forefinger in a circle—but for some reason I thought it would be funny if I grabbed my throat with both hands and stuck my tongue out and made horrible noises and staggered around the cafeteria until I collapsed and rolled around on the floor, making my legs jerk back and forth.

So I did.

All the nurses sprinted over to help me. There was a lot of yelling and people running back and forth, and the doctor raced out of the booth and yelled "goddamn it!"

Nobody had thought I was funny, especially Mr. Swell, the principal of Edison, who had called my mom and had made me stay after school for a week when he had found out I'd faked the whole thing.

But the shot protected me from polio. Mr. McDonald's son hadn't been so lucky.

"Martha told me that the McDonald boy caught polio back in '49," my mother said as she rinsed the rest of the plates. "There were more cases that year than any other previous year in American history. Over forty thousand. It's horrible for the parents. The mothers and fathers rush back and forth to the hospital at all hours, hoping for the best, always fearing the worst. Fearing their child might die. Always thinking . . ."

"Die?" I looked up and my dishtowel froze on the plate. "You can die from polio?"

My mother pulled off her rubber gloves and gave me a full-fledged everything-will-be-alright-mother-bear hug. "Oh, yes, Johnny Unitas, you can die," she said. "Not often, but sometimes."

"Is there any more coffee?" My father lumbered back into the kitchen.

My mom let the hug go.

My dad crossed the kitchen and emptied the dregs of the percolator into his coffee cup. "Maybe you could make another pot later."

My mother nodded.

I put a plate in the cabinet above the counter and reached for another one on the drying rack. "Mom was telling me about polio," I said.

"Polio? Why are ya'll still talking about that?" My father pulled a Pall Mall from the red pack, stuck the cigarette in his mouth, and flicked his lighter. "You get polio the same way you get any other disease," he said, torching the tip of his cigarette. "Germs. You get it from germs. You use public toilets and you don't wash your hands. Somebody sneezes on you. You handle other kid's stuff at camp. It's simple."

My mother took off her apron and hung it on the nail on the back of the pantry door. She leaned her back against the kitchen counter, folded her arms across her chest and cleared her throat. "Warren, I don't think so."

"Huh?"

My mother didn't disagree with my father often, and the tension in the kitchen was suddenly like when a teacher catches some poor guy cheating on a test. Everything got real quiet and uncomfortable and the air went all prickly.

"Everybody knows that cleanliness prevents disease," my mom said. "But polio only strikes in highly industrialized countries. Countries like the US or England, which are the cleanest countries in the world. Polio is almost unknown in Africa or India. If unsanitary conditions caused polio, the situation would be the reverse."

"Well, watch Mrs. Wizard." My father's sarcastic voice referred to the TV show where the guy explains science stuff. Between Mr. McDonald and my mom, my father had had a tough evening.

"Warren, listen. I went to the library and looked up some stuff on polio. Mothers want to know all they can. I know what I'm talking about."

My father frowned.

"Polio has only been a problem in this century," my mother said. "In past centuries when people lived in squalor and filth nobody got polio. Then suddenly polio hit like a biblical plague in industrialized countries. But never in poor countries. It's one of the great mysteries

25

of our time."

"I'm sure if anybody finds the answer, it'll be you, Miss Know It All." My father wandered over to the door. "And don't correct me in front of the boy anymore. He needs to think his old man knows something besides how to make a buck." He shoved the door open and stomped into the living room.

I hadn't realized I'd been holding my breath and was surprised when a bunch of air came whooshing out of my mouth.

How did the kid in the can next door get polio? Me and the kid breathed the same air. So did Sandra and Tommy Lee. We all lived on the same block. Was the shot in the cafeteria going to protect me? My father didn't want to know the answer, but I sure did. I promised myself I'd find out. One way or the other.

I decided not to think about getting polio or scary old Mr. McDonald telling my parents about my Big Secret. Either one of those things would end my world as I knew it.

My only hope was to push both of them out of my mind and jam them into the closet in the back of my brain. Shovel both of those suckers into the closet and slam the door tight. Then just don't think about them. No matter what.

Easier said than done.

CHAPTER FOUR

The best moment of any week, and I mean any week, was Friday afternoon. You couldn't beat Friday afternoon when the last bell rang and school was out for two whole days and there was nothing to do but stuff you love. Time seemed to stand still and grin at you on Friday afternoon.

Halloween was coming up in a couple of weeks and autumn was going full blast. The leaves made a crunchy sound when Tommy Lee and I stepped on them on our way home from school. The air felt crispy cold and stung my face a little.

Tommy Lee and I hiked through the woods that surrounded Edison, stopping to look in the creek for crawdads. We didn't see any. It was too cold. One of the real fun things about living in Kingwood was you had a bunch of creeks and lots of woods to horse around in.

Kingwood actually is a kind of a suburb, which is where you don't live in the city, but you don't live far enough out in the country to have horses and cows and pigs either.

Whoever built Kingwood thought it would be a hoot to make all the streets sound alike—Cherrywood, Valleywood, Koolwood. Pretty corny if you asked me.

Our house was on Pinewood, in the middle of what

my mom said was a fancy French name that must have meant "a handful of houses in a semicircle" because that's what it is—the McDonald's, then our house, then the Yancy's then Tommy Lee's then Sandra's—all in a semicircle at the end of the block.

On the other hand, one of the disadvantages of living in Kingwood was that you get creepy neighbors like Mr. McDonald. Since Tommy Lee and I had no intention of vaulting Mr. McDonald's wall and cutting through his backyard after I got chewed out, we took the stupid way home, walking all the way down to the big ditch and back up the hill.

We raced through the alley that connected Cherrywood and Luckywood as hard as we could because the garbage in the alley reeked like a bunch of dead cats. Cutting through the alley wasn't so bad in the spring when the sweet scent of the wild honeysuckle covered up the garbage stench. The honeysuckle smelled like ol' Mother Nature using her perfume to cover up her children's nasty mess. But in October it was still a good idea to run through the alley and hold your breath.

"Tell me again how Mr. McDonald cussed out your old man," Tommy Lee giggled as we reached the end of the alley.

"You wouldn't be laughing if you'd seen it," I said. "I thought Mr. McDonald might slug my dad. I think the old guy's crazy. No telling what he'd do if he caught us jumping the wall again."

"My old man says Mr. McDonald moved here because he finked on a bunch of other gangsters back east, and if they find him they'll mow him down with their tommy guns." Tommy Lee made a gun with his thumb and forefinger and gunned down a couple of garbage cans in the alley.

"Well, all I know is Mr. McDonald is terrifying when he's mad." I decided not to tell Tommy Lee that Mr. McDonald knew about our Big Secret. If Tommy Lee thought a grown up even suspected what we were doing he might chicken out and not do it anymore.

"Got ya. I ain't gonna cut through his yard anymore either." Tommy Lee stuffed his hands in the pockets of his windbreaker.

Tommy Lee's jacket was too small for him. Most of his clothes were too small because they had all belonged to his older brother, Mike. Mike had been little and skinny when he went to Edison, but Tommy Lee was big. Not big tall like I am but wide and muscly. He could whip anybody at school if he wanted to. Anybody except me. Not that Tommy Lee would ever want to call me out. He and I had been best friends since we were little kids. If we had a fight it would be like Batman duking it out with Robin or the Lone Ranger slugging Tonto. It wouldn't make any sense.

Tommy Lee Rush was a good guy. Even if he did look a little goofy with his hair stuck out like he had combed it with a mix master and his shirttail out, flopping around all over the place.

Tommy Lee didn't care. He didn't care for much of anything except basketball. Just like me. He and I were the top of the heap in elementary school. Star players in our last year.

But next year everything would change. Junior high. The seventh, eighth, and ninth grade. We'd be the rock bottom of the heap. Four elementary schools fed into the junior high. That's a lot of good seventh grade basketball players.

Tommy Lee's big brother, Mike, had been an All City player in junior high and more than anything Tommy Lee wanted to make the JVs when he got to the seventh grade next year. You had to be good to play JV, and the word around Lancaster Park was that most guys got cut after the first practice. One day and you're gone. Poof. No more hoops.

I wanted to make the JVs even more than Tommy Lee.

I wanted to make the JVs more than anything in the world. That was why I practiced all the time—shooting baskets in the backyard, dribbling a ball up and down the driveway, working on my footwork in my room when I was supposed to be doing my homework.

And that was why I was willing to risk being grounded forever by going up to the school ground every Sunday afternoon. Our Big Secret. That was what was gonna land me on the JV team. That or land me in military school

We crossed the Luckywood Bridge over the Creek. Other creeks in the neighborhood had names like Plum Bayou Creek or Oak Grove Creek. The Creek under the Luckywood Bridge didn't have a name because it was the only one that originated on the Lancaster Property.

The Lancaster Property sat facing the front of Edison School. Four square blocks of deep, thick, dark, scary woods surrounded by a high fence with barbed wire all over the top. In the middle of the property this real rich guy named Cantrell Lancaster had a giant mansion. At least that's what everybody said. Nobody had ever seen the house, but everybody said the Lancaster mansion was in there somewhere.

The first thing you learned when you went to Edison—I mean in the first minute of the first day of the first grade—was not to even think about going into the Lancaster Property. The older kids told you the stories—giant German Shepherd dogs who ate human flesh guarded the house or ghosts haunted the woods or old World War II land mines had been planted around the place or maybe there were bear traps dipped in poison hidden under the leaves and would snap your legs off if you went in there. Going into the Lancaster Property was something you didn't think about unless you were crazy.

When we reached my house, Tommy Lee said "so long" and headed on home to help his mom with her big "clean out the garage" project. My family always left the door unlocked so I let myself into the house, tossed my books on the table in the breakfast nook, and looked around for something to eat.

A plate of stale Oreos sat on the counter underneath a note. "Archie: I've gone to the drugstore to look at paperback books. Back in a bit. Save some cookies for your father. Love, Mom."

I got some milk out of the refrigerator and drank out of the carton while I ate half of the cookies.

The house was mine for a while.

I went in the living room and opened the top of the hi-fi. It was time for rock 'n' roll. I stuck the tube on the pointy cylinder so I could play my 45s and put on "Whole Lotta Shakin' Going On" by Jerry Lee Lewis. The song made you want to dance even if you didn't know how. Which I didn't.

The music always made me want to move, so while Jerry Lee sang "Come on over, Baby. . ." I pretended the top of the living room door was a basket, and I had a basketball and kept driving for imaginary lay-ups and shooting imaginary jump shots and grabbing imaginary rebounds. "We ain't fakin'. Whole Lotta Shakin' goin' on." Friday afternoons were the greatest.

Until somebody started pounding on the back door.

The records! Mr. McDonald! Oh, no!

What if I didn't answer the door? What if I crouched down behind the sofa and hid until he went away?

Bad idea.

That was the kind of thing you got in big trouble for. It was like the phone. No matter what you were doing, you had to answer the phone. That was the law. You couldn't just let the phone ring. Or let someone keep knocking on the back door.

So, finally, I took a deep breath and shuffled to the back door, taking my time, hoping—praying—that whoever it was had given up and gone away.

I opened the back door real slow, the way you open those little cans with a coiled snake in them, kinda ducking your head so the snake won't hit you smack in the face when it flies out.

"Hi. I'm Katherine McDonald from next door."

I had seen Mr. McDonald's wife a few times before, hanging laundry on the clothesline, once at Piggly Wiggly, but never up close. She was a puffy person, round and sorta swollen looking. She had on a faded blue housedress and a man's green sweater with a hole in the elbow. The sweater was way too big and seemed to swallow her up. Her hair was the color of dirty sand, and her eyes had dark circles around them. Teeny veins crisscrossed her nose. Mrs. McDonald was not a looker.

"I'm Archie Lane and I'm sorry I was playing my records too loud and I won't do it anymore. I promise." Everything came whooshing out all at once.

"It's all right, kid. Don't worry. That's not why I'm here." Mrs. McDonald had a glass in her hand. The glass had pictures of little red geese walking around the rim and was full of orange juice. My family only drank orange juice at breakfast. I guess Yankees did things their own way.

"I'm sorry my Joseph was rough on you and your father the other day. He didn't mean any harm. He's like that sometimes. If I didn't know better, I'd say some demon gets inside of him and gets him all riled up. You know what I mean?"

"I guess."

"That's not why I'm here though." Mrs. McDonald took a long gulp of orange juice. "I came to ask you to do me a favor." She looked down at her feet. I had never seen a grown up embarrassed in front of a kid before.

Yankees sure were strange.

"May I come in? It's kinda chilly out here."

"Oh, sure. Please." I pushed open the screen door and let her into the kitchen.

"It's really not much of a favor," she said. Her husky voice sounded hoarse, almost masculine.

"Listen, Mrs. McDonald. I'm real sorry about the records."

"Shhh." She took another long swig of juice and wiped her mouth with the back of her hand. "Call me Katherine. Mrs. McDonald reminds me of my late mother-in-law."

Katherine? No way. No grown up wanted some kid to call them by their first name. As my father said about a lot of stuff, "it's just not done." If Tommy Lee waltzed in here some afternoon and said, "Hiya, Warren, how's tricks? Hello, Terri, good to see ya," his folks would lock him in his room until we went to high school.

"Call me Katherine. I mean it."

"Okay . . . uh . . . Katherine." Her name stumbled off my tongue like some fat kid trying to do somersaults in gym class.

"And stop apologizing." She looked around our kitchen like someone who was thinking about buying the house. "I don't give a rat's behind how loud you play your music. Actually I kinda like some of it. 'Tutti-frutti, oh, Rudy.' Not bad. It's primitive, but fun. Joseph hates it, but then again, Joseph hates everything."

I wouldn't argue with that.

"No, what I came over to ask you is . . ." She cleared her throat and stared at her shoes again. Then she looked up. "Would you consider taking a few minutes and bringing some of your records over to my house and playing them for my son? He hears you playing them over here and wants to hear them up close. He's sixteen, but, as I'm sure you know, he can't come over here. Joseph won't let swing music in our house, but Joseph's in Memphis at the moment and what he doesn't know won't hurt him. And Roy, that's my son, would sure get a kick out of your records. Whaddya say, kid?"

"Now?"

Katherine smiled. "Sure. Why not? The only

records we have are opera and Fred Waring and the Pennsylvanians. That's pretty bleak fare if you're sixteen."

Talk about a pickle. I seriously didn't want to go over to the McDonald's house. What if Mr. McDonald came back all of a sudden and found me playing rock 'n' roll in his house? Not to mention being in a house full of polio. Who wants that?

"I guess I could come over now for a little while," I said. Believe me, Southerners are polite to a fault. We'd rather walk into a burning barn than hurt someone's feelings.

Katherine beamed. "Wonderful. Let's get a move on. I don't want to leave Roy for very long."

I shuffled back into the living room to get my records. Behind me, I heard the door open and Katherine following me into the living room. "I really appreciate this," she said, sipping her drink.

"I'm glad to do it," I lied as I pulled six records out of the little rack my mom gave me for my birthday.

Katherine stood by the door with her arms folded across her chest. "Do you know much about polio?"

I shook my head no.

"It's an old disease." Katherine said. "There is evidence that an Egyptian pharaoh may have had it."

"No kidding? We studied all about the pharaohs last year in Miss Harper's class. She never said anything about polio."

"It's not a well-known fact. Poliomyelitis didn't occur in large epidemics until this century. That's where the name polio comes from—poliomyelitis. The word means 'inflammation of the gray matter in the spinal cord.'" Katherine had a weird way of talking as if she was talking about one thing while she thought about something else. It kinda threw me off my game.

I nodded, trying to keep up. "My mom says polio only attacks children in clean countries like America." I felt like I needed to add something to the conversation.

Katherine's face lit up. "That's right," she smiled. "In 1949 when Roy caught polio, we lived in San Diego. Beautiful, clean San Diego, which had a high rate of polio. But across the border in Tijuana—dirty, grubby Tijuana, there were almost no cases. Isn't that amazing?"

I nodded. It was the same thing my mom had told me and it truly was amazing. "How does that happen?"

"Beats me." Katherine shrugged. "But I'm touched by your curiosity and I bet you're the kind of kid who'll find the answer some day. For now, let's you and I take those records over to my house and give Roy a taste of . . . what do you kids call this stuff?"

"Rock 'n' roll."

"Right. Rock 'n' roll." She saluted me with her glass and drained the rest of the orange juice. "Here's to rock 'n' roll."

I promised myself then and there that someway, somehow I would find the answer to why polio only attacked clean countries like America.

But for now I was trapped. Heading over to the house where mean, scary men and mysterious diseases lived. What a monumentally bad idea. My brain raced around, desperate to think of a way out of going next door with Katherine. Anything. I wasn't choosy.

I drew a blank. There was no way out.

The time had come to meet the kid in the can face to face.

CHAPTER FIVE

The inside of the McDonald's house was the creepiest place I had ever been in my life. Even creepier than the Junior Chamber of Commerce Spook House my mom took me to last Halloween.

Heavy, dark furniture filled every space in the living room like the movers had just delivered it but hadn't bothered to put it where it belonged. The drapes were closed, making the room feel like midnight. The only light came from these three giant red candles on the coffee table, which were flaming and smelling up the place like a burning Hershey bar.

It was a room that was never gonna smile.

Black-and-white photographs in thin red frames covered the front wall. The pictures were of GIs, standing in front of jeeps or tanks or sitting around in full battle gear in front of tents, smoking cigarettes, or eating off of little tin plates. The best picture showed these two army guys carrying this wounded soldier. You could tell they really cared about their buddy, and you knew without question they were going to save him.

The back wall was crammed with paintings of Jesus.

Big pictures. Little pictures.

Smiling Jesus. Frowning Jesus. Jesus walking. Jesus talking.

There were statues of Jesus on the floor by the picture window and on the coffee table and all over this fancy carved table in the corner. Big statues and tiny statues—an army of Jesuses waiting for the orders to move out.

Some of the statues showed Jesus hanging on the cross. Jesus suffering. Jesus in agony. Some of them looked like the real thing. Jesus' eyes were all bugged out. Nails were sticking out of his hands and feet, blood and sweat ran down the side of his tormented face. The crown of thorns stuck out in all directions like Tommy Lee's hair and Jesus' mouth was all twisted in a silent scream. The whole room throbbed with pain.

"Joseph and I are Catholics," Katherine said.

I wasn't sure what to say to that.

"We're Baptists," I finally mumbled. "My friend Sandra goes to Catholic school over at Holy Souls. But she's a Baptist too." I knew I sounded stupid, but try to come up with snappy patter in a room full of dying, crying Jesuses.

Katherine didn't seem to be interested anyway. She closed the front door and walked over to the fancy table in the corner. "Isn't this beautiful? It's all hand carved. It took over twenty years to make. Joseph's uncle made the table during his incarceration in the Boston Institute for the Insane. He worked on the table eight hours a day, every day for twenty years. It's beautiful, don't you think?"

I barely heard the question.

The Boston Institute for the Insane? An army of Jesuses in agony? A kid in a can? I wished I had never answered that knock at the back door.

"Uh, yeah. It's a neat table," I said when I realized

she was waiting for an answer.

"Well," Katherine said. "You didn't come over here to admire the furniture. Bring your records and come on back to the den. I'll introduce you to Roy."

I thought about just bolting out the front door and getting out of there as fast as I could. But my Southern manners wouldn't let me. Us Southerners were so polite we thanked the Devil when he opened the doors to hell for us.

The kid in the can was in the middle of the den.

There could have been a snarling tiger or a two headed grizzly bear in the corner of the McDonald's den and I wouldn't have noticed. As far as I was concerned there was only one thing in the room.

The can was this big, big cylinder, about six feet long and maybe three feet in diameter, resting on these skinny metal legs. Round porthole windows covered the whole thing. There were small doors and hoses and a thick bellows underneath. The can was a muddy green color and made a humming noise that sounded like Grandpa Lane snoring in the night.

The kid's head stuck out of one end of the can and rested on a little pillow. A mirror dangled above his head so he could see stuff going on behind him. At the moment he was asleep.

Beyond the iron lung, a sliding glass door looked out over the McDonald's walled in backyard. Some seriously goofy music played low on the hi-fi. A big orchestra and a woman yelling in a foreign language. The words to her song didn't even rhyme. I wondered how the kid in the can could snooze with all that racket going on.

"Don't be afraid. Come on in." Katherine patted

me on the shoulder.

I realized I had frozen in the doorway. I inhaled a deep breath and took a pair of cautious steps into the McDonald's den.

"Awful contraption, isn't it?" Katherine said. "It's nothing but a giant can with bellows and an electric motor." She caressed the iron lung like the machine was a beloved family pet. "But the thing keeps Roy alive. All of his body is paralyzed so the machine does all of his breathing for him. The rubber collar around his neck is airtight. At least it's supposed to be. We're always fighting leaks somewhere."

I stared at the head sticking out of the iron lung and tried to imagine what it would be like if it was me in the machine. Even my overactive imagination couldn't picture that one.

"A buzzer sounds when the pressure drops below a certain point." Katherine said as if she was reading from the manual. "We have to open the door for short periods to change the sheets or do other things. Roy can breathe for a couple of minutes on his own but if the door stays open too long he runs out of air."

There was nothing to say. I nodded and waited for Katherine to fill the silence.

Katherine brushed her fingertips across the boy's forehead. "Wake up, sweetheart. We have a visitor. He has a nice surprise for you."

The boy's head moved. By looking in the mirror over his head I could see his eyelids flutter. Suddenly he started making a clicking noise by popping his tongue against the roof of his mouth.

The sound spooked me and I backed up. I was way past my weirdness tolerance level.

"Roy doesn't get enough air to speak very loud," Katherine said, turning to me. "He makes that clicking sound to get my attention. It's a breath-saving device. A lot of iron lung patients use it. Chimpanzees talk to each other using similar sounds."

I wondered how Roy liked being compared to a chimpanzee.

"Come on over and meet Roy." Katherine motioned for me to join her.

I shuffled across the room like my veins were full of Novocain.

"Archie, meet my son, Roy." Katherine positioned me behind the iron lung, so Roy could see my reflection in the mirror. "Roy, this is Archie Lane, the boy from next door."

Roy's eyes fluttered open. He was about the same age as Tommy Lee's brother, Mike, who went to Central. Mike was big and strong and tan from working as a lifeguard over at the War Memorial swimming pool in the summer but Roy was shriveled and had skin that was the color of the paste we used in school to stick magazine pictures on construction paper.

To add to the weirdness, Roy seemed to be going bald. Like my dad. Roy's hairline had crawled back to the middle of his skull, making his forehead look like a pasty volleyball. The little hair he had left was brown and stringy and damp looking.

"Hi, Archie. Nice to meet you." Roy's mouth was round and too small for the rest of his face. His voice sounded like he smoked four packs of Pall Malls a day or he had been running sprints since breakfast. Little spit bubbles decorated the corners of his mouth.

"Hi." It came out in a squeak. Archie, the

Articulate Wonder of the Western World.

"I'd shake hands but I can't," Roy wheezed.

"No. No. That's okay. I mean I'm sorry you have to be in this thing. I mean it looks so gross." Oh, man. I was digging myself a hole. I wished I could stop talking. "I'm sorry. I mean it looks sorta uncomfortable."

"That's okay." Roy smiled. "I wish I could say you get use to living in this thing, but you don't. Not a day goes by that I don't hate it. Somebody has to bathe me and shave me. Do you shave yet?"

I ran my hand over my chin. "Nah, not yet." I made it sound as if I planned to start tomorrow. I thought it was a strange question until I realized Roy wanted to make me feel more at ease. If that was the case he had his work cut out for him.

"One of the worst problems is that when I have an itch I can't scratch it. That'll drive you crazy."

"I bet."

"Or watching baseball. You like baseball?"

"Sure. I love the Cardinals. I listen to Harry Caray on the radio every summer."

"Great. The Red Sox are my team. Ted Williams and Jackie Jensen and Jimmy Pearsall. Greatest outfield ever. My problem is sometimes I can't turn my head. When I watch a game on TV I have to watch it in the mirror, and when a guy gets a hit he runs to third base. That takes a little getting used to." Roy laughed and I laughed with him before I could stop myself. But the thought hit me that laughter was probably the very thing the House of Weirdness needed.

"I should love this cranky old iron lung," Roy said. "It does my breathing for me. Except every once in a while it'll leak and I'll pass out from lack of air. I think the machine does that on purpose to remind me how important it is to me. Like when you have a headache it reminds you how important your head is."

We both laughed.

"You like football?" Roy seemed excited to have some company.

"Sure. Everybody in Arkansas likes football. I listen to all the Razorback games on the radio. A&M, SMU, TCU, Texas. All of 'em."

"My dad was a big football star in college," Roy said. "He made honorable mention All American. He played fullback for Holy Cross."

"The Crusaders?" I thought I'd show off a little, thanks to Mom's Nickname Game.

Roy beamed. "Right. Wow. You're the only person around here who's ever heard of Holy Cross. That's great." Suddenly Roy choked on the last word and started making these awful noises deep in his throat. His face started turning purple as he coughed and gasped for air.

I stepped back from the iron lung, but Katherine didn't seem too concerned. I guess Roy got choked a lot.

"Roy's very proud of his father," Katherine said, giving Roy a chance to catch his breath.

"Sure am," Roy croaked out as he cleared his throat. "Dad also played lacrosse and was a champion boxer. Some promoters even asked him to turn pro. He went in the army instead. He fought in the Big War and in Korea too."

"My dad was in the army too." I said, hoping Roy wouldn't ask me to elaborate on my dad's war record.

"I wanted to play football too," Roy said. "Before I got sick. My dad had started teaching me how to box, but . . ."

Katherine leaned over and patted Roy's sweaty forehead. "Sweetheart, you've got more courage than a whole team of football players and boxers put together."

Roy smiled at his mom. I think he would have rather played football.

A long silence settled over the den.

Quiet makes me crazy. "How did your dad get that big scar?" My mouth appeared to be operating on automatic pilot, which happens when I get nervous or there's too much quiet. I bit down on the end of my tongue to limit the damage.

"Oh, man," Roy grinned, pleased that I had asked the question. "This is such a great story. Why don't you tell him, Mama? I'm getting a little winded." He made the strange clicking sound with his tongue and the roof of his mouth. This time it didn't sound so scary.

Katherine patted Roy's cheek. "Well, this is something Joseph never talks about. But I guess it would be all right to tell you. If you promise not to tell anyone else."

I nodded and crossed my heart, making a solemn promise.

"Okay then. I'll tell you the whole story."

CHAPTER SIX

"Back in '51," Katherine said. "Joseph was in the infantry during the Korean War. He joined up right after the Chinese Reds got into the conflict. His unit was fighting somewhere in the mountains near the border between North and South Korea. No matter what the US forces did they couldn't stop the Red Army. Joseph said the Chinese sent thousands of men into battle. He said they came at our guys in waves like a gigantic, stormy red ocean."

I got the feeling Katherine's story wasn't heading toward prison or a bear or any of the other stuff people in the neighborhood talked about when they wondered about Mr. McDonald's scar.

"Anyway," Katherine went on, "one day it was snowing hard and the Reds pulled a surprise attack and overran Joseph's unit. Our troops couldn't hold out any longer. There was no place to run. All of the men in Joseph's platoon were killed and he was wounded. A bullet grazed his temple and another one lodged in his shoulder. He fell and hit his head on a rock and got knocked out cold for several hours."

Roy made the clicking sound. His mom winked at him. She knew how much he loved the story.

"When Joseph woke up," Katherine gestured with her hand, "he was lying on the side of the mountain with about a dozen other GIs. Except all the other soldiers were dead. The Chinese Reds were walking around the bodies talking in Chinese and laughing at the dead Americans." She paused and took a deep breath. "Some of the Reds started scratching the faces of the dead GIs with the tips of their bayonets to make sure they were dead. Joseph lay still and kept his eyes closed and pretended to be dead too."

I was on the edge of my seat, this story was way better than prison or bears or anything else we'd thought of.

Katherine pressed her lips together as a shudder rippled through her body. Roy made another clicking sound, urging her to go on.

"When the Reds got to Joseph he was in incredible danger." Katherine put her hands on the side of the iron lung to steady herself. "He knew what they were doing, and when they ran the bayonet point down the side of his face . . . he didn't flinch. Not even a little." Katherine sucked in a quick breath. "He didn't move a muscle. The Chinese soldiers thought he was dead like the other Americans so they moved on to the next body. Later on, when the Reds were gone, Joseph got up and made his way back to the main American camp. It took him three days." She gestured again with both hands. "Alone in the snow with his face cut and bleeding. That's why it scarred so badly. The cut healed on its own without stitches. Joseph's a true hero."

Roy made another clicking sound. It sounded like an exclamation point.

"Wow. That's something," I said.

"I told you," Roy whispered. "My dad's a real hero. They gave him a bunch of medals and everything."

I couldn't see the mean, bullying, angry man who had chewed out my dad and me by the clothesline being this big war hero. I loved Katherine's story, but I didn't quite believe it.

Katharine pushed herself away from the iron lung. "Well, enough of the McDonald family history," she said. "Can I get you a Coke, Archie? All of you Southerners seem addicted to the stuff."

"Yes, ma'am. I'd love a Coke. Thank you."

Katherine headed for the kitchen that was separated from the den by a bar with three high stools. In a second I heard the refrigerator door open.

Roy made his clicking sound and I moved forward until I stood right behind his head and could see his face in the mirror. "Mama needs a drink after telling dad's story," he whispered. "She has to have her vodka every day. She mixes it with orange juice. She drinks so much orange juice I'm surprised she doesn't glow in the dark."

"My folks don't drink alcohol," I whispered back. "Baptists think drinking is a sin or something like that."

"That's why Mama drinks," Roy said. "She thinks she committed a sin. She thinks it's her fault I got polio. She let me go swimming on the beach at San Diego and started flirting with some guy and left me in the waterway too long. I got a chill. The doctors told her over and over that it wasn't her fault. But she still thinks it is."

"Geez."

"She thinks God is punishing her for what she did."

"Here we go." Katherine swept back into the den, carrying a small tray that held two Coke bottles with little yellow straws in them and another goose glass filled with orange juice. And vodka.

"Thank you." I took one of the bottles off of the tray.

Katherine held the other Coke to the side of Roy's head. He twisted his neck, and she placed the straw in his mouth. He took a long sip and said thank you with his clicking sound.

"Archie brought some of his records to share with you," Katherine said, taking a huge gulp from her own drink. "He and I thought it would be nice to introduce you to rock and roll up close."

I stuffed back a laugh. Katherine didn't say it right. She made "rock" sound like the most important part.

Katherine crossed the room and removed the record of the lady screaming in a foreign language from the hi-fi. She motioned me to come over and put on one of my records. I went with "Long Tall Sally" by Little Richard. If you're gonna play rock 'n' roll, play rock 'n' roll. The turntable started turning, the cylinder dropped the record, a scratchy noise filled the room, and then the McDonald's den came alive with the sound of Little Richard.

"Long tall Sally, she's real sweet, she's got everything that Uncle John need. Oh, baby. Wooooo, baby!"

Rock 'n' roll.

At first Katherine looked like she'd seen a dead rat, but then a little smile crept in around the corners of her mouth. She even started tapping her foot along with the music.

Next, I played Bill Haley's "Rock Around the Clock" and then the Everly Brothers' "Bye, Bye Love" and followed that up with Elvis Presley's "All Shook Up." Roy beamed the whole time.

As "All Shook Up" faded, Roy made his clicking sound, and Katherine and I both went over to the iron lung. "Play the 'Great Green Teddy Bear'," Roy whispered. "That's my favorite. I've heard you play the song over at your house."

The Great Green Teddy Bear? I didn't have any records called "The Great Green Teddy Bear." I had never heard of a song called "The Great Green Teddy Bear." I didn't have a clue what Roy was talking about. Maybe polio people heard stuff that wasn't really there.

"Uh, Roy," I stammered. "I don't have a record called 'The Great Green Teddy Bear.' Sorry." I had spent a chunk of the afternoon saying I was sorry.

"Sure you do. You were playing the record last Sunday. I heard you. You know . . . " Roy sucked in all the air his sick lungs could hold. "Oh, yes, I'm the great green teddy bear," he sang in a hoarse whisper. Then he broke into a coughing fit that made his face turn red and his nose run.

Katherine wiped Roy's nose with a tissue and gave him another sip of Coke. "Come on, Hon. Slow down now. You know you can't strain your lungs. If Archie doesn't have the song, he doesn't have it."

"I have the song," I said. "Only it's called 'The Great Pretender.' It's an older song by the Platters. I have it right here."

Roy grinned. His clicks indicated he wanted me to play the record. I walked back to the hi-fi and put on the song. "Oh, yes I'm the great pretender . . ." Well, okay, maybe it did sound a little like the great green teddy bear. Especially if you were lying in an iron lung, listening to the song all the way from the house next door.

When the Platters finished I walked back over to Roy.

"I guess I missed that one," Roy smiled. He wasn't embarrassed at all. "It's an even better song now that I know what the words are. Thanks, Arch."

I nodded. "Why don't you keep the record for a few days? Get your mom to play it for you while your dad's gone. I don't think he digs rock 'n' roll."

"Thank you, Archie," Katherine said. "Maybe you could help me make a list of some other records Roy might enjoy. I'll go to the record store tomorrow. What Joseph McDonald doesn't know won't hurt him." She gave me a conspiratorial wink.

Roy clicked his approval of the whole plan.

Great. Just great. I was now about to become a part of a plot to keep a big secret from the meanest, scariest man on the planet. A man who could blab to my parents about my own Big Secret. A man who held my future in the palm of his hand. Swell. Let's hide stuff from him.

Great plan, Archie.

Katherine patted Roy's forehead, which was soaked after his coughing fit. Then she turned to me. "You need to scoot now, young man. I don't mean to be impolite, but this has been the longest afternoon Roy has had in a long, long time. I know he's tired now. Maybe you could come back some other time."

"Yeah I'd like that," I said, shocked to realize I meant it. I turned back to the iron lung. "S'long, Roy. See ya around. Maybe next time we can listen to some more records or even check out a Razorback game on the radio."

"Bye, Archie. Thanks again. Come back real soon. Soon as you can." He made another clicking noise that I thought meant good-bye.

I gathered up my stuff and Katherine walked me back to the front door, past the army of Jesuses. "You're an angel," she said, as she opened the door to let me out. "This was the nicest thing that's happened to Roy since we moved here."

"I had fun," I said. "Roy's a good guy."

Suddenly, Katherine threw her arms around me. "Thank you," she whispered, crushing me in a bear hug.

"Maybe next spring I could come over and me and Roy could listen to a Cardinals' game," I wheezed over Katherine shoulder, hoping she would loosen her grip. "The Cards should have a good team next season."

Katherine gave me one last bone-crushing squeeze before holding me away from her and cradling my face between the palms of her hands. "Oh, honey." She sniffed back a flood of tears. "Roy won't be with us next spring."

Then she started bawling and bear hugged me real tight.

CHAPTER SEVEN

I slept late and had to scramble around to get ready for Sunday school and church. My dad tried to teach me to tie my tie for the umpteenth time, but every time I tied the old double Windsor the front wound up about a foot shorter than the back and I looked like Clarabelle the Clown.

Finally my father tied the stupid tie for me and swore that next Sunday we would get up earlier, and he would teach me how to tie the double Windsor.

Don't hold your breath.

My mom and dad and I piled into the blue Chevy and headed for the Kingwood Baptist Church.

As usual, Sunday school bored my socks off. Miss Crenshaw, our teacher, who had a face like Roy Rogers' horse, Trigger, and breath like a dog fart, read us a Bible story about this guy that tried to sell his donkey for too much money. Big woo.

I sat between my parents at the main service, which included an infinite string of impossible-to-sing songs sung in bored voices and an endless sermon about giving money to the church.

During the most boring part of the sermon, right when I thought my brain was about to buy the farm, my mom took a ballpoint pen out of her purse and wrote "Washington State" on the corner of her church program. I took the pen from her hand and scrawled "Cougars" on the opposite corner. Mom grinned and nodded.

"Yale?"

"Bulldogs." The Nickname Game.

Toward the end of the sermon old Reverend Brown snuck in something out of nowhere about how the Negroes ought to stay with their own kind the way God meant for them to. The people around us mumbled "amen" and nodded their heads in agreement. My mother scowled.

My dad had fallen asleep and missed the whole thing.

After church we went home and my mother served Sunday dinner—canned chicken, instant mashed potatoes, cold green beans, and Wonder Bread.

When we finished eating, my mom and I washed the dishes while my dad drifted into the living room and fell asleep reading the paper, which was pretty much his usual Sunday afternoon routine. Mom retreated to her bedroom to read and I went to my room and changed clothes. I hung up my Sunday suit and put on my old blue jeans and a faded gray sweatshirt. I laced up my black Converse basketball shoes real tight, took my basketball out to the backyard, and started shooting hoops on the goal my mom had put up for me summer before last.

The grass was still wet from the rain and the ball got damp and heavy. The sun played peek-a-boo with the clouds and a cool breeze reminded me Halloween was coming in a couple of days.

I shot around for a few minutes until I heard the screen door slam over at the Rush's house. I parked the ball on my hip and watched Tommy Lee cross the yard. He had his head down, shuffling along like he was going to prison. His toad-green sweater didn't even cover his belly button.

"We gonna do it?" I said as Tommy Lee ambled into our yard.

He leaned on the post that held up the basketball goal, his hands shoved deep into the pockets of his jeans. "We gotta stop, Arch," he said. "The whole town's in an uproar about this stuff. If we get nailed none of the kids at school will have anything to do with us. It'll be like we have leprosy."

"Most fun ever," I said, firing a jump shot at the goal. I missed and retrieved the ball. Dribble, dribble. Shoot. Rebound. Dribble. Shoot. I couldn't stand still. "We keep doing it, we make JV next year."

"If our fathers don't ship us both off to military school or exile us to Siberia."

"Only if we get caught," I said.

Tommy Lee shook his head. "Yeah. Only if we get caught."

"So let's don't get caught."

"No, Arch. Listen. It's too dangerous. It's . . ."

"Tell ya what," I said. "Gimme one shot. If I make it we go. If I miss, we hang around here all afternoon. Deal?"

Tommy Lee rolled his eyes. "Deal."

I dribbled to an imaginary free throw line, took a deep breath, and bounced the ball. I had taken to crossing myself before I shot a free throw. Last year I saw a guy over at Catholic High do it and then sink two game-winning free throws. So even though we were Baptists, I crossed myself at the free throw line.

Cross. Dribble. Shoot.

Swish.

Tommy Lee looked like he was heading for the dentist to have a tooth pulled. I was all smiles.

Instead of vaulting over the wall and cutting through the McDonald's yard, which would have been a whole lot easier, we went the long way round, dribbling the basketball down the center of the street, passing it back and forth, weaving in and out, dribbling with our left hands for practice, losing control and chasing the ball down before it rolled into the sewer pipe down on the corner.

We cut across the Luckywood Bridge over the creek and sprinted through the woods that surrounded Edison. We came out at the asphalt basketball court at the edge of the playground, where we started dribbling around and shooting baskets.

The Edison playground was deserted. The court, the jungle gym, the swings, the softball field all quiet and empty, surrounded by the deep woods on three sides and the brick school building on the fourth side. The woods were splashed with the reds and oranges and yellows of autumn.

The cool October afternoon belonged to us. Even the breeze stopped for a while like the whole world was holding its breath, waiting to see what would happen. The only sound in our universe was the ball hitting the asphalt and clanking off the metal backboard. The basket net was chain instead of twine, and when the ball went through the net it made a clinking sound. Thump, thump, boom, clink. .

"They're not gonna come," Tommy Lee said, firing a jumper from the corner.

"Can you blame 'em? Would you come over here?" I grabbed the rebound and put the ball through the basket.

"Hell, no." Tommy Lee had taken to cussing a lot lately.

I started to pivot and shoot a hook shot when I saw them. The ball froze in my hand. "It's a good thing they're not you," I said. "There they are."

Tommy Lee whirled around.

A pair of Negro boys stood at the edge of the woods, watching us. They were about our age although one of them was even taller than I was. He had on a plain white T-shirt and a pair of faded corduroy pants. He was the color of chocolate sauce, and his hair was cropped so short he looked bald. The smaller one had yellowish dark skin that faded into his yellow pullover.

We went through the same routine every Sunday— the colored kids hung around the edge of the woods while Tommy Lee and I shot baskets. After a while, they would cross the grass to the basketball court.

We never talked. I guessed they lived in the big housing project in Panky Town out on the highway. The project must have been a good five miles from Edison. I figured they walked down the highway and cut through the woods to the playground every Sunday afternoon, looking for me and Tommy Lee at the asphalt court.

I swished another jump shot, showing off.

Tommy Lee shook his head "If my daddy finds out what we're doing, I'm dead."

"Ditto but I don't want to think about it. Let's just have fun."

"Arch, I dunno."

"Come on. These guys are good. They're really players. You like playing 'em as much as I do. If we can beat them we can beat anybody." I retrieved the ball and launched another jumper. I could feel the familiar nervousness in my stomach I always felt before I played basketball. It was the best feeling in the universe.

"Ya'll want to play?" the smaller kid asked.

"Sure."

"Play to a 'undred?"

"Okay." I tossed the ball to him, thinking he and his friend might want to take a few warm up shots. But they never did. They just started playing.

The game always went to one hundred points, full court, me and Tommy Lee against the two colored kids. They took the ball out first and the smaller boy dribbled slowly up the court, getting a feel for the ball and the game. Tommy Lee picked him up when he crossed mid court.

I guarded the taller guy, who set up on the low post. As soon as he established position he raised his right hand, signaling for the ball and started this chant: "Bring it on home, bring it to Jerome." Over and over. "Bring it on home . . ." I guessed the guy's name was Jerome.

I could tell Tommy Lee was pumped up because he was down in a low defensive crouch, not letting his man move to either side. Tough D. The kid backed up a step and held his dribble. "You can't steal from the Phantom," he said, a grin widening across his face. He did a nice hesitation dribble and drove around Tommy Lee, stopped, and lofted a jump shot. The ball bounced off the front of the rim, and I pulled down the rebound.

I hit Tommy Lee with an outlet pass as he streaked up the court. But the Phantom got back to cover the break. The kid was quick. No doubt about it.

Jerome and I loped down to the other end of the court. I set up down low and Tommy Lee fed the ball inside to me. I faked to my left the way Mr. Sewell, our coach, taught me, but Jerome didn't buy it. I kicked the ball outside to Tommy Lee. He launched a two-handed set shot. Clink. The ball rattled through the chains and Tommy Lee waved his fist in the air. "Two–oh!" He yelled as he sprinted back down the court.

A second later, Tommy Lee stole the ball from the Phantom, drove the length of the court and hit a lay-up. "Four–oh."

Jerome sank a nice hook shot. "Four–two."

At the beginning of the game I kept one eye on the woods, praying nobody would suddenly appear while we weren't looking and see what we were doing. But after the score reached about twenty–twenty I forgot about watching the woods and drifted completely into the hoops.

"Bring it on home, bring it to Jerome."

Dribble, dribble, shoot, clink.

Another hook shot. A one-handed fade away.

Dribble, clink.

Thirty-six–thirty-four.

Jump shots. Rebounds. Fast breaks.

Bring it on home.

Fifty-two–fiftys.

Sweat poured through my shirt, dripped off my nose, and ran in rivers into my eyes.

Jerome's T-shirt was plastered to his body. Tommy Lee's face glowed; his hair clung to his forehead in damp ringlets. Sixty-eight–sixty-two..

A rebound basket by Jerome. A swisher from the corner by Tommy Lee. Back and forth. Back and forth, up and down the asphalt. The Phantom intercepted a pass and streaked down the court but he took off a little too early and banked the ball hard off the backboard. I was right behind for the rebound.

The Phantom, angry with himself for missing the shot, yelled "motherfucker!"

I froze with ball still in my hands in rebound position. There was no doubt in my mind that lightening was about to strike the basketball court and kill us all. The Phantom had just said the worst cuss word in the world, bar none. I had never heard anyone say that word before. And he had said it on Sunday. I knew we were all about to die an unspeakable death at the hands of a vengeful god.

Jerome shot passed me, a black comet streaking down the court. He grabbed the Phantom by the front of his shirt and shook him like a Raggedy Ann doll. "You shut yo mouth! You hear me? You say that again, I whup your ass good."

Tommy Lee and I looked at each other. Jerome was seriously terrifying when he was mad.

"I told you you can't be talkin' that way over here." Jerome gave the Phantom a last shake and let the smaller boy go. He stalked back to the court. "Seventy-six–seventy-two. Yo ball."

The Phantom trotted back to the other end of the court with his head down.

More jumpers, more lay-ups, more rebounds, more fun. Up and down the court. Soon the anger evaporated and me and Tommy Lee and Jerome and the Phantom were lost in the flow of the game. Our hands were caked with the dirt of the court and the ball felt thick and heavy. My legs began to ache and throb but we played on. Ninety-six–ninety-six.

Evening pushed Sunday afternoon aside, and the shadows of the trees reached across the court. The air felt like it had escaped from some giant freezer.

Jerome sank a turnaround jumper. Tommy Lee brought the ball up the court and whipped a pass to me along the baseline. I faked a shot and drove around Jerome. He recovered, stepped back and leaped to block my lay-up. Sensing his move, I hesitated in the air, brought the ball under the goal and banked in a reverse lay-up with my left hand.

"Good shot, man," Jerome muttered as we jogged back up the court.

The Phantom sank a driving scoop shot. Ninety-eight–ninety-eight. The next basket would win.

Tommy Lee fired up a long set shot. The ball spun around the rim and popped out. I boxed out Jerome and grabbed the rebound. With Jerome on my hip, I wheeled to the outside for my favorite turn around, fade away shot. When the ball left my hand, I knew we had won.

But the ball hit the heel of the rim and popped out.

Jerome rebounded and we sprinted to the other end of the court on tired legs.

"Bring it on home, bring it to Jerome."

The Phantom tried to feed the post but I knocked the ball away.

Tommy Lee turned around and the ball hit him in the back and ricocheted straight to the Phantom.

My best friend had lost his man. Unguarded, the

Phantom banked in an easy lay-up. One hundred–ninety-eight.

It was almost dark.

Tommy Lee's hands covered his face. "I'm sorry," he whispered.

"It's okay," I said, trying to keep the disappointment out of my voice. "We'll get 'em next time. I promise."

Jerome and the Phantom started walking toward the woods, Jerome's arm draped over his buddy's shoulder. "Good game," he called back toward the court. "Ya'll are good. Real good."

That was it. The two Negro kids disappeared into the trees behind the playground. That was how My Big Secret worked. Sunday afternoon, show up, play to a hundred, take off. No promises about next Sunday. Just hope and pray my father would never find out.

The whole world was watching Little Rock try to keep colored kids and white kids apart, and if my father found out we were playing ball with colored guys every Sunday . . .

Tommy Lee and I headed home, our heads down, the bitter taste of losing stinging our tongues. I tucked the basketball under my arm. No more dribbling or passing. We were too tired. We cut through the woods and emerged on Luckywood Road. The streetlights lined our walk with flickering florescence and dim shadows.

"Halloween is just around the corner," Tommy Lee said after a while. "I can't wait. I've already swiped a can of shaving cream from my old man. We'll get some eggs and stuff and tear this town apart. It'll be the best Halloween ever."

I nodded my agreement and kicked a bunch of pebbles up the street, still thinking about the fade away shot I missed that would have won the game for us. I promised myself I wouldn't miss the next time. I'd work on the shot on the goal in the backyard until I had it perfect.

"I hate losing to them," Tommy Lee said. "It's a lot worse than losing to white guys over at Lancaster Park. You ain't supposed to lose to colored guys."

"They're good players," I said. "I don't care what color they are. Jerome and the Phantom can play."

Tommy Lee frowned. "You just can't keep doing something this bad without getting caught. I mean nobody can get away with something like this for long. Not with all that stuff going on over at Central."

"What d'ya think would happen to Jerome and the Phantom if they got caught?"

"They'd probably get lynched," Tommy Lee said.

Tommy Lee had called it. We were all like little kids playing with matches. We were either gonna get caught or else we were going to burn down the house.

I kicked more pebbles. "We can take 'em, Tommy Lee. I know we can. Next Sunday. We'll play hard from the start. Get a couple of fast break baskets. Work the ball. If I can set up just a little closer to the basket."

Slowly the bitterness of defeat faded into memories of bright moments on the court—good passes, good shots, good rebounds—and the sure and confident knowledge that the next game, which is always the best game, would belong to us.

CHAPTER EIGHT

School was a big pain on Monday.

Tommy Lee and I raced into the Quack's room and my stomach knotted just like it did every morning. One of these days I was going to walk through the door and puke. That's the way our teacher, Miss Quackenbush, affected me.

"Archie! You and Tommy Lee are late!" the Quack snapped as we scrambled into our seats.

"No, ma'am. Not yet. The tardy bell hasn't—" The bell rang.

The Quack shot me a dirty look and sat down at her desk in front of the room. We all sat in desk units, which were long desks of two stations shoved together to make blocks of four kids. The Quack said this setup was supposed to be a lot better than individual desks all facing the teacher. Mom said Miss Quackenbush was real up on modern education.

I was in a unit with Harry Foster and Nancy Atlee and Connie Campbell. Tommy Lee's unit was on the other side of the room.

"Did you hear what happened over at Central yesterday?" Nancy said as I sat down at my desk.

"No."

"Susan Lott's sister is a sophomore over there," Nancy said. "She told her mom that two of the Negro boys asked her out on a date. Can you believe that?" Nancy loved gossip like moles love darkness.

I didn't believe Nancy for a minute. Rumors like that were always flying around town.

"I'd kill those clowns if they ask my sister for a date," Harry said. "Negroes and whites got no business being together. Not in school. Not on dates. Not anywhere."

I wished we could change the subject. Besides, the possibility that any colored guy would ask Harry's sister out was pretty slim. Same for any white guy. Harry's sister went to junior high over at Forest Heights and looked like a tackle for the Chicago Bears.

"Harry's right," Connie said. "My daddy said he'd take an ax handle to any Negro boys he saw hanging around with white kids."

"Give me an ax handle and I'd be right there with him," Harry said.

Race seemed to be the only thing anybody wanted to talk about since the troops hit Little Rock. The conversation made my stomach hurt. I mean what was so bad about colored kids and white kids playing together?

"Alright, boys and girls. Let's recite the pledge." Miss Quackenbush stood up and faced the American flag next to the window. We all stood at our desks and placed our hands over our hearts. "I pledge allegiance to the flag of the United States of . . ."

While we said the pledge, I snuck a look at Miss Quackenbush. She had short muddy-colored hair and wore real red lipstick. She was chunky and had a chubby nose with little round nostrils. She might not be that bad looking if you were a guy around her age. She had nice white teeth and big bosoms.

" . . . and to the republic for which it stands . . ."

Miss Quackenbush hated all the boys in our class. Sandra went to Edison last year, and she told me it was because when the Quack went to Hendrix College up in Conway, an ex-soldier had given her some kind of horrible disease that had made it hurt when she peed.

"With liberty and justice for all."

Everybody took their hand off their heart and sat down. Outside, slate gray clouds covered up the sun. I hoped it wouldn't rain out basketball practice.

"Shirley, would you read our Bible verse this morning?" The Quack always asked Shirley Bell to read the Bible because her father was a preacher at the little Methodist church up on the ridge.

Shirley prissed up to the front of the room, picked the big Bible up off Miss Quackenbush's desk and opened the book to the place where the Quack had left her little red bookmark. She took a deep breath and started to read in her wheezy voice. "And yet there were still adulterers among them and . . ."

I rested my chin in the palm of my hand and tried to listen. It was no use. Too much other stuff was going on inside my head.

I couldn't decide if I wanted to tell Tommy Lee about meeting Roy. Meeting Roy was really cool, but I wasn't sure Tommy Lee would think so. I felt like one of the Hardy Boys. I had solved a big mystery. All the guys in the neighborhood knew the kid in the can lived next door, but nobody knew anything about him. The Mystery of Kingwood. And for sure, nobody knew the kid in the can liked baseball and rock 'n' roll. Nobody except Archie the Ace Detective.

But Tommy Lee might not see it that way.

And, of course, my brain never let me get too far away from My Big Secret. How could it? Kids like Nancy and Harry talked about race all the time. Federal troops were all over the place. Integrating Central left the whole town in an uproar. You couldn't get away from the question of coloreds and whites mixing together. The whites all thought everybody would go to hell if white kids hung out with colored guys.

And if anybody found out we were actually playing . . .

"Archie!"

"Huh?"

"Pay attention!" The Quack's voice rained down on me like thunder from the mountain. "These are the words of the Good Book. Pay attention!"

"Yes, ma'am. Sorry."

Shirley peeked over the top of the Bible and gave me the stink eye. Then she went back to her reading. "And yea, though . . . blah, blah, blah."

Going to school with colored kids didn't seem so bad. I just didn't get it. I mean lightening hadn't struck me for what we were doing on Sundays up at the school ground.

But even so, if my dad found out I'd be heading for military school. Cadet Archie reporting for duty. Yuk.

"And the evils that they saw . . . ," Shirley droned on.

And if all that hadn't fried my brain, I was losing the Race of Life.

The Race of Life was the Quack's way of motivating all of her students to work hard.

At the beginning of the year, Miss Quackenbush taped this giant roll of white paper all the way around our classroom. The paper was marked off with a bunch of lanes and we all drew in stands with spectators and flags and pictures of real race cars we cut out of magazines. The whole thing was supposed to be like the Indianapolis 500.

The first day of school, every kid made his own race car out of construction paper and pinned it in one of the lanes at the "starting line." My car was red with a drawing of a skull and crossbones on the side. I called it the Pirate.

As the year went on, if you did real well on a math test or a book report or something, you got to move your car a couple of spaces. Five spaces were the most you could move. At the end of the week, the kids that didn't talk or chew gum or fart got to move their cars five more spaces.

When somebody's race car crossed the "Finish Line" first they would win The Prize, which was a whole book of tickets to the War Memorial amusement park, which was a great place to ride rides and play carney games and horse around. The Quack said our cars were symbols of the Race of Life, which was a big deal adult thing.

"When the Pharisees heard it they said . . ."

It was only the middle of October and Vivian Smith's green racer had already cleared the back wall. Susan Boling's blue car was right behind her. There was a small cluster of yellow and brown cars and then the pack—Tommy Lee and Harry Foster and Lewis Goodman and Fat Jerry Booker and Sid Martin. Way back, and I mean way back, the Pirate had stalled out near the starting line. I could spit further than the Pirate had traveled in the Race of Life.

Even when I did stuff I got counted off because Miss Quackenbush said something about my handwriting being messy or she found a coke stain on my homework. Big deal.

The Quack said stuff like "Vivian, this is excellent work. You may move your racer five spaces. Archie, I don't think this kind of messy work earns any spaces in the Race of Life. Do you?"

"An evil and adulterous generation seeks for a sign, but no sign shall be given." Shirley closed the Bible like she thought the book might blow up in her hand.

"Thank you, Shirley," Miss Quackenbush said. "Now everybody get out their arithmetic workbook and let's see who can move forward in the Race of Life."

The school day had started.

CHAPTER NINE

Saturday morning lasted forever. A chilly autumn rain hammered the windows in my room and the sky stayed cloudy all morning. As if time decided to lie down and die. Tommy Lee had to go visit his aunt down in Arkadelphia, so he couldn't come over. My mom planted herself in the overstuffed living room chair with a Frank Yerby paperback and her cigarettes and coffee. As usual my dad went to work.

The rain made a pinging sound on the windowpane like a thousand little needles rat-a-tat-tatting on the glass. Through my window I could see Arnold, Tommy Lee's cocker spaniel, messin' around with an old tennis shoe. The rain didn't seem to bother Arnold at all. He had about as much to do as I did.

I got out my basketball and dribbled up and down the hallway until my mom hollered at me to stop. I went back to my room, turned my back to the door of my closet, faked left, then spun inside, and banked the ball through an imaginary basketball goal that hung above the door frame. I saw this guy over at Central do that move last year in a game against Pine Bluff. I couldn't wait to try it in a real game. I shot a few imaginary hook shots, pretending I was Neil Johnson of the Philadelphia Warriors. Rebounds, jumpers, free throws. I was a dozen different players with a dozen different moves on a rainy Saturday morning.

When my mom yelled at me to "stop all that racket" I thought maybe I should go outside and chew on a tennis shoe.

Instead, I fished my baseball cards out of my nightstand drawer. Sitting cross-legged on my bed, I lined up the Cardinals in their batting order— Blasingame at second, Dark at short, Musial at first, Boyer at third . . . Roy kept popping up in my mind, so I dug out my Red Sox cards. I wondered if Roy would like to see my collection or if he was too old for baseball cards? Nah. If you loved the game you would never get too old for baseball cards.

I promised myself I'd take my cards over to Roy's house the next time I went.

I turned on my little plastic radio on the nightstand. I used to listen to Big John and Sparkie every Saturday morning. I love "The Teddy Bears' Picnic" song. But I guess I got too old or something. Now I listened to this crazy disc jockey. He played some good songs and made all these stupid noises and then he said "and now here are the ball scores—eight–two, four–three and nine to zero." He never mentioned the teams. Just the scores. That always cracked me up.

I finally stuffed my baseball cards back into the drawer and got down to business. I picked up one of the books my mom and I had checked out of the library yesterday, curled up on my bed and started reading. I was determined to learn all about polio.

Talk about tough going. These books weren't exactly The Hardy Boys or Chip Hilton. Some of the paragraphs in these books took up a whole page. A whole page of big words. But I kept plowing. Some of the stuff might as well have been in Chinese. But some of it made sense and I got the main idea. At least I think I did.

I took a break, stretched out on my back, and tossed a tennis ball in the air, caught the ball and tossed it again. And again and again. It's what I did when I thought.

Suddenly I heard a car door slam over at the McDonald's. Then I heard angry shouting. I jumped off the bed and crawled over to the window, where I got on my knees and rested my elbows on the windowsill. That way I could look right into the McDonald's carport, about ten yards past our clothesline.

The DeSoto had pulled into the McDonald's driveway behind the T-bird in the carport. Through the drizzling rain I saw a roundbelly in a wrinkled brown suit standing in the carport, talking to Joseph McDonald.

The roundbelly clutched a little black bag in his hand and you didn't have to be Nancy Drew to figure out he was a doctor. Mr. McDonald looked mad. He shook his finger in the doctor's face. His own face was a big, red ball of mad. The doctor kept shifting the bag back and forth from one hand to the other. You could tell he was scared of Mr. McDonald. Just like my dad.

I wondered if anyone in Kingwood wasn't afraid of Mr. McDonald.

Katherine came out the screen door and walked meekly into the carport, her shoulders slumped. She had a glass of orange juice in her hand, and she stood off to the side, listening to her husband chew out the doc. She tried to put her arm around Mr. McDonald, but he pushed her away. Then Mr. McDonald yelled at the doctor. I couldn't hear what he yelled because of the rain. Katherine said something to the doctor and he shook his head no.

A terrible thought crashed into my brain. What if Roy had died? I mean people did die. Even in the suburbs.

Katherine took the doctor by the arm and guided him toward the house. They disappeared through the screen door. Mr. McDonald stood in the carport, glaring at the rain; his face twisted in a snarl like he could stare down God and make the rain stop falling. When the rain started falling harder, he whirled around and went into the house.

I kept watching for a while until I realized nothing else was going to happen.

I went back to my tennis ball.

What if Roy had died? Or as my dad said, what if we had lost Roy? The way we lost Uncle Charles, dad's brother, a couple of years ago. My dad always made it sound like we could go out and find Uncle Charles down by the river or out in the woods.

Or maybe Roy had gone to his reward. What did that mean? Or bought the farm. Or croaked. For some unknown reason, nobody wanted to say somebody died. I guess it sounds too permanent.

I thought about Marcia Gibson, this girl from my first grade class. She got hit by a car and died. I still remember her with her pigtails and missing tooth and little Bugs Bunny lunch box, heading down the hall on her way to first grade. Now I guessed she was in heaven. I wondered if I saw her in heaven if she'd still look the same way she did in first grade? A girl in heaven with a Bugs Bunny lunch box.

But what if I didn't die 'til I was old? Like forty-five? Would I be this old man in heaven talking to this little girl? Would Marcia know me?

I started tossing the tennis ball faster and faster.

What if there wasn't any heaven? I mean how did they know heaven even existed? Had anybody ever been there and come back and told about it? Didn't think so.

Maybe somebody had just made it up a long time ago.

Like a zillion million years ago, somebody's old Uncle Bob bought the farm. Or got lost. Or crossed over or passed or whatever. And somebody asked, "Where did old Uncle Bob go?" And everybody shook their head and mumbled 'cause nobody had a clue.

Then this real smart guy said, "Wait a minute. I know where he went. Old Uncle Bob went to . . . went to . . . Heaven. Yeah, that's it! He went to Heaven. Right this minute he's playing golf or softball or just having a good time messing around in heaven. Yeah. That's where Dead Uncle Bob is. In this great place called Heaven where they eat lots of ice cream and go to ball games and fish and don't do anything but fun stuff."

Then everyone smiled and nodded. They figured the smart guy must know what he's talking about. I bet that's how it all started.

But what if you died and there was nothing. Nothing but nothing. Not even a dream or anything. What if being dead meant nothing . . . forever?

"Archie, phone call."

"Achhhh!" I whirled around and the tennis ball hit me in the head.

"Sorry, Arch. Didn't mean to scare you." My mother's head peered in through the open door.

"Mom! Out the window. Over at the McDonalds' house." My breath came in little gasps. "The doctor came and Mr. McDonald yelled at him and Kath . . . Mrs. McDonald was crying. Mom. Did . . . Roy . . . the kid in the can. Did he . . . die?

CHAPTER TEN

My mother folded her arms across her chest and leaned on the door frame. Then she gave me this weird look. She pushed herself away from the doorway, crossed the room, sat down on the edge of the bed, and pushed my hair off my forehead. "It's okay, Archie. Roy didn't die during the night," she said. "But he almost did."

"What happened?"

"I talked to Sandra's mother this morning and earlier she spoke with Mrs. McDonald." My mother peered down at me through her glasses, which made her eyes look large and wise. "Martha said that the boy's iron lung developed a leak and he blacked out. Thank heaven, Mr. McDonald figured out a way to stop the leak. He's very mechanical."

"So why was he yelling at the doctor?"

"Martha said Mr. McDonald is angry because the doctor was supposed to get a new iron lung for Roy last month, but for some reason the machine hasn't been delivered."

"Mr. McDonald has a terrible temper," I said.

"We'll talk some more about it later, Arch. I promise. Right now someone is waiting for you on the phone."

Knowing that Roy was all right gave me that same feeling you have on the last day of school before summer vacation. That hunch that everything was gonna be peachy for a long time. I hoped Roy's mom had bought him the records I told her about and hoped his dad would never find out. I didn't care if Mr. McDonald had been a big football star and a big war hero. He shouldn't go around hollering at everyone.

I hopped off the bed and ran to our phone, which sat on this little table out in the hallway. "Hello?"

"Hi." It was a throaty, whispery voice. "This is Marilyn. Marilyn Monroe. I'm looking for a new boyfriend and hoped you might be interested."

"Naw," I laughed. "I'm sweet on this little blonde down the street. Once she gets her braces off, she'll be a bigger star than you. You wait and see." I heard a familiar giggle on the other end of the line.

"So you DO think my braces make me look ugly."

"I didn't say that. I said when you got them off you'd be a bigger star than Marilyn Monroe. I meant it too."

"You'd tell me if you thought they made me look ugly. Promise me you'd tell me."

"I promise. I'll walk right up to you and say, 'Sandra, your braces make you look uglier than the south side of a dog's butt.' How's that?"

"Thanks for nothing. What are you doing right now?"

"Talking to you."

"I meant before that."

"Not much. How 'bout you?"

"Going twelve rounds with my dad." There was no more laughter in Sandra's voice. "The man must love rules more than anything else in the world. He's always making up new ones. Why don't you meet me out in the

Playhouse? I need some company. Okay?"

I never passed up a chance to see Sandra. "Sure. Be there in five minutes."

"See ya later, alligator." Sandra hung up the phone.

By the time I got my black Converses and my windbreaker on my mom was back into her book in the living room. I sprinted out the back door and raced off into the freezing downpour. I cut through Tommy Lee's backyard and slipped through the high shrubbery that divided the Harrison's yard from the Rush's yard. The Playhouse was on the other side of the hedge.

The Playhouse was a neat little house in the Harrison's backyard that looked like something straight out of the illustrated version of *Heidi*—white clapboard with a pointed green roof, green shutters, and green flower boxes on the windowsills. The tiny structure had one room and didn't have a bathroom or a kitchen but it had electricity and an old sofa and a hi-fi—the important stuff. Sandra's favorite word for the Playhouse was cozy, and I think the little house was the only place she ever really felt safe.

"Come in before you drown," Sandra said from the doorway of the Playhouse.

I stepped inside and stopped to catch my breath. Water cascaded off my windbreaker, making dark spots on the tan carpet. Sandra didn't seem to mind.

"Hi," I grinned.

"Hi, yourself." Sandra closed the door in a way that made me think she was shutting out more than just the rain.

I tossed my wet jacket on the back of a chair. As I turned around Sandra stood right next to me. "I can't believe you're taller than I am," she said. "I've always been taller than you. It's not fair."

Sandra was wispy thin with a long blondish ponytail and sad eyes that were the color of a Hershey bar. She wore a pair of black pedal pushers and a white dress shirt with the sleeves rolled up and the shirttail hanging out.

Sandra Harrison was a looker. No question about it.

"I hear you're a big basketball star these days," Sandra said as she moved over to the hi-fi.

"Where'd you hear that?"

"Jeff Morrison told me. Don't look so surprised. Jeff plays on the JVs over at Holy Rosary. He said you've been the star at the Saturday pickup games in Lancaster Park this fall. He said you might even make the JVs at junior high next year."

I tried not to look pleased.

"Oh, don't look so pleased," Sandra said. "You know you're good. You guys at Edison might even win the City Christmas tournament this year."

I nodded. I didn't want to say anything and jinx our chances.

Sandra thumbed through her stack of records, which was even bigger than mine. She put on "Searchin'" by the Coasters. She said something else but I missed whatever it was because I was trying to look down the front of her shirt. I'd been doing a lot of that lately.

"Sit down. Take a load off." Sandra sounded like Jackie Gleason's wife on *The Honeymooners*.

My heart was beating so loud I was afraid Sandra could hear it. Looking down her shirt had that effect on me. Actually I had been thinking about Sandra a lot the last few weeks. Sometimes thinking about Sandra was more fun than thinking about basketball. That couldn't be right. Could it?

"My father is so upset about the colored kids over at Central." Sandra flopped on the sofa, tucking her legs under her. "He can't get over the idea that the Negroes go to Central now. He's so scared the whole thing is going to ruin his business. As if the whole integration crisis is nothing but one big plot to ruin Harrison Real Estate."

"My dad's not too happy about it either," I said, sitting down on the faded yellow camp chair facing the sofa.

"My dad's taking it out on me," Sandra said. "He hates colored people even more than Tommy Lee does and everybody knows Tommy Lee and his whole family are a bunch of rednecks."

"I thought they were Pentecostals."

"Very funny." Sandra jumped up and changed the record. The sound of the Coasters' "Youngblood" filled the Playhouse.

"So what's been going on with you?" Sandra headed back to the sofa.

I was glad to get off Tommy Lee and his redneck family. Tommy Lee was my best friend. I felt disloyal talking behind his back. "I met the kid in the can," I said real casual. I knew Sandra would be wowed.

"No!" She stopped pacing and stared at me, her eyes as big as two full moons.

"Yeah. I even went in his house. No lie. Roy and I are friends now."

Outside, the sky got even darker and the rain pounded the roof of the playhouse.

"Weren't you scared you'd catch polio? Standing right next to him and all."

"Nah," I said with authority. "Roy's not contagious anymore. Besides, I've had the Salk vaccine."

Sandra looked impressed so I delivered the knockout punch. "Do you know why only children in clean countries get polio and not kids in dirty places like Africa and China?"

Sandra pressed her lips together. She liked to figure out stuff for herself. One of the reasons Sandra was my second best friend was because she always wanted to know how things worked or where they came from. She was curious. Just like me.

She thought for a minute. "Wow. That's tough. I give up. Bet you don't know either."

I crossed my legs the way I'd seen my dad do when he talked business on the phone. "Yeah, I do. I read all about polio in these books I got in the library." I paused for what my mom called dramatic effect.

"Well, don't just sit there, silly, tell me."

"Okay, here's why." I leaned back, balancing the chair on its back legs. My mom would have a cat if she saw me do that. Luckily we were safe from parents in the Playhouse. "When babies are born they have this thing called an immunity, which keeps them from catching diseases, but the immunity only lasts a little while."

Sandra nodded.

"If the baby gets exposed to the polio germ while it has the immunity, the immunity gets stronger. But if the baby never gets around the germs then the immunity just goes away, figuring it's not needed. Since American babies are born in nice, clean hospitals where they wash everything a kajillion times, the babies never get exposed to the polio germ."

"So later when the baby gets to be a kid and runs into the polio germs, the kids don't have any immunity and they get polio." Sandra beamed. She caught on to stuff quickly. "You're pretty smart for a basketball jock."

I liked to share stuff with Sandra. "I also learned that Jonas Salk, the guy who invented the Salk vaccine, was only twelve years old when he went to high school. There's a chance he may have been smarter than you and me."

Sandra crinkled up her nose. "Maybe. Maybe not." Sandra never made anything but straight As. "But I'll bet you have a better jump shot than Jonas Salk."

Probably so.

"I heard that President Roosevelt had polio and wore braces on his legs." Sandra didn't like to be outdone. "He couldn't walk by himself but nobody knew it."

"No kidding? While he was President? Wow."

I loved talking to Sandra about this kind of stuff. Tommy Lee was fun in a lot of ways but nobody ever learned anything talking to Tommy Lee.

Sandra got up and put on "Don't Be Cruel." When she came back I told her about Roy and the iron lung and how he almost died the night before. Sandra said she wanted to meet Roy sometime. I said it could be arranged.

She was super impressed.

We talked for a while about Holy Souls and one of Sandra's teachers, who had been on this TV quiz show called *The Big Payoff* and how the show had never sent any of the prizes the teacher had won on the air.

After a while, Sandra got up and reached way back into the hi-fi cabinet and pulled out a crumpled pack of Viceroys and a book of matches. "You want one?"

"Sure." I took the pack and the matches and lighted Sandra's cigarette and then mine, trying to be suave like Clark Gable in the movies. Sandra didn't inhale. She faked it. She put the cigarette in her mouth for a while and then waved it around like she knew what she was doing, blowing smoke all over the place. It looked kinda cute.

I listened to the rain pounding away on the roof. It refused to let up.

Sandra and I smoked in silence. We didn't talk. Sometimes just being with Sandra was enough.

CHAPTER ELEVEN

Monday at school, we broke up into little groups for our reading class. The Quack called our reading groups the Redbirds, the Bluebirds, and the Blackbirds. I didn't know why. Everybody knew it was the Smartkids, the Okaykids and the Dumbkids. I was in the Blackbirds. Me and Fat Jerry and Harry Foster and Sid Martin who was the dumbest kid in the class.

I did my spelling worksheet right, but the Quack said I wrote outside the lines. So the Pirate stayed put. At this rate I'd be twenty-five years old before my racer finished the Race of Life. My mom said Miss Quackenbush put me in the Blackbirds to teach me a lesson. I guess I hadn't learned it yet.

At recess we played kickball. Miss Hopkins, the PE teacher, loved kickball. She had short dark hair and a body like a fullback. She always wore a tan shirt and tan pants, which was pretty much what all PE teachers wore.

Miss Hopkins liked kickball because the girls could play. I never really minded it when the girls played. Connie Campbell could run faster than most of the boys, and Ann Koch could kick the ball into the next county if she wanted to.

We never played teams. Everybody got a turn to kick the ball and the rest of us rotated positions in the field. Miss Hopkins pitched to each batter to keep things fair. Nobody won and nobody lost. It was weird.

"I want to go over to Central and see what it's like," I said to Tommy Lee from my position at first base. He was lined up at second and we were just a few feet apart.

"Why would you want to do that?"

"I want to see history. The paratroopers and the mob and everything." This idea had been percolating in my brain for a while. I'd been reading *Huckleberry Finn* and I wanted to have an adventure of my own.

"You're crazy."

"No really. Think about it. It's history. Right here in Little Rock. Where nothing ever happens. We ought to check it out."

The day was clear and cool. Fall lurked just around the corner. Beyond the outfield, the leaves were turning red and orange and yellow.

"Only crazy people want to be over at Central." Tommy Lee hitched up his jeans. "Mike says it's a zoo over there."

"All your brother does is go to class. I want to see what's really going on." Archie the Ace Reporter.

Eloise Kelly kicked the ball right at Tommy Lee, who knocked it down and tossed it to me at first base.

"Way to go, Tommy Lee. Nice play." Miss Hopkins clapped her hands. She made everything sound like the last out of the World Series. She had half-moons of sweat under her arms.

Tommy Lee rolled his eyes. We rotated positions and Tommy Lee moved to shortstop and I took over at second base. Eloise went to right field and Lewis came in from left to play first base.

I pulled a piece of Double Bubble out of my jeans pocket, tossed it in my mouth, and started chewing. Nothing tastes better than bubble gum.

"All right. Let's look sharp out there," Miss Hopkins yelled to her fielders as Fat Jerry took his position behind the plate to kick the next pitch.

"How would we get over there?" Tommy Lee said.

"I dunno. On the bus maybe."

"Sometimes I worry about you, Arch. You get these goofy ideas and then I wind up in trouble."

I knew he meant our games with Jerome and the Phantom.

Fat Jerry charged the kickball like he planned to kill it but he mistimed his kick, whiffed the ball, and fell on his butt. Some of the kids laughed and Miss Hopkins shot them a dirty look. I didn't bother. It was Fat Jerry.

"Nobody would even know we were there," I said. "We'll just walk around and see what's up. It'll be exciting. We can tell our grandchildren we were there."

"If we get caught over at Central, we won't have any grandchildren. We'll still be grounded."

"Cluck, cluck, cluck." I flapped my arms like chicken wings.

"Come on Jerry. Keep your eye on the ball." Miss Hopkins rolled the kickball toward home plate so slowly I thought it might stop before it got to Jerry.

"You're crazy, Arch. Crazy." Tommy Lee shook his head.

Fat Jerry kicked a weak dribbler down to Lewis at first and waddled down the line. Lewis picked up the ball and hit Jerry in the back with it. He didn't throw it hard.

Tommy Lee moved to third and I took over at short.

Ann Koch came up for her turn at the plate.

"At least think about it," I said.

"Are you talking about skipping school to go over to Central?" Tommy Lee suddenly seemed more interested in my idea.

"Maybe."

Ann kicked a screaming line drive over second base just out of my reach. The ball fell in the outfield, and Ann rounded first base and never slowed down. She made it to second by the time the guys in the outfield got the ball back in. She stood on the bag and grinned at me. I grinned back.

Ann had on a white blouse and a navy skirt. She had short blonde hair held in place by emerald berets. She had a million freckles on her face. Sandra Harrison may have been the cutest girl on the planet, but Ann Koch finished a close second.

Tommy Lee went in for his turn kicking the ball, and I moved over to third. I knew my idea sounded nuts. But so much had been going on lately, I thought a new adventure might just be the ticket to get me out of the doldrums. Like Huck Finn floating down the Mississippi with Jim.

Tommy Lee kicked the ball deep into right field and drove Ann home for a score. The outfielders fumbled the ball, and Tommy Lee raced all the way to third. He stood on the bag, panting like a dog.

"So are you in?"

"It would be a great adventure," Tommy Lee said.

"Maybe the greatest adventure ever."

"I don't know how you do it, Arch. You can sell

anything. Okay. Count me in. I just hope we're not making a big mistake."

I gave Tommy Lee the okay sign and ran in for my turn at kicking the ball. The thought of our big adventure fired me up so much I kicked the thing over all the outfielders' heads, all the way into the woods.

Ann Koch couldn't stop clapping.

CHAPTER TWELVE

"You wanna meet the kid in the can?"

That drew silence from the other end of the line. I sat on the hallway floor, the phone receiver balanced between my shoulder and my ear, unwrapping a Clark bar. I had on a new pair of jeans and a pressed blue checked shirt, and keeping the chocolate off my clothes was a high priority.

"Are you serious?" Sandra finally said on the other end of the line.

"I kid you not. It's all set up. I saw Katherine . . . Mrs. McDonald out hanging up the wash. I had some new 45s and thought I'd share them with Roy. I went over and talked to her and she said Mr. McDonald went down to Texarkana, and after lunch would be a great time to stop by."

"But what about . . .?"

"I ask her if I could bring a friend to meet Roy. She ate that up. So we're all set. You wanna go?"

"My hair's a mess."

"Somehow I don't think Roy will care."

"I'll need to change clothes."

"No sweat. Meet me out in front of the house in ten minutes."

More silence. I bit off a chunk of the Clark.

Chocolaty goodness.

"You're an amazing guy, Archie Lane."

"I like to think so." I took another bite from my candy bar.

"Okay. Make it fifteen minutes and I'll meet you at the bottom of the driveway."

"Until that time, Marilyn." We both burst out laughing.

*   *   *   *

"Oh my. What a lovely young girl you are. Please come in."

Katherine wasn't just wolfing. Sandra looked like a million bucks. She had on a pair of navy blue pedal pushers and a pink sweater that fit snug around her little bosoms that weren't so little anymore. Contrary to what she told me earlier, her shiny clean hair cascaded over her shoulders.

"Thank you for inviting us," Sandra said. "I'm looking forward to meeting your son."

Katherine beamed. She stepped aside and we paraded through the McDonald's living room. Sandra stared at all the Jesuses but didn't say anything.

"I brought my new records," I said. "Buddy Holly and Chuck Berry and Elvis Presley. I think Roy will like them."

"I'm sure he will," Katherine said. "He's about worn out "The Great Pretender," the one you left last time. Come on back. Roy's excited to see both of you."

When Sandra saw the iron lung she drew in a sharp breath. Without thinking I took her hand and gave it a squeeze. She squeezed back.

Across the den, Roy made his clicking noise. "Hi Archie. Come on in."

"Hey Roy. How ya doing?" I brought a friend of mine over to meet you." I saw Roy smile in the mirror above his pillow. I pointed Sandra toward the mirror. She nodded and squeezed my hand again.

We positioned ourselves so Roy could see both of us in the mirror. "This is Sandra. She lives down the street and goes to Holy Souls. She's pretty cool. For a girl."

Sandra shot me a playful elbow in the ribs. "It's nice to meet you, Roy. Welcome to the neighborhood."

"Any friend of Archie's is a friend—" Roy broke into a coughing fit. "Sorry," he said when the coughing subsided.

"No problem," Sandra said. "Archie brought you some new records. He said you were a bopper."

"That sounds cool. Yeah. I guess I am. I love the music. Even the slow stuff."

"Me too. Have you heard the Fleetwoods' 'Come Softly to Me?'"

Roy made a clicking sound, indicating he hadn't.

"Archie's got it in his stack," Sandra said. "It's the most romantic song I've ever heard. I just love it." She looked around and spotted the McDonald's hi-fi in the corner. "May I put it on for you?"

"Please."

In a minute the soft harmonies of the Fleetwoods flooded the McDonald's den. "Doobie-do, dum-dum, dum-do-dum-doobie-do. Dum-dum."

Roy smiled. His eyelids fluttered in time to the music.

"I've got a lot more good songs," I said.

Roy grinned and made his clicking sound.

Katherine appeared out of nowhere and served Cokes in bottles with little yellow straws and a plate of Oreo cookies.

Sandra held Roy's Coke to the side and guided the straw to his mouth as if she did it every day.

"How come you don't go to public school like Archie," Roy asked.

"I did until this year," Sandra said. "But my parents were afraid there would be a lot of turmoil over integration."

"Looks like they were right," Roy said. "I watch the news on TV every night. I bet those nine colored kids are really scared. Mobs trying to keep them out of the school. Soldiers all over the place with guns. I don't know if I'd be brave enough to do what they're doing."

I took a giant sip of my Coke. It had never occurred to me that the nine Negro kids might be scared. I had never stopped to think how they might feel about being the guinea pigs for integration. Of course they were scared. They were risking their lives.

"I imagine you know something about being brave," Sandra said, giving Roy another sip from the Coke bottle.

A little smile crept into the corners of Roy's mouth. I could tell he liked Sandra. Who wouldn't?

When the Fleetwoods finished "Come Softly to Me," I put on Buddy Holly's "Rave On."

Sandra and Roy and I talked a little more about the crisis at Central. Sometimes when people talked about that stuff I felt like a criminal because I played ball with Jerome and the Phantom. Fortunately we changed the subject and talked about rock 'n' roll for a while,

Sandra was arguing that Elvis Presley was the best ever. Roy and I liked Buddy Holly and Jerry Lee Lewis a little better.

"Hey," Roy said. "Halloween's coming up. Do you guys still dress up and trick or treat?"

"Sure," I laughed. "That's always fun."

"I love it," Roy said. "When I was little I liked to dress up like a pirate. I had a real thing for pirates. I always thought I'd end up sailing the seven seas and stealing the booty from other ships. Har-Har, mateys." Roy's smile could break your heart.

Sandra gave him another sip of coke. He clicked his thanks.

I glanced over toward the kitchen where Katherine sat on one of the bar stools, watching us and sipping orange juice. She always looked so sad, but at that moment she looked really happy. She smiled and tapped her foot to the music.

Finally Roy started using his clicking sound more and more and sweat broke out on his forehead. He had had enough for one afternoon. Sandra and I said good-bye and promised to come back soon. I left some of my records and told Katherine I'd pick them up later. She walked us to the door.

As we stood in the doorway she threw her arms around both of us. "You kids are something special," she said. "And you, dear," she said to Sandra "are going to have the young men lined up around the block to ask you out."

Sandra blushed.

"And you," Katherine gave my shoulder a squeeze, "should be first in line if you have any sense."

I blushed too.

*   *   *   *

Back in the Playhouse, Sandra lost it.

She dug out a crumpled pack of Old Golds and matches, and we were both smoking, winding down from our visit with Roy.

"Oh, God. He looked so sad." Sandra waved her cigarette around, leaving a trail of blue smoke. "I had no idea the iron lung would be like that. Can you imagine living in that thing? I could see the pain in his eyes." She started pacing around the Playhouse.

"You said you wanted to meet him."

"No. No. I'm glad I met him. He's the sweetest, bravest boy in the whole world."

"I knew you'd like him." I took a drag on my cigarette. The tobacco had gone stale, stuffed in the back of the hi-fi.

"Look at us. We're so lucky." Sandra crushed out her cigarette in the empty tuna can she used for an ashtray. "You're a basketball star and I take ballet and piano, and poor Roy will never get to do any of that stuff."

When Sandra got wound up like that all I could do was nod.

"I just wish we could do something to help him. Make him well so he could run and dance and do all the other stuff we do."

"Not much chance of that," I said. "But we can be his friends. I think that helps."

Sandra let out a long sigh. "Thanks, Archie. Thanks for taking me over there. I owe you one."

I smashed out my cigarette butt in the tuna can. "I

think Roy had fun and I know I did."

Sandra let out another sigh. "You still going shoe shopping with your mom this afternoon? She told my mom you've already outgrown your school shoes."

"Basketball shoes too. I'm gonna be a big boy someday," I laughed.

"You're already a big boy." Sandra threw her arms around my neck and crushed her face into my chest. She let out some little crying sounds. I didn't have a clue what to do, so I patted her on the shoulder. Her body felt really nice all nestled in next to mine.

"Thanks again for taking me to meet Roy," Sandra said without moving her face from my chest. "You're the sweetest guy in the world."

I patted her shoulder some more. Then i held her even closer. We just stood like that for a while. Holding sandra had to be the best thing that had happened to me in a long time.

CHAPTER THIRTEEN

My mother had been replaced by Dorothy on her journey to Oz.

Her hair was in pigtails, oversized penciled freckles marched across her cheeks and nose, and her short dress and stockings were right out of *The Wizard of Oz*. Standing around in our tiny kitchen I expected the Lion and the Tin Man to show up any minute.

My mother loved any excuse to dress up and be somebody else. She loved evening clothes and costume parties and wearing church clothes to the Piggly Wiggly. She always said she liked to dress up because sometimes she got tired of being Terri Lane of Pinewood Road in Kingwood. So, for her, Halloween was the greatest night of them all.

"Dorothy" and I ate dinner early since my dad was still down at the office. After supper we washed the dishes and carved a jack-o-lantern with scraggly teeth, stuck a candle inside the hollowed out pumpkin, and put the thing on the windowsill in the hallway. From the outside I was sure our house looked like the Castle of Dracula.

Then my mother helped me make my costume for the night. She let me have an old suit coat of my dad's and a battered old brown fedora. Then she put this powdery stuff all over my jaw and chin, which made me look like I needed a shave. When she finished, Mom stepped back and clapped her hands, delighted with her handiwork. She said I was a dead ringer for the old bums that camped over by the river and stole rides on railroad cars.

The doorbell started ringing about five thirty. All the little kids from the neighborhood trick or treating before dark—cowboys and ballerinas and ghosts and skeletons and spacemen—all about two feet high. The tiny creature's parents hung around in the street, talking to each other and smoking cigarettes and telling each other how cute their little goblins were.

After the kids yelled "trick or treat!" I dropped a Chunky from the basket in the hallway into their paper sacks. Some of the little guys were scared when a tramp answered the door. I loved it. They'd giggle, take the candy, and scamper on down the block.

Our phone rang as I opened the door. When I finished passing out the candy and returned to the hallway my mom was still on the line. Things were not well in Oz.

"Oh, Warren, for God's sake. It's Halloween. Come home. Help me pass out the candy to the little trick-or-treaters. They look so cute. We can make some candied apples. It'll be fun. Please come home."

I refilled the basket with more Chunkies and Tootsie Rolls.

"Oh, bull, Warren. Bull!! Bull! Bull!! You used to know how to have fun." Mom shouted. "Of course I want you to get ahead. I just don't think spending one Halloween at home is going to wreck your precious career. Oh, all right! Come home as soon as you finish the stupid accounts." Mom slammed down the receiver like she wanted to smash the phone.

I ran back down the hall to answer the doorbell. Mom huffed off to the kitchen.

The Creature from the Black Lagoon lurked in the doorway.

Actually it was Tommy Lee in this incredible green rubber mask. The thing covered his whole head and, except for the fact that he had on Mike's old junior high letter jacket, he was the mirror image of the Creature.

I led him into the kitchen where he snarled and growled and put his claws out just like the monster in the movie. My mom was sitting in the breakfast nook, smoking. In more ways than one.

She started laughing at the Creature and acted scared. Mom should have been in the movies. Tommy Lee started laughing too and pulled off the mask because he said it made his head sweat.

"It's neat out," Tommy Lee said, helping himself to a Chunky from the basket in my hand. "You can see all the stars and it's not cold and all the little ghosts and goblins are running around all over the place. It's kinda spooky and kinda fun at the same time."

My mom blew smoke through her nose. It looked funny to see Dorothy puffing on a Kent on her way to Oz. "You look wonderful, Tommy Lee," Mom said. "You fellows enjoy yourselves. Stay around the neighborhood."

Tommy Lee and I headed for the front door.

"Archie?"

"Yes ma'am?"

"Home by nine, okay?"

"Nine? Aw, Mom, come on. It's Halloween. That's just when everything gets good. Just a little later.

Please?"

"All right. Nine fifteen."

I looked pained.

"Okay. Nine thirty. And not one second later. That's my last word. You have school tomorrow." My mother could be tough as a snake when it came to being home on time. "And stay away from any vandalism. I mean it. I know vandalism has always been a big part of Halloween in Little Rock, but this whole town is on edge because of the integration crisis over at Central. So be extra, extra careful. Understood?"

"Gotcha. We'll just trick or treat a little. We'll stay in the neighborhood. Promise." I thought about trying for a ten o'clock curfew but the look on Dorothy's face let me know that I'd better be back in Oz by nine thirty or else.

Outside, Tommy Lee picked up two cans of shaving cream and a carton of eggs he had stashed in the shrubs in front of our porch. "Ol' Terri's pretty cool," he said. "She's not snotty like my mom. You're lucky." He handed me one of the cans.

"Yeah. Terri's okay," I said, getting a charge out of calling my mom by her first name. Tommy Lee and I both giggled at the sound of it. We started walking across the yard and into the street. Parents and little goblins swarmed over the neighborhood. We walked past Sandra's house, where a full-sized scarecrow in a cowboy hat sat in a chair on the front porch. It was almost dark.

"How come you didn't tell me you met the kid in the can?" Tommy Lee asked as we left the cul-de-sac. He didn't sound mad or anything. Just curious.

"Where'd you hear that?" I felt silly talking about

Roy with the Creature from the Black Lagoon.

"It's on the grapevine. I can't believe you actually went into creepy old Mr. McDonald's house and didn't tell your best friend about it. What's the story?"

"It was no big deal." I shrugged. I wasn't sure why I hadn't told Tommy Lee. I guess sometimes I wanted to have stuff between me and Sandra. "I only stayed a couple of minutes. The kid in the can, his name is Roy, is in this gross iron lung thing. He's a real okay guy though."

"So you gonna be hanging around with gimps now?" Suddenly a little edge crept into Tommy Lee's voice.

"No way, man. It was just a one-time deal. Honest."

We walked down Cherrywood not fast, not slow. Just taking in the sights.

"I heard you took Sandra over to the gimp's house." Now Tommy Lee sounded steamed.

I had hoped he wouldn't find out. "Yeah, I did."

"You took Sandra but not your best friend?"

"It wasn't like that. I didn't think you'd want to go."

Tommy Lee thought about that. "I wouldn't. I don't hang around with gimps."

"There you go. See, no big deal. Sandra and I dropped some records off. We only stayed a couple of minutes."

"That's good, 'cause I don't want to be best friends with some gimp lover. Know what I mean?"

My heart sank. I had thought about telling my best buddy about taking Sandra, but Tommy Lee's mind was sealed tighter than a deep-sea diver's air hose. "No sweat." And I should have gone to bat for Roy, but I didn't want to ruin our night on the town. " Everything's jake. Hey, it's Halloween. Let's go squirt shaving cream on Sid Martin's mailbox. What d'ya say?"

Tommy Lee paused. He didn't want to have an argument with me on Halloween. "I say let's have the best Halloween ever!" Then he burst out laughing. But there was something different and strange about his laugh.

I felt like I had dodged a friendship bullet. We ran the rest of the way down Pinewood, enjoying the heady sense of freedom that only Halloween night could bring. That night when nobody is who they really are and nobody knows what's going to happen next.

I squirted some shaving cream in the Martin's mailbox on the corner, and Tommy Lee left a long white streak of shaving cream on the Thompson's black Ford that was parked in front of their house. With Tommy Lee's crankiness behind us and my encounters with Roy McDonald forgotten for the time being, we both laughed and charged after more fun.

"Listen, you're not gonna believe this," Tommy Lee said as we hiked down Valleywood Road toward the big ditch. "You know Larry Castle? Donna Castle's big brother?"

"Yeah. He's in the ninth grade over at Catholic. Plays ball at Lancaster Park some."

"Right. He's fifteen. And get this. He's got his grandfather's pickup truck tonight. His grandfather is visiting and he and the Castles went out somewhere and the grandfather left the keys to the truck and his folks and grandparents won't be home until late and Larry's gonna take the truck downtown." Tommy Lee was so excited he spewed out his words in a single long breath and danced around like there were firecrackers in his pants.

"No lie?"

"No lie, Sherlock. And get this. Larry said you and me could ride in the back of the pickup if we wanted. Can you believe it? You and me downtown on Halloween. Is that not the coolest thing ever?"

I nodded yes, but it was not the coolest thing ever.

Downtown Little Rock on Halloween night had the reputation of being wild and scary, and people did all kinds of crazy, insane stuff. Going downtown on Halloween night was something you were supposed to wait to do until you were in high school. With all the awful stuff that had been going on over at Central, venturing into downtown Little Rock on Halloween night was definitely not the coolest thing ever.

Not by a long shot.

CHAPTER FOURTEEN

"Castle told me he wanted to get the truck back by nine," Tommy Lee said. "So you'll be okay with your mom. We gotta hurry though. We don't want to miss out."

"Right. We don't want to miss out." Nobody wants to be a chicken on Halloween night.

We raced down the alley, which cut through to Koolwood Road. Dried cornstalks were stacked around the lampposts, which made the street look different and scary. We were both puffing and panting by the time we reached the top of the hill.

Tommy Lee pulled up so fast I ran into him. "Look," he said. "There it is." The pickup truck was parked under the streetlight right where Tommy Lee said it would be, a hulking chariot of fun.

Larry Castle's grandfather must have been a farmer because the pickup was old and rusted and crusted with dirt and smelled like horse manure. A handful of guys were hopping in and out of the truck, yelling and laughing and whooping it up like school had been snowed out.

What little excitement I felt for the whole thing headed south when I saw Bobby Sanderson among the guys in the truck. Bobby was the closest thing

Kingwood had to a real hood. He was in the eighth grade and wore his hair in a greasy ducktail with a spit curl in the front. He was chunky and had pimples all over his chin and wore a black leather jacket. Even in the summer. Several kids at Edison told me that he smoked cigars and carried a switchblade.

Bobby's two best friends, Calvin Mashburn and Ricky Thorn were in the back of the truck ready to go. Their parents wouldn't let them wear ducktails, but they tried to act tough and cussed a lot and followed Bobby around everywhere. Rumor held that their fathers were in the Ku Klux Klan and Bobby and his buddies were known around the neighborhood as the "Little Klan."

If the sight of Bobby and Calvin and Ricky wasn't depressing enough, Tommy Lee and I were the only kids wearing costumes. I felt like a big baby. Fortunately none of the other guys—not even Bobby and his crew—said anything about our costumes. They were too fired up about going downtown in the truck.

A couple of minutes after Tommy Lee and I got there, Larry Castle jumped in behind the steering wheel of the truck. "Let's rock!" he yelled. "Let's tear this town apart!"

Everyone yelled and cheered.

Tommy Lee ran across the street and hid his creature head in the bushes next to this little house. That left me as the only kid in a costume.

I found a spot behind the cab where I could look through the window. Larry Castle was a lot shorter than I remembered. He could barely see over the steering wheel.

The bed of the truck was packed with guys, and I noticed most of them had egg cartons and cans of

Barbasol. They were all laughing and talking and yelling and hardly paid any attention to the fact that Larry was having a tough time with the stick shift of the pickup. The old truck bucked forward, stopped, then bucked again. The pickup finally lurched away from the curb, tossing us around like fruit salad, but nobody cared because we were falling all over each other, laughing and squirting the other guys with shaving cream.

After a few blocks, Larry got the hang of the stick shift and we started for downtown. The truck passed by Edison and the spooky Lancaster Property, bucked through the Kingwood subdivision, and clunked by Edgehill, the old neighborhood where all the rich people lived. Then we started down the steep, curvy hill that led to downtown Little Rock.

Riding in the bed of the pickup was like being on one of the thrill rides at the state fair. Larry whipped around the curves, making us hold on to whatever we could grab or get banged against the sides of the truck. The wind, full of early winter cold, lashed our faces.

At the bottom of the hill, Larry pulled up behind some cars at a stoplight and gunned his engine like a race car out at the Benton Speedway on the highway. The truck needed a new muffler.

Up on the sidewalk, this old colored guy was waiting for the bus. He had on a fedora that was in worse shape than the one I had on and he had on dirty, baggy pants that didn't match his suit coat.

Bobby Sanderson stood up and started yelling at him. "Jigaboo! Stupid coon!"

The colored man must have been hard of hearing because at first he didn't even look over at the truck. At last, he glanced up at us and grinned. Then he gave us a big, friendly wave with his whole arm.

Bobby went nuts. "Jigaboo! Jigaboo!" He started grabbing eggs out of his carton and throwing them at the man as hard and as fast as he could. "Jungle Bunny! Jigaboo!" Calvin and Ricky started yelling and throwing eggs as fast as they could get them out of the cartons.

Eggs rained on the poor guy.

Tommy Lee jumped up and took up a position next to Bobby. He started heaving eggs at the man and yelling "Dirty Coon! Go back to Coontown!" Bobby looked down at Tommy Lee and grinned. Tommy Lee grinned back.

Some of the eggs hit the man on the shoulder, and the shells shattered and the yellow stuff ran down the front of his suit. He kept smiling and waving even with all the egg goo running all over him. He kept grinning and waving like if he stopped something even worse would happen to him.

The light changed and the truck lurched forward. Tommy Lee and Bobby rushed to the back of the truck and kept throwing eggs at the man as we pulled away. When Tommy Lee finally came back to where I was sitting behind the cab, he was laughing his head off.

"What'd you do that for?" I asked.

"'Cause he's a coon and because it's Halloween. That's why." Tommy Lee sounded irritated. "We gave it to him good. Me and Bobby. Yeah!"

"Why?" I was surprised at how mad I sounded. "The old guy didn't do anything to you. How could you do something so mean Tommy Lee?" I lowered my voice until it was almost a whisper. "You know . . .

after playing ball with Jerome and the Phantom and all."

"Shhh! What's wrong with you?" Tommy Lee looked around to make sure none of the other guys had heard me. "Don't ever say anything about that out loud. You hear? Do you know the hell we could catch from these guys for doing that? Keep quiet."

"I still think what you did was mean."

"It's Halloween. You're supposed to do mean stuff. Geez, Archie. What's wrong with you?"

Good question. Only I didn't know the answer. But something had soured inside of me. I didn't like going downtown on Halloween. I didn't like what Tommy Lee and Bobby had done to the colored man. These were not guys I wanted to hang around with. I missed plain ol' trick or treating. Tommy Lee was right. There was something wrong with me.

I didn't say anything else as the truck made its way into Little Rock's main downtown business district. Larry turned onto Main Street and I stood up, holding on to the cab for support to take a look around. The wind whipped my face, but I hardly noticed. Beyond the pickup the strangest sight imaginable unfolded in front of me. The whole place was definitely a candidate for the Creepiness Hall of Fame.

Downtown Little Rock looked like the landscape of a lost city—a city inhabited by hundreds of night creatures that darted in and out of doorways and alleys. Skeleton creatures, cowboys in black masks, devils with red tails, and black clad witches in pointed hats, carrying broomsticks. Hundreds and hundreds of them, scurrying around the buildings and alleys and parking lots, running wild in the streets.

The creatures carried small cylinders. They stopped, aimed the cylinders and squirted foamy lines on the windshields of parked cars or on the front windows of stores or over the parking meters that stood like embalmed sentries in neat rows along the streets.

Small fires, started by the creatures, blazed from trash containers up and down the street, casting flickering shadows on the sides of the buildings and stores, lighting the mindless assaults of the masked inhabitants of the lost city.

The truck rambled past the Center Theater, where *Jailhouse Rock* was playing. Bobby and Ricky and Calvin and some of the other guys egged the life-sized cutout of Elvis Presley that stood in front of the theater. Elvis looked seriously stupid with gooey egg all over him.

When the pickup stopped at the next light some of the guys jumped out of the truck and sprayed Barbasol over the window of the Haverty's furniture store next to the Center. Then they egged a new white Cadillac parked on the corner. Everyone howled with laughter. Bobby Sanderson unzipped his fly and peed on the Elvis cutout.

In downtown Little Rock on Halloween night the rules didn't count. You could do whatever you wanted.

I glanced down into the back window of the cab. Larry Castle was chugging a can of Falstaff beer.

I felt lost and out of place.

We rode around a while, jerking and lurching, egging and emptying cans of shaving cream and throwing eggs all over downtown. Bobby and Calvin scrawled dirty words all over the front of the Worthen Bank building. More Barbasol, more gooey eggs. More laughing. Happy Halloween.

I didn't have a watch, but I began to get worried that I was going to be late getting back to Kingwood. I wasn't about to tell anyone I had to go home even though I knew my mother would be in orbit if I got home late.

I was near panic when Larry honked the horn to get everybody back to the truck, and after all the guys piled into the bed of the pickup, he peeled out and roared through downtown. I felt relieved the whole stupid adventure was almost over. Maybe I could still make it home on time. No harm, no foul.

Tommy Lee couldn't sit still. He kept squirming around and giggling and pounding his fists on the side of the truck. Halloween pranks were Tommy Lee's idea of heaven.

All I felt was disappointment.

As we started up the Cantrell hill somebody yelled, "What time is it?"

Larry stuck his head out of the cab window. "Ten after nine," he shouted into the wind generated by the truck.

If I hustled I might make it. Everything might turn out okay. I settled back and watched the houses fly by as the truck went faster and faster. Through the cab window I saw Larry open another Falstaff with a church key. He didn't know how to do it and beer spewed all over the cab of the truck.

A couple of blocks from Edison, Larry went into a left turn. Suddenly a bunch of little masked Halloween goblins leaped out from behind some hedges and eggs rained on the back of the pickup. Egg goo splattered all over the bed of the truck, all over us, all over the windshield. The goblins roared with laughter.

Bobby Sanderson scrambled to his feet. "You dumb little turds!" He shook his fist at the goblins. "We'll kill you! Stop the truck!"

Larry tried. Except he hit the accelerator instead of the brake and the truck surged forward, going way too fast to come out of the turn. The pickup banked into the hill that made up the grassy yard on the opposite side of the street. The left wheels lifted all the way off the pavement, slamming everyone in the back hard against the side of the truck in a pile.

Time froze and I could see what was about to happen. So could Tommy Lee. He reached toward me and whispered "Oh, no" in this little boy voice.

I threw my arm around my best friend's shoulder and held on tight, as Larry Castle's grandfather's pickup truck turned over.

CHAPTER FIFTEEN

It was the weirdest scene ever.

The pickup truck lay on its right side, the wheels on the left side sticking up in the air, still spinning. The guys who had been in the bed of the truck were sprawled all over the grassy yard or scattered over the street like broken dolls. Some of them were crying. Some of them weren't moving.

All these dwarfish skeletons and devils and vampires stood around gawking, their eyes wide beneath their masks. Larry Castle sprawled on the ground a few feet from the truck with this enormous gash across his forehead. Dark red blood covered his shirt and jacket. His upper front teeth were missing, and he was bawling and shaking all over.

Porch lights had come on all up and down the block, and a lot of people had come out of their houses and rushed over to the truck. Two men squatted down and used a blue bath towel to stop the blood from gushing out of Larry's head and mouth, but the towel wasn't working too well. The other people were trying to help the guys sprawled in the street.

Ricky Thorne and Bobby Sanderson were writhing around on the ground, the wind knocked out of them. Their mouths kept trying to suck in air, making them look like a pair of fish out of water. Their eyes were wide and panicky. Other guys were bleeding and bawling.

I had hit the ground and rolled into the hedges. I was lucky. It was no worse than falling off the top of a jungle gym. My elbow hurt and the back of my head throbbed, but the rest of me seemed okay.

I recognized Rusty Wisenhunt's mom and dad in the crowd. And Harry Foster's grandfather too. Rusty and Harry were a couple of our teammates on the Edison basketball team. Vivian Smith's mother was running around telling everybody what to do, but nobody paid any attention to her.

A few minutes after the truck flipped, a black-and-white police car screeched to a halt across the street. The car's red roof light was flashing, throwing reddish beams over the injured kids and the ghouls and goblins and the frantic parents, which made the scene even weirder.

Tommy Lee had landed in the shrubbery and was slowly crawling out. He looked okay. We untangled ourselves from the bushes and stood in the driveway, watching the eerie scene in front of the house.

Everybody was talking loud and some of the kids were telling the policemen what had happened and the goblins that threw the eggs were telling anybody who would listen that the wreck wasn't their fault. The red police car light kept flicking over the whole scene.

"I gotta go home," I whispered to Tommy Lee.

Tommy Lee sucked snot into his nose and nodded.

"My mom will kill me if she finds out I was in that truck," I said.

Tommy Lee sucked in more glop. His lower lip

shook like it might fall off of his face.

"I'm already late. Come with me. Nobody will notice. We're not bleeding or anything. We can just mosey over to the end of the yard and then quietly slip down the block. Nobody will notice. There's too much going on."

"Okay." Poor Tommy Lee's lip wouldn't stop quivering.

We acted real casual and circled the crowd and the overturned truck and the police car until we got to the end of the hedges. Then we strolled down the street, looking over our shoulders about every other step to see if anyone saw us. No way. Everybody was looking at the truck and at Larry Castle who was gushing blood and bawling.

Tommy Lee and I broke into a trot, and I held my breath and waited for somebody to holler at us to stop and come back. When nobody did, Tommy Lee and I started sprinting down the middle of the street. I mean we were motoring. We were both rattled from the accident and scared that our folks would be pissed because we were late. Terrified that they might find out we had been in the pickup and had gone downtown. That was a giant helping of fear. You can really run fast when you're scared.

We raced down the south side of the Lancaster Property, turned into the school ground and hurdled the creek behind the basketball court. It was hard to see, but the moon was bright and Tommy Lee and I had crossed the creek twice a day for the last five years so we knew where to jump and where to land. After we cleared the creek, we flew through the dark woods, our internal radar warning us when low branches were approaching.

When we came out of the forest at the corner of Koolwood and Cherrywood. I took a hard left, my arms and legs pumping.

"Where are you going?" Tommy Lee yelled, gasping for air.

"Home. This is the quickest way. Come on." I slowed down. My breath came so fast I had trouble talking.

"Are you nuts? You're heading straight for the McDonald's backyard." Tommy Lee bent over and put his hands on his knees. His whole body heaved from a lack of air.

"I've got to get home," I gasped. "Right now. My mom goes nuts if I miss my curfew. Come on. The stupid McDonalds are probably in bed. They'll never know."

Tommy Lee straightened up and licked his lips. "I . . . I can't, Archie."

"Why not?"

"Mr. McDonald. I really don't want to mess with him. He's scarier than Frankenstein or Dracula or the giant ants in *Them*. You told me what he was like when he chewed out your dad. He's killed people. I'd rather face my mom than Mr. McDonald. He warned us to stay out of his yard and . . . I'm not gonna jump the wall again. Not ever. I just can't do it."

"You're going all the way around to the bridge?" I could see the fear in Tommy Lee's eyes in the moonlight. I knew he wasn't going to vault the wall. "That'll take ten minutes even if you run as hard as you can. If we cut through the McDonald's yard we'll be home in five minutes. Tops. Come on."

Talk about lost causes. "Mr. McDonald is gonna

kill you. Don't do it, Arch."

"I got to. Do what you want, Tommy Lee. I gotta go. See ya." I spun around and bolted up the nearest driveway. When I reached the corner of the house I slowed down and looked back at my best friend. He was still standing in the middle of the street, silhouetted in the glow of the streetlight, looking at me like it was the last time we'd ever see each other.

Driven by the fear that I was in the worst trouble of my life, I jumped the gully and scrambled up the rise that ended at Mr. McDonald's wall. My house was only a few feet away. All I had to do was vault the wall, run as fast as I could across the McDonald's backyard, hurdle the wall on the other side of the yard, and I'd be home. Piece of cake. I could do the whole thing in ten seconds. Maybe less.

I didn't even slow down when I reached the wall. I leaped forward, put my hands on the top to make my vault and . . . nothing happened. My body froze. My brain screamed. "Go! Move!" But my arms and legs screamed "No way!"

What if Mr. McDonald was in his backyard? Or what if he had set bear traps? What if Tommy Lee was right?

My body wouldn't move.

What if Mr. McDonald did see me? So what? Big deal. I was a kid. Nobody would hurt a kid. Oh, sure he might yell. I could take yelling. Kids can take a lot of yelling. Besides, why would he be in his backyard this late at night? On Halloween.

So I vaulted the wall.

I hit the ground hard and pitched forward, catching myself with both hands. No problem. I jumped up and glanced around. The harvest moon was still bright, and I could see everything clear as day. No Mr. McDonald.

So far, so good.

All the lights in the house were off except in the den. The curtains inside the sliding glass door were closed, but the door itself was open. That was weird. Winter was right around the corner. Why would the door be open?

The wind ruffled the drapes, billowing them back into the den.

I heard the woman hollering in a foreign language coming from the hi-fi in the den behind the curtains. Opera. I think.

I also heard a groaning noise. It was the same sound Sid Martin made when he broke his ankle sliding into third base in Little League.

In between groans I heard Roy McDonald's clicking sound. It was so faint I could hardly hear it.

As I scrambled to my feet the moaning faded. Instead of racing across the yard the way I had planned to do, I tiptoed toward the wall next to my house. Whatever was going on in the McDonald's house was none of my business. I had to get home. Every second counted. The groaning and clicking had absolutely, positively nothing in the world to do with me. Nothing. Not my problem.

The clicking started going real fast like playing a record on the wrong speed. I tiptoed as fast as I could across the yard. But when I reached the wall next to our property, when our clothesline came into view over the top of the wall, my stupid pill kicked in. My brain completely took a vacation. I felt like I had to check on the McDonald's house. Check on Roy. Surely I couldn't be that stupid.

No one could be that stupid.

I *was* that stupid.

I turned around and tiptoed back to the patio next to the McDonald's house, where I hunkered down in a catcher's crouch across from the curtain.

A slit in the gauzy curtain let me see into the den when the breeze rippled the drapes. I couldn't see all of the room but I could see the sofa, where Mrs. McDonald—Katherine—was sleeping, sprawled on her back with her mouth wide open, snoring like a mastiff. Her hair stuck out in all directions like Tommy Lee's and drool rolled down the side of her chin like Niagara Falls.

The groaning and the clicking came from the other side of the room. I couldn't see what was going on because the wind died down and the curtain went limp. I waited for a few seconds, holding my breath and finally a tiny breeze parted the curtain again.

I caught a quick glimpse of the iron lung and Roy and Mr. McDonald before the drapes went slack again. I waited a few more seconds. Then the wind pushed back the drapes.

The iron lung was open! The whole side was up.

The opera stopped and the scratchy end of the record started. Mr. McDonald's back was toward me, but I could hear his voice, low and pleading.

Mr. McDonald was stroking Roy's forehead. "It's better this way. Believe me."

Roy shook his head no. He could barely move.

"It wasn't your fault," Mr. McDonald pushed Roy's hair off his forehead. "You've already suffered so much. It isn't fair. I'm sorry. I can't stand it anymore. Oh, God I'm sorry."

Click. Click. Click.

I watched Roy's whole body go rigid. He made this awful sound from deep in his throat and then he just kinda relaxed all over. I didn't need to be a genius to know that Roy McDonald was dead.

"I'm sorry," Mr. McDonald said softly. "I know you're better off now. We all are." He closed the door of the iron lung like the thing weighed ten tons. He turned to the side and I caught a glimpse of his face. The Scar looked like a snake that had attached itself to his cheek. He had on a tank-top undershirt and his muscles glistened with sweat.

Then, as if my night couldn't get any worse, a gust of wind parted the curtain really wide for an instant. Just for a second or two. Long enough for Mr. McDonald to look right at me before the curtain swept back and covered the glass door.

I jumped up from my catcher's crouch and sprinted across the backyard, my sneakers barely touching the grass. I vaulted the wall and landed in our side yard, where I crashed to the ground and rolled. I scrambled to my feet and staggered and stumbled under the clothesline, heading for the safety of our house.

But just before I reached the house, I heard this noise behind me. A rustling sound. I couldn't tell what it was and I was too scared to care. All I wanted to do was get in our house where I'd be safe.

Our house was totally dark except for the jack-o-lantern in the front window. Not even the hall light was on. The whole place was pitch-black. Weird. Super weird. I hurdled the steps and landed on the front porch, grabbed the doorknob and twisted it with all my might.

Somebody had locked the front door! We never locked the front door. Never ever. I mean we live in the suburbs. Why on earth would you lock your door in the suburbs? I pounded on the door. I held the doorbell down. I attacked the door with both fists. "Help! It's me! It's Archie! Mom! Please! Open the door! Right now! Please! Somebody open the door!"

Bam! Bam! Bam! I hit the door with my fists as hard as I could.

Nothing happened.

Something rustled through the shrubs at the side of the house.

I leaped off the porch and raced round the driveway into our carport. The car was gone. My dad still wasn't home.

The noises in the shrubs got louder.

The carport door to the house was locked too. What was going on? We never locked the doors. I twisted the handle back and forth but nothing happened. The shrubs rattled some more.

I fumbled around in the dark carport until I found the spare key we always kept on a nail by the toolshed. I scrambled back to the side door and started jabbing the key at the keyhole, but my hand was shaking so much I couldn't get the key in the lock.

I heard a sound by the driveway. That made my handshake even more. The key just wouldn't go into the lock.

Then Tommy Lee's stupid cocker spaniel, Arnold, bounded out of the shrubbery and took off toward the Rush's house down the block.

The key finally slipped into the hole and the lock snapped with a quick twist. For a second I thought I heard another sound in the bushes. I didn't wait around to check it out. I threw open the door, scrambled into the house and slammed the door behind me. I locked the door from the inside and leaned my back against the heavy wood. My heart was thumping about nine jillion beats a second and sweat poured off of me like it was ninety-eight–ninety-eight in a game to a hundred with Jerome and the Phantom at high noon in July.

I was going crazy.

I forced myself to get control. Sorta. I mean I was in my own house. The doors were locked. I was in the safest place in the universe—our house in the suburbs in Kingwood. There was nothing to worry about.

Then I heard it.

This strange, bizarre sound. At first I thought the noise came from the carport. I pressed my back tight against the door, held my breath and listened. I heard a low moaning noise. And it wasn't coming from the carport or the shrubs or anywhere outside.

The sound was coming from inside our house.

CHAPTER SIXTEEN

It sounded human but it was so choked with agony and suffering all I could think of was when Joe Knight's collie got run over by a car in front of our house and lay out in the middle of the street, kicking his legs in the air and making these awful groaning noises. That's pretty much what I heard coming from somewhere inside our house.

I tiptoed through the dark living room and crept down the hallway past the glowing jack-o-lantern on the windowsill, listening as hard as I could, trying to figure out what was going on. Finally I traced the sounds of pain to my parents' bedroom.

It was my mom's voice.

I felt so relieved I charged down the hallway, threw open the door, and burst into the room without knocking. "Mom! Next Door! Roy! Mr. McDonald killed him! He left the iron lung open on purpose! He kept the door open until Roy died! I saw the whole thing! Mom! We gotta do something!"

My mother lay curled up on her bed, her face pressed into her pillow. When she looked up she had this goofy, dazed look on her face. Her hair had broken free from the little girl pigtails and her freckles ran down her cheeks, washed away by a steady stream of tears. Dorothy looked like she had been in another tornado on the way back from Oz.

"Mom! Did you hear me?"

My mother looked up at me like I was some strange kid that had walked in off the street. Like she couldn't quite remember who I was.

"Archie? Are you alright?"

"I'm okay. Honest. I'm fine. Mom, listen. I'm serious. Next door. I saw the whole thing. I was crouched down out on the patio and the wind blew back the curtain and Roy was clicking like crazy to get his dad to close the door of the iron lung and—"

"Oh, sweetheart. Vivian Smith's mother called me and told me about the accident. She said you and Tommy Lee were in the back of a pickup truck when it overturned. She said you disappeared and nobody knew where you were. Oh, God. I've been worried sick."

She wasn't listening to me.

"Please, Mom. Listen. This is more important. This is more important than anything. I mean it. Next door. Roy is dead."

My mother sat up and let her legs dangle off the side of the bed. She blew her nose into a tissue. "Oh, Honey, you must be mistaken. You're all upset from being in the wreck. Oh, God, I hope you didn't hit your head. Is your head alright, Archie?"

"Yeah, sure. My head's fine. Mom, please . . ."

"Vivian's mother said they took little Larry Castle to the hospital with a gash in his head and probably a broken arm and a concussion." She paused and wiped her nose. A cloud seemed to move over her face. "Archie Lane, were you in that truck?"

I couldn't stand still. I felt trapped in Crazy World. "Yes. I was in the truck. But I'm okay. Really. But that's not the important thing. Mom, listen—"

"I don't know whether to hug you or slug you." My mother pushed her hair back off her forehead. "Larry Castle is fifteen years old. He doesn't even have a driver's permit. Vivian's mother said he had been drinking. What on earth were you doing in that pickup truck?"

Mom and I were like two strangers who spoke different languages and neither one of us had a clue what the other one was saying even though we both had something important to communicate.

"Mom, I saw what he did."

"Oh, Honey. You're all upset. You must have hit your head in the wreck. Oh, Christ, I know it must have been awful. Do I need to call the doctor? Are you dizzy or anything? Seeing spots? Maybe you have a concussion like Larry Castle." She jumped off the bed and pulled me to her in a big hug. "My baby was in a car wreck. Oh, my God."

She wasn't going to listen.

I had seen this awful, horrible thing and I couldn't get my mother to listen to me. She just didn't want to hear about it. The whole world seemed upside down.

"Everything's alright now." My mother stroked my head the way she had when I was a little kid. "This has been such a horrible evening. Your father called and said he had to work late and he and I had the most awful fight . . . and you've been in a car wreck and . . . I was so angry with you because you were late . . . and . . ." She broke into sobs. Her whole body shook as tears streamed down her cheeks.

I didn't know what to do. The best plan seemed to be to just wait until my mother calmed down and then try to tell her what happened. Again.

Or maybe wait and tell my dad when he got home.

"Now you listen to me, young man!" My mother surged back to normal. "You're going to be punished for disobeying me. For being late and not telling me where you were. You know better than to leave our neighborhood after I told you not to. Not to mention getting into that truck when you knew Larry Castle wasn't old enough to be driving anywhere."

She was gathering a pretty good head of steam and actually, I was glad to see it. This was my mom. I didn't know that person who collapsed on the bed in tears. My mom was a fighter.

"The very idea of you riding in a truck with a fifteen-year-old driving and all that drinking going on. Now that I know you're safe, you're in big trouble, mister."

That didn't make a lot of sense but I was too happy my mom was back to normal to care.

"Just you wait until your father gets home." She sucked in a deep breath and the storm passed over her face. "The creep!" She buried her head in her pillow and started crying again.

I didn't know what to do so I wandered over to the dressing table. A framed wedding picture filled up the corner—my dad in his army uniform and my mom in her white wedding dress. They were walking down the aisle as people threw rice at them. They both looked ecstatic.

I got a box of Kleenex off the dresser and put the tissue next to my mother. She looked up and nodded her thanks. Her eyes had this dull, glassy look. I waited for a while, but Mom just kept crying into her pillow so

I slipped into the hallway and went to my room. I couldn't think of any place else to go.

* * * *

I felt the most alone I had ever felt in my life, standing around in the dark not knowing what to do. Everything seemed the same—my bed and my dresser and my drawing board where I drew cartoons and did my homework. It all seemed different though. Nothing felt quite right.

I took off my tramp outfit and put on my blue pajamas. I didn't brush my teeth or wipe off the hobo beard on my chin. I climbed under the covers and curled up in a ball.

My body felt exhausted but my brain wasn't sleepy. All these thoughts kept roaring in and out of my head like a posse chasing some bad guys in a cowboy movie. I had seen Mr. McDonald kill his own son. I had seen him do it with my own eyes. Right there in the den of their suburban house in Kingwood. Mr. McDonald had ended Roy's life by leaving the door of the iron lung open. Then Mr. McDonald had seen me and chased me home. I played the scene over and over and it never changed so it must have been real.

My mother wouldn't listen to me. That was really weird. She was all shook up. But nothing ever shook up Terri Lane. She had waited until the worst thing in my whole life had happened to come unglued. Great. Just great.

I pulled my knees up in to my chest and hugged my pillow tight. It felt like if I let go I might go spiraling down into some big deep hole with no bottom.

Maybe my mom was right and I had hit my head when the stupid truck flipped over. Coulda happened. But what I saw was so real.

I must have dozed off because when I heard my dad come in the back door, my head snapped off the pillow. I started to get out of bed to go tell him what I saw but he and my mom got into this awful fight right after he walked into the house. They stood in the kitchen yelling and screaming at each other. I couldn't understand what they were saying, but the fight went on for a long time. One of them dropped a glass and I heard it shatter. A few minutes later everything got quiet.

I decided to wait until morning to tell my dad about Roy. I just couldn't face him after such a big fight with my mom. I stayed curled up in my bed, burrowed in like a little mole kinda sleeping, kinda not sleeping. I heard the floor furnace kick on and smelled the burning smell that told you heat was on the way. I burrowed down deeper in the covers.

I heard the car just before I fell asleep. I opened my eyes in time to see the headlights sweep over the ceiling of my room as the car pulled into the McDonald's driveway. The car engine went dead and the headlights went out. I heard two doors open then slam shut.

I got out of bed and tiptoed to the window. The hardwood floor felt like a block of ice so I knelt down on the knees of my pajamas and rested my chin on the windowsill. The moon shone brightly over the ridge, and the stars just sat way up in the sky all twinkling and still. The windowpane had frost in the corners and felt like a Popsicle when I touched it.

Peering through the window, I saw this crazy

looking car in the McDonald's driveway. From the light in the carport I could see that the car was shiny black like somebody had washed it an hour ago and looked like it couldn't make up its mind if it wanted to be a car or a van. Whoever had been in the vehicle had already gone into the McDonald's house.

I kept watching and after a while two strangers came out of the house. One guy was short and fat and the other was taller and balding. They wore neatly pressed black suits and reminded me of Abbot and Costello. They were carrying this giant hanging bag that looked like the ones men used to carry their suits and sport coats on the train. Only bigger. Whatever was in the bag was heavy because Abbott and Costello were both struggling and straining to wrestle the thing into the back of the car.

Mr. and Mrs. McDonald followed them out of the house. He was wearing a bulky white sweater, blue slacks, and tennis shoes. He talked to Abbott nonstop. Mrs. McDonald hung back by the door to the house. I shrank down until just my eyes and forehead showed over the windowsill.

As Abbott and Costello hoisted the bag up, Mr. McDonald put his hand on it and just held on. He didn't want to let go. Costello patted him on the back and said something. Mr. McDonald shook his head no. I could see their breath in the cold air. After a while Costello removed Mr. McDonald's hand. Mr. McDonald nodded and finally let go of the bag so the men could close the back door. Abbott and Costello piled into the front of the car.

In a minute the headlights came on and gray smoke poured out of the tailpipe as the car backed down the driveway. Mr. and Mrs. McDonald stood in the middle of the carport. Mr. McDonald put his arm around Katherine's shoulder and drew her next to him. They stood that way until the car vanished down Pinewood Road. Katherine cried softly. Mr. McDonald look down at the driveway and shook his head.

When he looked up the Scar seemed to glow in the moonlight like the mark of the devil. I shrank down even lower.

All of a sudden he whirled around and glared at our house, devouring it with his eyes. What was he looking at? Goose bumps broke out all over my body.

The more Mr. McDonald stared at our house the more I knew I was in deep, bad, serious, awful trouble—the kind of trouble you shouldn't get into until you were grown.

I was in the kind of trouble that could mess up your life forever.

CHAPTER SEVENTEEN

The morning after Halloween I tried my best to tell my dad what I had seen in the McDonald's house the night before. I acted calm and tried to let him know I had something important to say.

No sale.

As usual, Dad was running late to work and told me to talk to Mom about my problem, whatever it was. He gulped his whole cup of coffee and ran out the door. So much for Plan B. I didn't have a clue what to do next.

For the time being, doing nothing seemed to be the only option.

Two days of school raced by in a blur. Larry Castle wound up in the hospital and everybody said Larry's dad planned to ship him off to military school as soon as Larry got out.

Tommy Lee wouldn't look me in the eye. I think he felt embarrassed about being too chicken to vault the wall.

Mom grounded me for two days for disobeying her on Halloween—I had to come straight home and do chores and homework—but I didn't care. Not after what I'd seen on Halloween night.

One thing was for sure. Roy McDonald was really dead. I knew he was really dead because my mom and I went to his funeral the following Saturday morning. They held the service at the Healy and Roth Funeral Home downtown instead of at a church. The inside of the funeral home reminded me of a church—all dark and quiet and full of creepy organ music. The place also had wooden pews and a wine-colored carpeted aisle down the middle and a pulpit up in the front. So it might as well have been a church.

The coffin that held Roy's body sat right in front of the pulpit. The coffin was bronze and covered with purple and yellow and white flowers and . . . the top half was open. I couldn't make something like that up. Fortunately we were sitting near the back and I couldn't see into the casket. Not that I tried or anything.

My mom and I went to Roy's funeral with Sandra and her mom but not many other people showed up. That made me sad. I guess Roy didn't have any friends since he came from Boston and lived in an iron lung and couldn't go to school or get out and meet other kids. From the size of the turnout, it didn't look like Roy's folks had many friends either.

I mean they could have held Roy's funeral in our living room it was so small. Mom and I and Sandra and Mrs. Harrison sat by ourselves on the next to last row. Looking around, I recognized the doctor who came to the McDonald's house, sitting a few rows down to our left. He had the whole pew to himself. Right behind him, this old guy with a shaved head sat with this younger man who had shaggy hair and a beard. He looked like a Beatnik. They both had on dark blue suits and red ties, which made them look like a vaudeville team on TV—Harry and Baldy.

That was the whole crowd. Everybody who cared

that Roy McDonald had died or cared that he had lived. Seven people.

Well, there was another guy who played the organ, but I figured they paid him to be there so he didn't count. He played a bunch of slow, sad hymns that just made everybody feel worse. I kept wishing he would play "The Great Pretender" because Roy loved the song so much. The organ guy never did though.

Sandra got bored and leaned over and started whispering to me. She must have swiped some of her mom's perfume because she smelled like honeysuckle in the spring.

"Look at the old guy over there." Sandra indicated Baldy.

I nodded.

"That's Cantrell Lancaster. *The* Cantrell Lancaster. You know, the real rich guy who owns the Lancaster Property across from Edison.

"No way."

"Way. He still lives in the mansion in the middle of the woods on the property. He lives with his son, the bearded guy next to him. My mom told me all about it. The son went nuts in the Korean War. Now somebody has to look after him all the time. Mom said creepy ol' Mr. McDonald was big buddies with Cantrell Lancaster's son over in Korea. She thinks Mr. McDonald saved his life. Mom says that's why the McDonalds moved to Little Rock in the first place. Old Man Lancaster wanted Mr. McDonald close to his son, so he set up Mr. McDonald's photography studio up in the Heights. I'm not lying. Mom told me the whole story."

The thought of Mr. McDonald saving anyone's life

struck me as pretty far-fetched. I mean I had watched him kill his own son.

Not that anybody cared or would even listen to me.

After what seemed like all morning, the preacher got up behind the little pulpit. He was an old guy with gray hair and veins all over his nose. He talked in a deep voice about how Roy's death violated the natural order of things, how parents should never have to bury their children and stuff like that.

It didn't sound like he actually knew Roy at all. I mean he didn't mention the Boston Red Sox and how much Roy liked them or how Roy played football before he got sick or how he liked rock 'n' roll or anything that made you remember Roy.

He got paid too.

Off to the preacher's right, in a little separate room, I could hear Katherine crying. I knew it was her because she sounded just like she did the day I played my records at her house.

Even though I couldn't see him, I knew Joseph McDonald was back in the little room with Katherine. I could just feel him in the funeral home like a lurking evil.

The minister read a bunch of long verses from the Bible and I tuned out. Too many "thees" and "thous."

While the preacher droned on, I thought about the conversation I had with my mother before Sandra and Mrs. Harrison picked us up to take us to the funeral home. My dad had gone to work and my mom and I had been sitting in the living room all dressed up. I had on my blue suit. My hair was slicked down with Brylcreem and my mother had on her church dress with the white lace around the collar, her brown hat and a pair of white gloves.

"You're still mad at me, aren't you, Archie?" my mother said.

I scrunched down in the pillows of the sofa and shoved my hands into my pants pockets. "Yeah. Kinda."

"You want to talk about it?"

"You still don't believe me," I said. "Roy's dead and you still don't believe me even after I told you what happened. You won't even listen to me. Neither will Dad."

"Do I need to remind you of the last time you were the little boy who cried wolf?"

I gritted my teeth. She was talking about this thing that happened in Florida. It was the reason my parents wouldn't listen to me and it was the last thing I wanted to hear about.

My mother lit a cigarette and exhaled the smoke out of her nose. "Honey, what you say you saw on Halloween night didn't happen. You were upset and frightened because you were in a car wreck. It was Halloween night and you were spooked and your imagination got carried away. That's all. That's the story. That other thing—Mr. McDonald deliberately leaving the top of the iron lung open on purpose and killing poor Roy—Archie, that didn't happen."

"That's what I saw."

"Sweetheart, there was a leak in the iron lung. It had been on the fritz for weeks and Roy ran short of air and got choked and died. Mrs. McDonald told Martha Harrison all about it." My mother paused to pluck a piece of tobacco off her lower lip.

"Katherine doesn't know what happened," I said.

"She was asleep on the sofa the whole time. Nobody saw what happened but me. Honest."

"Katherine?" My mother arched one eyebrow.

"She said it was okay."

My mother smiled and patted my leg. "Archie, listen to me. This is important." Her voice got all solemn and serious. "Do not tell anyone what you told me you saw. I mean it. Not a soul. Not even your father. Not Tommy Lee or Sandra or anyone. This is a time of tremendous grief for the McDonalds. If you start spreading rumors that Mr. McDonald was in some way responsible for Roy's death, it could destroy their family, and Archie, I simply won't have it. Not a peep. Do we understand each other?"

"Yes, ma'am." There had been a sharp tone in my mom's voice that I had never heard before; a hardness that had let me know this was not negotiable. This was a promise I had to keep. Even if it was totally unfair.

But if I did what my mother told me, nobody would ever know what happened that night.

Nobody except me.

"You may view the body."

Back in the funeral home, the preacher finished his little talk and stepped down, directing everybody to the coffin. My stomach jumped into my throat.

"Do we hafta look?" I grabbed my mother's arm.

"Not if you don't want to," Mom said. "But some people do it as a way of saying good-bye to the person who has passed away. It's the last time you'll ever see them."

I did not want to see a dead body. Not Roy's. Not anybody's. I had never seen one. I mean it just didn't come up.

I watched Harry and Baldy and the doctor shuffle past the casket. They didn't really seem all that interested. I guess all grownups have seen a dead body. Not a dead body on TV or in the movies. A real one. So I figured I'd have to see one someday. Sometime. Somewhere. The more I thought about it, I did sorta wonder what a dead body looked like. What exactly did a person look like when they weren't there anymore?

It was our turn. Sandra shook her head no like someone had insisted she eat a turd or something. Her mother patted her hand and told her she didn't have to go look if she didn't want to.

I took a deep breath. I must have sucked half the oxygen in the funeral parlor into my lungs. Then I stood up and exhaled louder than I meant to and Harry and Baldy turned around and stared at me. My mom and I walked to the end of the row and down the aisle toward the coffin. My legs were shaking so badly I could barely walk.

When we got to the casket I planned to keep my eyes on the minister, who was standing off to the side, and then go back to my seat and make up something when Sandra asked me what the body looked like.

But curiosity overcame me and I looked right smack into the coffin.

It wasn't Roy.

At least it didn't look like him at first. When I looked closer though I recognized him. His eyes were closed like he was asleep, and his whole face looked like someone had covered it with the clear glue we used at Edison to stick the little stars on the ceiling for our Christmas pageant. Roy had on a black suit and a blue tie, and his face seemed rounder than I remembered.

Even though he was all waxy looking, Roy looked like he might open his eyes any minute and make his clicking sound. I mean he almost looked alive, but not really. I even had this weird feeling that somehow, at that very moment, Roy knew I was there. He knew I was right next to the coffin, looking in at him. He understood that I had come to say good-bye.

I could almost see his lips move and make his clicking sound.

Tell them! Tell them what you saw! You're the only one who knows. Please tell them. Tell them for me.

I felt dizzy and hot and sick to my stomach.

"Are you alright?" My mother guided me back to our seat. My whole head broke out in a big sweat.

Tell them! Tell them what you saw.

Sandra smiled at me and I tried to smile back, but it's hard to grin when you're a couple of seconds away from puking.

*   *   *   *

When the service ended we all went outside into the parking lot and I leaned against the Harrison's Ford and sucked the cold autumn air into my lungs. My stomach felt like I'd eaten a zillion too many Twinkies. But believe me, the last thing in the world I wanted was to upchuck with Sandra Harrison watching me.

"You look awful," Sandra said.

I was afraid of what would happen if I opened my mouth so I waved my hand in a gesture that meant I felt fine. The look on Sandra's face told me she didn't buy that for a minute.

My mother came up behind me and put her hand

on my shoulder. I jumped. "Martha and I are going to speak with the McDonalds," she said. "Why don't you two wait in the car? We won't be a minute."

Relief washed over me like a wave at the ocean. I wouldn't have to see Joseph McDonald face to face. Sandra didn't want to see the McDonalds either. She jumped into the car and I scrambled into the back seat with her.

We sat for a while, watching the shoppers across the street from the funeral home drift in and out of the stores. They carried shopping bags and walked briskly to avoid the cold. Saturday was a big shopping day on Main Street in downtown Little Rock. It seemed strange to watch all those people scurrying around to buy shoes and ties and stuff and know that none of them even knew that Roy had died and the funeral home people were about to bury him forever and ever.

Last summer, Mr. Harrison left a watermelon in the trunk of the Ford and the melon rotted when the sun beat down on the trunk and made it hotter than the hottest oven. The stinky sweet smell still haunted the back seat. I cracked my window. The rotten watermelon wasn't helping my resolve not to puke in front of Sandra.

"Do you think I'm a chicken because I didn't go look at the body?" Sandra kept her eyes on the shoppers.

"Nah. It doesn't matter if you do or you don't. Dealer's choice."

"I wasn't scared. It's just that I've never seen one."

"It's okay."

"Thanks." Sandra leaned back and crossed her arms over her chest. She was mad at herself.

"To show you I'm not a 'fraidy cat," Sandra said. "I'll go with you and Tommy Lee next Thursday. Even though I think you guys are nutty as fruitcakes to think of something that dangerous. But count me in. Okay?"

I had invited Sandra to go with me and Tommy Lee on my crazy adventure, the one I had sold Tommy Lee on when we were playing kickball. I had almost forgotten about it. I never imagined Sandra would actually go.

"You sure? Might be tough going for a girl."

"I can do anything Tommy Lee Rush can do," Sandra said, snapping her white gloves off her hand, finger by finger. "Count me in."

"Great."

Sitting there in the quiet of the Ford, I really wanted to tell Sandra what I saw on Halloween. If I didn't tell somebody soon I was gonna go nuts. But I'd promised my mom I wouldn't tell anyone, and somehow I knew that had been more than a promise.

"My dad has this book," I said, mostly because I was afraid I was about to blurt out what I had seen at the McDonalds' on Halloween night in spite of my promise. "I thought the title was *How to Buy Socks*, and I thought that was a stupid thing to write a whole book about. But last night I looked at the book again and it's actually called *How to Buy Stocks*. My dad buys stocks, whatever they are, to make extra money."

Sandra giggled. "My dad does too," she said. "Only I think his stocks always lose money. He's always cussing about how he lost some money in the market. I thought he meant the Piggly Wiggly."

We both cracked up.

"Maybe he should borrow your dad's book."

Sandra bit her tongue to stop from laughing.

"At least he'd have nice socks," I said.

We both lost it and our giggles turned into big belly laughs.

When our moms got back to the car, Mrs. Harrison was talking nonstop, the way she always did. She blabbered on about how Mr. McDonald had left the church because of Roy's polio and how weird it was they didn't have the funeral in a church and what a handsome man Mr. McDonald was, even with the Scar. Blah, blah, blah.

My mom didn't say anything. She had that don't-bother-me-I'm-thinking look on her face.

Mrs. Harrison drove out of the parking lot and turned on Main, her mouth going ninety miles an hour. I slouched down in the backseat and looked back at the funeral home.

Tell them what you saw! You're the only one who knows.

CHAPTER EIGHTEEN

"What's the matter, Arch? You been quiet as the cat all morning." Tommy Lee ripped open a pack of baseball cards and stuffed the stale stick of bubble gum in his mouth.

We had just left the Heights Variety store where we'd stocked up on jawbreakers, Neccos, and baseball cards. We'd turned right and started ambling down the sidewalk that constituted the main drag of the little shopping area known as The Heights. The sky was overcast and a faint smell of rain filled the air.

"I dunno." I opened my Neccos and ate one. Strawberry. My favorite. "I can't get Roy's death out of my mind." I wasn't about to tell Tommy Lee about what I'd seen Halloween night or how I'd felt Roy's presence at the funeral. Tommy Lee had always been my best friend, but I had a feeling if I told him that stuff, he'd just laugh at me.

"Yeah," Tommy Lee said. "That hurt. You and I don't know that many people that have . . . you know . . . bought the farm. My grandpa croaked last year down in Arkadelphia, but I didn't really know him all that well. I guess you didn't know Roy McDonald all that well either. You only talked to him once. And that time you and Sandra went over there."

I could tell Tommy Lee was still miffed I'd taken

Sandra to meet Roy. We walked on through The Heights past Corder's Model Market and Boshears cleaners. I didn't feel like talking about Roy with Tommy Lee.

"The guy's probably in Gimp Heaven by now."

"What?"

"Roy McDonald. He probably went to Gimp Heaven, where all the people in wheelchairs go. And all the Special Ed people. The ones with big heads that drool on themselves and all the club foots and guys with hooks for hands. And—"

"Shut up, Tommy Lee! That's garbage and you know it."

Tommy Lee opened another pack of baseball cards and stuffed more gum in his mouth. He reminded me of a cow chewing a monster cud. "I knew it," he said with a smirk.

"Knew what?"

"You're a gimp lover."

"Bite me."

"You can say anything you want to me, but when we hit junior high next year you better not let guys like Bobby Sanderson or the Barton twins know what a wuss you are. They can smell guys like you coming."

"Guys like me?" I stopped in the middle of the sidewalk and whirled around to face Tommy Lee. The sudden movement startled him and he took a step backward.

"Are you talking about people who feel sympathy for guys like Roy who can't help what happened to them?" I barked at Tommy Lee. "People who feel for guys that have to fight every minute of every day just to get by?"

Tommy Lee's eyes narrowed. His jaw assaulted his gum with a vengeance. "They're gimps," he said. "Cripples. Retards. They ain't like you and me. They ain't ever gonna be like you and me. They're the people God hates. That's why he did that stuff to them. Quit trying to be their champion or whatever it is you're trying to be. You're starting to sound like stupid Sandra."

My whole body shook. I started clenching and unclenching my fists. Best friend or not, Tommy Lee had pushed the limit. "Listen you jerk. I liked Roy and I don't care what you or Bobby Sanderson or his crowd thinks about that. Roy was the bravest guy I ever met. I'm not talking about taking a dare brave. I'm talking about real life brave. You don't know what you're talking about so shut up. You got it?"

Tommy Lee's eyes went to the pavement. "Yeah. Okay. I got it. No more."

We hiked past the Heights Theater where Tommy Lee and I went every Saturday morning to catch the double feature—Roy Rogers or Zorro or Hopalong Cassidy plus a Commando Cody serial.

Neither one of us said a word as we circled the block and headed back for Hall's drugstore on the corner. Best chocolate milkshakes in Arkansas.

Tommy Lee opened another pack of baseball cards. "Ah, damn," he said. "I got two Ken Boyers. Out of three packs. Can you believe that? Two Ken Boyers and I'm still looking for one Johnny Temple. Then I'll have the whole Reds' infield."

He had already forgotten all about Roy. Nothing was going to change Tommy Lee's world. But my world had changed. What I saw in the McDonald's house on Halloween night had changed everything. I had seen someone murdered. Roy didn't deserve what happened to him. And I was the only one who knew the truth of what happened. I had to let the world know that truth. I had to find justice for Roy. I had to make it right. But I didn't know how.

"Let's get a shake," Tommy Lee said as he approached the drugstore. That had become our once a week ritual—the variety store, a walk around the Heights, and a milkshake at Hall's. It had always been fun. Only now I didn't want any more of Tommy Lee.

"Not today," I said. "I gotta go home. Do some stuff for my mom."

Tommy Lee stiffened. "Suit yourself," he said, opening the door of the drugstore. "I'll see you around." He went inside without turning around.

I trudged on down Kavanagh Street, my head down, my hands thrust deep in the pockets of my jeans. Gimp heaven? Where did my best friend go?

CHAPTER NINETEEN

"In the name of God, whom we all revere, in the name of liberty we hold so dear, in the name of decency, which we all cherish, what is happening in America?"

That was our governor on TV last night.

They canceled *I Love Lucy* so Governor Faubus could go on television. Everybody knew his speech was serious. I mean they never cancel *I Love Lucy* for anything. Mom had been telling my dad and me for a week that the speech was coming. She said Faubus wanted to get elected governor again so he wanted to keep all the white people upset and angry about the nine black kids over at Central.

"The federal authorities are in complete control," the governor said, staring sad eyed at the TV audience. "The will of the people no longer matters. School attendance at bayonet point is not compatible with the American way of life." Faubus had this long droopy face that always looked like a dog begging for table scraps.

The bayonets the governor talked about belonged to the 101st Airborne Division, the Screaming Eagles, that put the Negro students in Central and made the mob of white people leave them alone. Now the troops stood guard at the school every day. It had been in all the papers and on TV and everything.

Mike, Tommy's Lee's brother, who went to Central, said the soldiers didn't come into math class or guard football practice or anything like that. He said their job was to patrol the grounds outside and stop people who wanted to hurt the colored kids.

Anyway, Mom said Governor Faubus was acting all innocent, but he really wanted people to challenge the soldiers who were guarding the school. She said things had kinda quieted down, but now the governor wanted to stir everything up again. That's why he was on TV instead of *I Love Lucy*. Mom says Faubus doesn't want white people to get used to the idea of colored kids and white kids going to school together.

All my dad ever said was that any white kid who hung out with Negroes ought to be hauled out to the woodshed and straightened out. Not much wiggle room there.

Despite my dad's attitude, I knew the time had come for our big adventure, the one Tommy Lee and I had planned on the kickball field. I knew the governor was going to go on TV Wednesday night, so I figured that Thursday something important was probably going to happen over at Central. Something so big and super it might be in the history books or even on TV.

So we decided to be there.

The adventure was a super idea for a lot of reasons, not the least of which was that I needed something big to get my mind off of what happened to Roy on Halloween night. What I had witnessed haunted me like a ghost. I had to find a way to get justice for Roy, but I didn't even know where to start.

I thought about telling my dad in spite of my promise to my mom, but he was putting together this big deal so the Royal Laundry, where he worked, could wash all the sheets for the new motels out on the highway, and when he got home from work he was always so tired all he did was lay down on the living room sofa and stare at the ceiling. So I bagged the idea of telling him.

I also hoped a big adventure would patch things up between me and Tommy Lee. I wouldn't take back anything I said up in the Heights, but I wanted us to go back to being best friends.

So a big adventure was just what the doctor ordered.

Tommy Lee and I never mentioned gimp heaven or what went down in the Heights. Instead we worked out our plan to see history over at Central as if we were going to attack Inchon in Korea or pull off the D-Day invasion. Walking home from school every day, we worked out all the details so nothing could go wrong.

Basically, me and Tommy Lee and Sandra decided to skip school the day after Governor Faubus' big TV speech and take the crosstown bus over to Central.

Tommy Lee and I left for Edison in the morning like always. But Sandra called Edison and talked like our moms and told the girl in the office that Tommy Lee and I were sick and couldn't come to school. Then Sandra sent a note that looked just like her mom wrote it over to her school with Abbie Nolton, this friend of hers who went to St. Mary's. The note said Sandra had the flu.

My mom and Mrs. Harrison left early to go over to North Little Rock to play bridge with my Aunt Jane.

The coast was clear.

Sandra had on a plaid skirt and a starched white

blouse with a blue sweater over her shoulders. She had washed her hair and pulled it back in a ponytail.

We all left our books and school stuff in Sandra's Playhouse, then the three of us walked all the way to the Piggly Wiggly at the end of Durwood, where we caught the crosstown bus. All the lawns in Kingwood were a wintery brown color, but the sky was clear and the day felt too warm for winter. I even started sweating under my windbreaker.

"The Cadillac Seville has the greatest fins ever," Tommy Lee said as the half-empty bus rumbled down Hayes Street. Most of the people on the bus were colored maids going to work for the rich families over in Edgehill. They barely looked as us and sure didn't seem to care that three white kids were out of school on Thursday, riding the bus in the middle of the morning.

"Yeah, but I'd take a T-bird anytime over a Caddy." I stood in the aisle, holding on to the straps that hung from the bar. Tommy Lee and Sandra sat in the seats facing me. I was thrilled about being tall enough to reach the straps. Last year I didn't come close.

"The best one of all though," Sandra said, "is gonna be the new '58 Chevy Bel Air."

"Girls don't know anything about cars," Tommy Lee snapped at Sandra.

"Shut up, Tommy Lee," Sandra barked back. "I know the Bel Air has a turbo thrust V-8 that will outrun any car you'll ever have." She beamed like she had just won the city spelling bee.

A turbo thrust V-8? I was impressed.

Tommy Lee gritted his teeth. "It's a coon car," he growled. "I wouldn't drive one if you gave it to me."

Sandra whirled around in her seat and faced Tommy Lee. "Stop using that word! It's a redneck word! You say it all the time and I don't want to hear it anymore. You sound like trailer trash."

"Woo." Tommy Lee shook his hand in front of him the way Ralph Kramden did on TV.

"Knock it off, you guys," I said. Sandra and Tommy Lee were my two best friends in the world, and it made me feel weird when they carped at each other.

The bus turned on 12th Street and headed east. Off to the left I could see the zoo and the municipal swimming pool and the ball park where the Travelers, Little Rock's minor league baseball team, played in the summer. Central High was only a few blocks away.

We passed a billboard that said "Who Will Build Arkansas if Her People Do Not?" Underneath the billboard, a pair of uniformed soldiers sat in a jeep. They had their rifles out. The maids in the back of the bus pointed at them and shook their heads. One of the maids smiled.

Tommy Lee, Sandra, and I got off the bus at Park Street and started walking through the neighborhood toward Central like we did this every day.

I'd been to Central a bunch of times to see Mike play football and basketball for the Tigers. They had a beautiful stadium right next to the school, and I couldn't wait to go to Central. Mike told me and Tommy Lee over and over how cool it was to be a Central High Tiger.

The houses in the neighborhood around Central looked like the setting for an Andy Hardy movie. They were old and small but most of them were well cared for, freshly painted with neatly trimmed lawns.

A couple of blocks from the school we passed a man raking leaves in his front yard. He wore patched green pants and a T-shirt and an old faded black-and-gold letter jacket from Central that had a little football on the LR and '48 on the gold sleeve. The man needed a shave.

"Hey! Where do you kids think you're going?" The man sounded angry.

Tommy Lee looked at me, indicating that I had been elected spokesman for our group.

"Nowhere," I said.

"You're not heading over to the high school, are you?"

"No sir," I lied.

"You better not. That's no place for young folks like you." He sounded a little more friendly. "There's a big crowd of angry people at the front of the school. I hear it's a real mob. The governor's speech on the television last night got 'em all riled up. They're looking for trouble and there's no telling what they're liable to do. Ya'll stay away, you hear?"

"Aren't the soldiers there to protect everybody?" Sandra piped up.

"Yeah, they are," the man said. "Toughest bunch I've ever seen." He shook his head. "And I saw some tough outfits over in Korea. The 101st can handle the crowd, no doubt about it. But still . . . there's no telling what might happen. You kids stay away, ya hear?"

The three of us nodded our solemn agreement.

The man scratched his head. "How come you kids ain't in school? What's going on here?" He tossed his rake into a pile of leaves and walked over to the edge of the yard. "What's your name, boy?" He looked right at

Tommy Lee.

"Run!" Tommy Lee yelled, as he whirled around and took off, sprinting down the sidewalk. Sandra and I followed right behind him and the three of us dashed down the block and turned into a narrow alley. Behind us we could hear the man in the letter jacket yelling. We raced through the alley and cut across a bunch of backyards full of doghouses and laundry on the clotheslines and stumbled out from behind a white clapboard house, pausing in the driveway to catch our breath. When I looked up I realized we were right across the street from Central High School.

What a scene.

The giant blond brick school building hovered in the background, while in the front dozens of armed soldiers in combat helmets stood at attention on the sidewalk, clutching their rifles across their chests. About half a block away hundreds and hundreds of people spilled over into the street. There were so many people, cars couldn't even get past if they tried.

There were all kinds of people: men wearing suits and neckties and fedoras; women in dresses and hats; younger men in jackets and chinos and sport shirts; workers in uniforms with their names over their shirt pockets; guys in overalls; old men. You name it.

And every last person in the crowd was somewhere way, way past furious. You could feel their anger in the air around the school, feel it crawling on your skin like some kind of radioactive dust. A lot of the people were yelling and cussing and pointing to the school building and talking to each other in loud voices. They couldn't stand still they were so mad. Their faces glowed red and big veins pulsated on their necks.

Some of them shook their fists at the soldiers. The soldiers held their rifles at their sides and looked straight ahead as if the mob wasn't even there.

The whole atmosphere crackled with anger and fear and hatred. We had made a bad, bad mistake. Sandra and Tommy Lee and I had no business being in front of Central, surrounded by an angry mob and a company of armed soldiers.

History suddenly felt like someone had lit a fuse to dynamite, and everything was about to blow sky high.

CHAPTER TWENTY

The leader of the soldiers paced back and forth along the front walk of the school, talking to the crowd through this big megaphone like the ones the cheerleaders use at football games. "The 101st Airborne is here to enforce the law," he shouted into the megaphone. "You are hereby instructed to disperse and return to your homes."

"Go to hell!" A man in a brown cap and blue windbreaker yelled at the soldiers.

"Disperse and return to your homes immediately."

Suddenly a helicopter appeared over the roof of the high school. I had never seen a real helicopter before and I found the sight scary and unreal. The copter looked like a giant flying bug out of a science fiction movie. I could see two soldiers inside the chopper, pointing to the crowd and talking into microphones that were strapped to their heads. The helicopter made a terrible, loud whirring noise that drowned out the roar of the mob.

"Geez, Arch. Look at that!" Tommy Lee shouted as he shielded his eyes from the glare of the sun and pointed to the helicopter. He had never seen one before either.

"Disperse immediately!"

The chopper circled the crowd.

"You can't make us!" The helicopter seemed to drive the man in the cap completely nuts. "We're American citizens minding our own business. This is our school! You disperse!"

Lots of people in the crowd clapped and cheered the man and he seemed to draw energy from the crowd's approval. "This is our school! Our children are in there! We can go in Central High anytime we want!"

"Yeah, yeah!" Clap, clap. "Atta boy! You tell 'em!"

"Not today, you can't." The soldier with the megaphone barked at the man.

"Get out of my way! I'm going in!" The man in the cap took a couple of quick steps toward the school. Several people in the crowd surged in behind him. The whole mob was going to charge the soldiers to get at the school building and then, I suppose, the black kids inside.

A young soldier stepped out of formation, whipped the butt of his rifle around, and slugged the guy in the cap square on the side of the head in one dazzling motion.

The crowd reacted as if the soldier had hit each one of them individually. They stopped like they had been playing a giant game of "Freeze." Everyone gasped as the man in the cap sank down on one knee and grabbed the side of his head. The blow had cut him and dark red blood oozed between his fingers and trickled down his hand and dripped all over his windbreaker. He looked dazed as he stared in disbelief at his own blood.

Beside me, Sandra let out a little gasp. Her face had turned white. I reached over and took her hand and gave it a big squeeze. Sandra squeezed back so hard I thought she might break my fingers. Neither one of us could take our eyes off of what was happening in front of the school.

"Disperse and return to your homes." The leader of the soldiers repeated like a record that had gotten stuck on the turntable.

Knocking the guy down vaporized some of the crowd's angry energy. People retreated back across the street and started milling around in the front yards and driveways. A couple of men helped the cap guy to his feet and led him back across the street, where he sat down on someone's front steps and bled some more.

"This is . . . is . . . something," Tommy Lee whispered.

Everybody stood around like they were waiting for the next thing to happen.

They didn't have to wait long.

"They found a jig reporter over yonder!" A fat woman in a red print dress waddled past us, shouting at the crowd like a chubby Paul Revere. "He's with all them other Yankee reporters."

"Where? Where's he at?" The crowd forgot about the man in the cap. New energy surged through the mob.

"Over yonder! Around the corner! Follow me!" The fat woman broke into an awkward gallop and the crowd surged after her as her thick legs propelled her down the street like her underwear was on fire. People broke into rebel yells and shook their fists at the soldiers as they moved toward the end of the block.

Curiosity got the best of us. Tommy Lee and Sandra and I fell in with the crowd and ran down the middle of the street. Like some kind of monster caterpillar with hundreds of legs, we all made a wide turn at the corner and about halfway up the block everybody screeched to a halt and formed a wide circle in somebody's front yard. Rebel yells filled the air.

"I can't see," Sandra gasped. "There's too many people. They're too tall. What's going on, Archie?"

"Up here." I grabbed Sandra's hand and led her toward an old black Oldsmobile that was parked by the curb. The car was dusty and looked like it had been parked there since the Korean War.

"We can't stand on somebody's car," Sandra said.

"We can until they make us get down." My heart pounded with excitement that seemed to have become a part of the very air we were breathing. I went first, stepping on the back bumper and propelling myself onto the roof of the Olds with one quick step. I caught Sandra's hand and helped her scramble onto the top of the car. Tommy Lee followed right behind.

With the three of us standing on the roof, I could feel the metal sag under our weight. I knew we would get in real trouble for standing on someone's car, but when I looked at what was happening in the center of the circle of angry people I realized nobody would give a hoot if three kids were playing hooky and standing on the top of an ancient Oldsmobile.

In the middle of the circle, this well dressed colored man clutched a flash camera in one hand while he tried to reason with two angry young white guys. The young men had greasy ducktails and short sleeve shirts with the collars flipped up.

The taller of the two guys clinched and unclenched his fists, and I could tell that any second he planned to slug the colored man. The crowd pressed in around the three of them. The guy shoved the Negro, who backed up and held up his hands like he didn't want any trouble. Fat chance. The guy shoved him again.

The mob ate it up. They all waved their fists and cussed at the colored man, whose eyes grew wide with fear. Rebel yells rained down on him. I couldn't blame him for being scared.

Sandra grabbed my arm and pulled herself close to me. She was really frightened. So was I.

"Kick the coon's butt!" Tommy Lee danced around on the roof of the car.

"Stop it this minute, Tommy Lee!" Sandra roared like the drill sergeant in this movie I saw last summer.

"Make me!" Tommy Lee didn't even turn around. "Kick his black butt!" Spittle sprayed out of Tommy Lee's mouth. "Hit him! Hit him hard!"

"Don't be a jerk, Tommy Lee. Cut it out." I couldn't listen to my best friend anymore.

Sandra pulled me even closer.

An older man in a white dress shirt and tie jumped out of the crowd and knocked the camera out of the colored man's hand. The mob cheered as the camera hit the ground and shattered. The colored man held up his hands as if to say it's okay to break my camera but just don't hurt me.

The taller young man attacked the Negro reporter and slugged him right in the face. When the man spun around to avoid the blow, the other guy kicked him in the back. The crowd screamed its approval. People clapped and yelled. The two young guys circled around like boxers with their fists in fighting position, waiting to throw more punches. The crowd kept up a steady roar.

Then suddenly, from behind us, this strange rhythmic noise silenced the mob.

Clomp, clomp, clomp, clomp. Louder and louder.

I turned around and saw about two dozen soldiers of the 101st Airborne Division, their combat helmets pulled low on their foreheads, their rifles clutched tight across their chests, trotting down the middle of the avenue in two neat lines. They were double-timing down the street, their faces locked in serious, grim masks.

Clomp, clomp, clomp, clomp.

The mob parted to let the Screaming Eagles through. The two young men who had attacked the reporter saw the troops and faded into a group of people who retreated across the street. A pair of soldiers broke ranks and helped the colored man to his feet. The thugs had ripped his jacket and blood had splattered all over his shirt.

The troops had frightened the mob and most of the people broke away and drifted down the street in twos and threes, glancing over their shoulders to make sure the soldiers weren't coming after them.

"Man! They gave it to the jig! They showed him!" Tommy Lee punched the air like Rocky Marciano.

"Shut up, Tommy Lee!" I had never yelled at Tommy Lee before in my life. "Shut your stupid redneck mouth!"

I had a lot more to say, but I stopped cold. No more words would come out. My blood had turned to ice water. I couldn't move, let alone talk because as the crowd moved away, I saw him in a front yard across the street, leaning against a tree.

Mr. McDonald!

His gray slacks, white shirt, and blue blazer looked out of place at the mob scene. His arms were folded across his chest and his mouth worked double time on a big wad of gum.

But the really awful thing, the thing that made my insides go icy, was the fact that he wasn't paying any attention to the troops or the colored man or the young punks or the mob.

Mr. McDonald wasn't watching any of that. His eyes were glued to me.

CHAPTER TWENTY-ONE

I didn't go to the school ground Sunday afternoon to play ball with Jerome and the Phantom. In fact, I didn't go anywhere. Somehow, my mom found out Sandra and Tommy Lee and I skipped school Thursday. So I had to kiss the weekend good-bye. No TV, no phone, no basketball, no fun. I was confined to quarters.

Fortunately, my mom didn't find out where Tommy Lee and Sandra and I went when we played hooky. Thank goodness. If my parents ever found out we went over to Central my goose would be cooked for good.

For one thing it was dangerous. There were soldiers with rifles running around all over the place. Not to mention mobs of white people who were so mad they were liable to do anything. Some of them were probably carrying guns or knives. There were rumors of bombs hidden in lockers in the school. I couldn't blame my parents for not wanting their kid in the middle of all that.

That's why, on the bus ride home, Sandra and Tommy Lee and I took a blood oath never to tell anyone where we went that day.

That was the only time I said anything on the ride back to Kingwood. The sight of Mr. McDonald leaning against the tree, smacking his gum, and watching me left me feeling so scared I could barely think. He had delivered his evil message.

Right after I spotted Mr. McDonald, things moved pretty fast at Central. The soldiers who rescued the colored reporter scared the people in the mob, and the crowd vanished into the neighborhood. More soldiers showed up and the helicopter came back.

Suddenly a half dozen ducktailed hoods appeared out of nowhere. One of the hoods, a stocky, muscular guy in his early twenties attacked one of the soldiers with a baseball bat. He swung the bat like Mickey Mantle and caught the soldier on the shoulder. The soldier dropped his rifle and screamed in pain.

Then things got wild. One of the other soldiers tackled the hood and drove him to the ground. The rest of the hoods tried to help their buddy but more soldiers jumped in, swinging their rifles like clubs.

The mob reappeared.

Everyone was yelling.

Tommy Lee and Sandra and I scrambled off the hood of the car. We were trapped. The mob was surging down the street on one side of us and more troops were charging down the other side. There was no way out.

I turned left, toward the soldiers. I thought Tommy Lee and Sandra were behind me but when I glanced over my shoulder they were gone.

The soldiers in the front line looked straight ahead, their faces set in a series of grim frowns. They were coming right at me at a full trot. I was penned in the middle of the street.

Until Mr. McDonald appeared.

He popped out from between two parked cars. He was still smacking his gum, unfazed by the troops. My heart shot up into my throat.

When he raised his hand I thought Mr. McDonald was going to grab me but all he did was motion between the parked cars. He looked like he was going to say something but he didn't.

I darted past him, raced between the cars, and sprinted up a driveway on the other side.

When I reached the end of the driveway and slowed down, I spotted Sandra and Tommy Lee in the yard a few houses down. They waved and pointed to an alley that ran down the side of the block. I took off again and didn't look back.

The three of us charged down the alley, the shouting from the troops and the mob echoing in our ears.

We didn't stop until we were a long way from Central High and history.

Tommy Lee and Sandra hadn't seen Mr. McDonald, and I didn't mention him on the bus ride back to Kingwood.

I didn't know what to think. The only thing I could figure out was that Mr. McDonald had planned to grab me as I ran between the cars but I had been running too fast.

I had seen Mr. McDonald murder Roy on Halloween night, and Mr. McDonald knew I had seen the whole thing. And now he wanted me to know I'd better keep my yap shut. He knew I was the only one who could find justice for Roy.

With the possibility of being murdered on my mind I welcomed the chance to be grounded and spend the weekend in my room because that was the one place on the planet I felt safe.

Also being stuck in my room gave me a chance to think about all the weird stuff that had been happening lately. My life was starting to feel like I was riding in a bus with no driver.

The number one thing in my brain was what I saw on Halloween night and what I was going to do about it. I saw Mr. McDonald kill Roy and Mr. McDonald knew I saw the whole thing. So now he was following me around trying to scare me or worse so I wouldn't tell anyone.

How could I make Mr. McDonald stop following me? Who could I tell what I saw? I gotta tell somebody or my brain's going to explode. I needed to find somebody to help me bring Mr. McDonald to justice. I couldn't just let him get away with what he did.

If things hadn't changed I'd tell Tommy Lee. But everything had changed. Tommy Lee hated all the Negroes. I didn't get it. We both wanted to improve our game and make JV next year so Tommy Lee didn't mind playing ball with the Phantom and Jerome on a deserted court—he loved the game too much to miss a chance to play against really good players—but then he just hit the hate button when we got away from the playground.

All that hate was making me feel weird. It took everything I had to forgive Tommy Lee for the way he acted up in the Heights and over at Central. He was still my best friend but sometimes I wondered.

But you know what? The more I thought about it, the more I didn't think there was anything wrong with playing ball with Jerome and the Phantom. Or going to school with colored kids for that matter. I mean what's the big deal?

I didn't care what my dad or Tommy Lee thought, but I wished the whole thing wasn't turning me into a big liar. Sneaking around to play ball on Sunday afternoons, skipping school and going over to Central, going downtown on Halloween night when my mom told me to stay in the neighborhood. I mean all these lies are going to blow up in my face one of these days. Right?

I needed a plan.

I thought about telling Sandra about Jerome and the Phantom. Maybe even about Mr. McDonald. She wasn't like Tommy Lee. She understood stuff. I knew she was a girl and all that but lately every time I was around her I felt . . . different. Sandra would know what to do. Sometimes I thought she was the best thing in my life.

Her and the school basketball team.

We would open the season in a couple of weeks with the big City Christmas Tournament. Every school in Little Rock would play in the tournament, and if you won the thing your school would get this neat gold trophy with a little basketball player on top. Edison had never won the Christmas Tournament. Mr. Sewell, our school principal and coach, wouldn't say it, but he hinted around sometimes that he thought we could win the whole thing this year. Wouldn't that be something?

Last week we played a practice game after school against the Wilson School. We killed 'em. Tommy Lee fed the ball to the guys inside and even hit a couple of outside shots. Harry Foster grabbed a bunch of rebounds. Even Lewis Goodman, who was not much of a shooter scored a couple of baskets. I tried out this cool spin move I picked up from watching Jerome and it worked every time. The Wilson guys couldn't stop me and I wound up with sixteen points, which was the most anybody had.

During the game, Mr. Sewell's wife stopped by the gym. She was going to have a baby any second. Her stomach looked like she swallowed a basketball. She brought Coach a sandwich, then stayed to cheer for our team.

The game was the most fun I had all week. Basketball is like that. When you're really into it, the game was all you thought about. You forget all the bad stuff for a while. Wish I could play basketball all the time.

With that thought on my mind, I ran outside with my ball and shot hoops on my backyard goal until my muscles ached and my brain stopped swirling.

Basketball was great. No doubt about it.

What was not great was the dance at the Community Hall next Saturday. I'd never been to a dance. I didn't know how to dance. I didn't particularly want to know how to dance. None of my friends knew how to dance. But a bunch of parents got together and decided it would be a good idea to have a dance for a bunch of kids who don't know how to dance. Figure that one out.

My mom said the parents wanted us to learn social skills, whatever that meant. So the parents rented the Community Hall, and next Saturday night would be the Big Dance.

It was one too many things to think about. So I let it slide.

But Saturday night finally rolled around, and I got dressed in my Sunday suit, slicked my hair with

Brylcreem, and polished my penny loafers. My dad even let me wear some of his stuff that you put on your face to make you smell good. I splashed on a lot. No one wants to stink at a dance.

My mom offered to teach me how to dance in one easy lesson. She loved dances. My mom said they're the most romantic things in the world. She thought that because that was where she had met my dad. Mom grew up across the river in North Little Rock, but she had gone to junior college here in Little Rock, where she had belonged to a girls club called the Battlecriers. During the war, the Battlecriers had set up this little place where they had sold candy and sodas and had kept the GIs company over at Camp Robinson. The soldiers at the camp were training to fight the Japs and the Germans.

One night, all the soldiers and all the Battlecriers had this dance at a big ballroom called the Rainbow Room, on top of this fancy hotel that overlooked the Arkansas River. Mom said she danced with a bunch of soldiers, and then she went outside on a balcony to get some air and look at the river in the moonlight.

And there was my dad. In his army uniform, smoking a cigarette and looking at the moon like Clark Cable or Humphrey Bogart. (That's the way my mom tells the story.) So Terri and Warren introduced themselves and talked and looked at the river in the moonlight. Later they went back into the ballroom and danced with each other the rest of the evening.

The next day all the soldiers had shipped out.

Now don't get me wrong, my dad didn't exactly ship out to the front. I mean we're not talking Iwo Jima here. Actually my dad went to this big army base in

New Jersey, where he helped with the army's laundry. I'm not saying he washed dirty clothes or anything. He figured out how much washing all the clothes cost and stuff. Kind of like what he does now for the Royal Laundry and Cleaners. He was the laundry boss. He doesn't talk about it much except to say that he did important work and helped win the war.

Before the war ended, Dad had gotten a leave from the army and had come back to Little Rock, had found my mom and they had gotten married. Just like that. The second time they had ever seen each other.

Even I think that's pretty romantic.

I wasn't feeling romantic at all the night of the community hall dance. Not knowing how to dance would do that to a guy. Good thing my mom came to the rescue. She pushed back the furniture in the living room and put a Percy Faith record on the hi-fi and tried her best to show me how to waltz.

"You can't go wrong if you know how to waltz," she said. "All you do is hold your partner around the waist with one hand and hold her other hand up in the air and walk around in this imaginary box."

At first I felt stupid. There I was in my suit and my mom was wearing a pair of khaki slacks and a ratty old blue sweater of my dad's and she and I were walking around the living room in a bunch of imaginary boxes while she counted out loud. One-two-three-four. One-two-three-four. At first our knees bumped and I stepped on my mom's foot a couple of times before I finally got the hang of it.

"Mom," I said as we glided around the living room floor. "What would you do if Mr. McDonald tried to kill me?" I couldn't tell my mother about Mr.

McDonald following me all the way over to Central, but the meanest man in the world was following me and I had to do something.

"Oh, Archie, stop it." Mom had a big smile on her face. She still didn't believe me. "One-two-three-four. I know what you going to say next—all that ridiculous nonsense about Halloween. I don't want to hear any more about it. Mr. McDonald is not trying to kill you. I'm sure he's a very nice man inside that gruff exterior. In fact, I hear he's something of an artist with his photography, and artists don't kill people.

"Mom. Please. Just listen."

"Besides," my mother said, ignoring my plea, "we live in the suburbs and no one ever gets killed in the suburbs." She took the lead and we swirled across the living room like ol' Fred and Ginger in the movies. Then Mom paused and looked out the front window with this goofy, dreamy look in her eyes. "In fact, nothing ever happens in the suburbs," she mumbled.

We waltzed past the couch and danced around the TV set. It was dark outside and frost was forming on the window. My mother was not going to listen to me about Mr. McDonald no matter what.

Mom changed the record and showed me this dance called the fox-trot. Pretty stupid name for a dance, huh?

The fox-trot was harder than the waltz. I really had to concentrate. While we shaped up my fox-trotting skills we talked about school and basketball and the City Christmas Tournament and stuff like that.

I finally got the hang of the fox-trot. Sorta.

Then somebody started pounding on the back door. BOOM! BOOM! BOOM!

My heart jumped up into my throat and my whole body shuddered. I jumped away from my mom. "It's him," I whispered. I know it. It's Mr. McDonald. He's come to kill me."

CHAPTER TWENTY-TWO

"Calm down, Archie." Mom gave me one last whirl, curtseyed, and thanked me for the dance. "I told you. We live in the suburbs. Nothing bad can happen here. Trust me." Then she left to answer the door.

It was Tommy Lee.

Mom gave him a hug and invited him into the living room.

My best friend looked awful. He had on an old tan summer suit of Mike's that had a catsup stain on the lapel. Tommy Lee had tied his tie in a square knot, and he had enough gunk on his hair to grease the axles of my dad's Chevy.

"My mom said she would drive us to the Community Hall," Tommy Lee announced. "She said we could walk home."

"That sounds fine." My mother smiled, trying not to look at Tommy Lee's hair. "Archie's dad and I are going out for the evening. Our first evening out in a month of Sundays." She stepped back and looked at us with a broad grin. "My two handsome boys. You guys will be the toast of the ball. Every young lady in Kingwood will be dying to dance with you."

"I hope not," Tommy Lee mumbled.

My mother laughed.

Tommy Lee's mom drove us to the Community

Hall in the Rushs' truck. The Rushs were the only family in the neighborhood that had a panel truck since Mr. Rush needed it for his house painting business.

The inside of the Rushs' truck smelled like paint and sweat, and I hoped it wouldn't rub off on me on the way to the dance. I wished I'd splashed on more sweet smelling stuff before we left.

The Kingwood Community Hall was located on the other side of the Lancaster Property from Edison, next to the little store where all the kids used to stop after school for cokes and candy until last year when the old guy that ran the store did something to Randy Pringle in the storeroom and the police closed the place down. Now it's a flower shop.

All the lights were on inside the Hall and the building looked like an enormous jack-o-lantern that was sucking in a bunch of kids from the neighborhood, all wearing their Sunday best. We were all nervous and everybody walked like miniature zombies heading for the Voodoo sacrifice, our legs stiff, silly grins on our faces.

Inside the Community Hall, the parents who were chaperoning the dance had set up folding chairs along both sides of the wooden floor and strung red and white crepe paper all over the ceiling. At the end of the hall we found a table with a punch bowl full of pink liquid and stacks of Dixie cups. Powdered bakery cookies and red napkins were fanned out over the end of the table.

In the opposite corner a hi-fi played Sam Cooke's "You Send Me," but nobody paid any attention to the music.

Everybody was dressed up. All the guys had on suits or sport coats, ties, and white socks. Dark socks are too weenie to even talk about. The girls wore dresses with stiff ruffles and lace collars. They all clustered together on the left side of the room and the scent of their collective perfume smelled like a giant flowerbed overflowing with mysterious blossoms.

We had all known each other since the first grade. We had been in Cub Scouts and Brownie Scouts together, copied each other's homework, spent the night at each other's houses, played together at Lancaster Park every summer, eaten a bazillion lunches together in the Edison cafeteria. We knew each other about as well as a group of kids could possibly know one another.

Yet the minute I walked into the Community Hall for the first dance of our collective lives, I felt like I had entered a room full of total strangers.

All the boys huddled by the punch bowl, stuffing their faces with cookies and talking real loud, trying not to look at the girls—the same girls they saw every day in school. The girls giggled and talked to each other and worked hard at not looking at the boys.

Nobody danced.

Tommy Lee and I got some punch and stood around with Harry Foster and Lewis Goodman and talked about our practice game with the Wilson School. Talking about basketball made us all feel normal.

Across the room, I saw Sandra talking to Vivian Smith. Sandra looked like a movie star. She had on an emerald green dress with a yellow belt, and she had fluffed out her hair, which was all shiny and pretty. I casually moved in front of Harry so I could still talk to the guys and look at Sandra at the same time.

Vivian's mom, who was one of the chaperones,

came over to our group and asked if we wanted to dance with the girls. We all nodded and said, "Yeah, fine, great, sure. In a minute. Soon as I finish my punch." Yeah, right. We'd all dance as soon as pigs soared with eagles.

So nobody danced.

After a while, Sandra stood up. She whispered something to Vivian and Vivian shook her head yes. Then Sandra turned and walked slowly across the empty dance floor all by herself. She headed straight for our group, and from the look on Sandra's face, I knew I was about to go down with the ship.

"Archie, would you come and dance with me?"

The other guys laughed.

"Wooo. Big man with the ladies."

I vowed to strangle Harry Foster the first thing Monday morning at school.

"Please, Archie."

"Wooo. Lover boy."

I planned to kill Lewis right after I strangled Harry.

"Don't listen to them," Sandra said. "Come and dance with me. It'll be fun."

My mouth was so dry I couldn't swallow. "Okay." I was as surprised as anyone in the group when "okay" fell out of my mouth.

Sandra held out her hand. I took it and we wandered onto the dance floor. Out into No Man's Land. I took a deep breath. The conversations had stopped. Everyone was looking at us. We were monkeys in the zoo. Sandra and I just stood hand in hand all alone in the middle of the silent Community Hall dance floor. Waiting.

"Tragedy" by Thomas Wayne came on the hi-fi. I

thought that was a truly appropriate song for what was about to happen.

"I hope you know how to waltz," I whispered. "It's the only dance I know how to do."

Sandra held up her right hand and put her left hand over my shoulder. "I love to waltz," she said.

I slipped my hand around her waist and took her right hand in my left hand. We were ready to waltz. Only suddenly everything my mother had taught me earlier in the evening took a vacation. I couldn't remember which foot to start on or which direction I should go if I did remember. I knew I looked like the village idiot. I heard Tommy Lee and Harry snickering over by the punch bowl.

I thought about grabbing my stomach, falling on the floor, and pretending I had a horrible cramp or something.

"Count," Sandra whispered.

So I counted. One-two-three-four and Sandra and I circled around the dance floor, walking in our imaginary box as my mother's instructions slowly returned to my brain.

"When did you learn this?" Sandra grinned.

"About an hour ago," I said. One-two-three-four.

"Way to go, Archie." Sandra couldn't stop smiling.

We waltzed round the dance floor for a minute or so. Just me and Sandra. All by ourselves with everyone watching.

As we passed Vivian Smith, Sandra nodded. Vivian nodded back, grinned, got up and lumbered across the dance floor. The guys by the punch bowl acted like she had some dreaded disease. They backed away, headed for the bathroom, started deep conversations with each other. But it was too late for Harry Foster. In the blink of an eye Vivian and Harry were out on the dance floor, waltzing around in their own imaginary box.

Becky Jamison, responding to some incomprehensible desire, crossed the floor and, like a hunter who had bagged her prey, returned to the floor with Sid Martin, the King of the Weenies. Nancy Pat Carney and Connie Campbell sprinted past us and in a second had Gerald Hardy and Billy Wolfe waltzing to the fading strains of "Tragedy."

"Be-Bop-A-Lula" by Gene Vincent came on the record player. There's no way on earth you can waltz to "Be-Bop-A-Lula." Trust me. My mom's fox-trot? Not even close. I knew a treasure trove of useless dances, and, as a result, I was dead in the water in the middle of the Community Hall dance floor.

"Do you know how to jitterbug?" Sandra asked.

I shook my head.

"Can you do the Push? It's sorta like the Jitterbug."

"I can fox-trot," I said, knowing how pointless that sounded.

All around us the other kids were swaying and hopping around to the music, dancing in various imitations of what older brothers and sisters had taught them or what they had seen on American Bandstand.

"Just do what I do." Sandra refused to give up. She took my left hand in her right hand. "Push on my hand whenever you feel me pushing on yours. In the meantime, shuffle your feet. Keep time to the music. That's all there is to it. You don't have to be Gene Kelly or anything. Just shuffle and push easy."

So I danced.

Sorta.

My moves probably didn't look any worse than what anyone else was doing. They played more records and Sandra and I kept at it. The music sounded great. Rock 'n' roll. Dancing was kinda fun after you got the hang of it. It helped that all the other kids were doing it too.

All the other kids except Tommy Lee. He sat in a folding chair by himself, sipping pink punch, wearing his mad face. I wished one of the girls would ask him to dance but none of them did.

After about a dozen records, one of the chaperones called for an intermission. Sandra was sweating a little and so was I, so we fell in line for the punch bowl.

We took our punch cups over to the hi-fi and thumbed through the records—"Long Tall Sally," "Party Doll," "Don't Be Cruel," "Johnny B. Goode," and "Peggy Sue." How could anyone ever get tired of listening to such great music?

Tommy Lee crossed the dance floor and joined us.

"Hey," I said, smiling as he walked up.

"Well don't you two look great doin' the jigaboo bop."

"Oh, come on Tommy Lee," Sandra said. "We were just dancing. Having fun."

"My daddy warned me they might play that music here. He says it's all a Communist plot against the youth of America."

"Your daddy thinks everything is a Communist plot against the youth of America." It came out a lot harsher than I intended.

"Go on," Tommy Lee said. "Do the dirty jig bop. But both of you will go to hell for it and you know you will. It's in the Bible. Look it up."

"What are you talking about?" I was getting sore at Tommy Lee. That seemed to be happening a lot lately. "Where are you getting this junk? Stop it. You and I are best friends."

"Not anymore. I can't be best friends with somebody who does the dirty bop in front of everybody. You're gonna have to go to hell by yourself."

"Tommy Lee, you're just mad 'cause Archie is dancing with me and not sitting in the corner talking to you about basketball or cars," Sandra cut in.

"Shut up, Sandra!" Tommy Lee bared his teeth like a hungry vampire.

"Come on, buddy, settle down." I draped my arm around his shoulder. "Forget all this crazy stuff. Let's be friends like always."

"Leave me alone!" Tommy Lee shrugged my arm off his shoulder. "Go on. Dance to the Devil's music. Not me. I'm going home. You can walk home by yourself. See if I care!"

He spun around and sprinted across the empty dance floor toward the front of the Community Hall. Everyone stopped what they were doing and looked at him. Then, before I could say anything else, my best friend disappeared out the door into the night.

CHAPTER TWENTY-THREE

After the dance, Sandra rode home with Ann Koch and Susan Pettit and Connie Campbell in Connie's dad's station wagon. Connie's dad offered me a ride, but I didn't want to ride in a car full of girls, so I said no thanks.

I started walking down the street toward Edison. I hiked past the Lancaster Property, down to the school, and cut through the woods. Even without crossing the McDonald's backyard, which I had absolutely no intention of doing, I could be home in twenty minutes. Tops.

The walk was lonesome and cold without my best buddy. My shoes crunched on the dead winter leaves and the smell of decaying foliage filled my nose. My breath clouded up the air in front of me. I flipped up the collar of my suit coat but that really didn't warm me up much.

I had my hands stuck down deep in my pants pockets when I jumped The Creek so when I landed on the bank on the other side I lost my balance and fell down on one knee. My knee hurt and I stopped for a second to rub the spot. The pain made me think of Roy.

I missed him. He understood a lot more than any average kid. Maybe being trapped in the iron lung let him see things in a different way. He knew stuff. I think we could have been good friends and just seeing him in that iron lung and hearing him talk about baseball and music gave me a sense of courage. If Roy could face life in an iron lung surely I could face my problems with his dad. But first I needed to find justice for Roy. Someway. Somehow.

With or without Tommy Lee. The two of us had always been like one, but this new Tommy Lee wasn't the same guy. This new Tommy Lee liked hanging around with creeps like Bobby Sanderson and the Little Klan.

But maybe I wasn't the same guy either. I liked playing ball with Jerome and the Phantom. That didn't seem wrong at all. They seemed like good guys. And I did like Sandra. A lot. Things had changed and it looked like this New Me would have to tackle junior high and the future by myself.

I stumbled over a rock and kept from falling down by grabbing a low tree branch. I stopped and caught my breath.

That's when I heard it.

I froze and held my breath. Then I heard it again. A crunching noise like somebody walking on crumpled paper. Or dead leaves. Crunch-crunch-crunch. Slow and steady. There was somebody in the woods behind me. No doubt about it.

I jumped up and turned round in a circle, looking everywhere, but it was too dark to see much. Crunch-crunch. The noise got louder.

"Tommy Lee? Is that you? What are you doing?"

Nobody answered.

Crunch-crunch-crunch. Footsteps crackling on dead leaves. The forest closed in around me. Everything seemed extra dark and extra cold and extra quiet. My whole body had the shaky shakes. I couldn't tell if I had the quivers because I was cold or because I was scared.

"Tommy Lee!"

Nobody answered.

I started back up the path. I wasn't running but I wasn't walking either. When I got to the top of a little hill I stopped and listened. Crunch-crunch-crunch. I looked behind me but I still couldn't see anybody. Crunch-crunch. Whoever it was speeded up.

I speeded up too. It was hard to run in penny loafers but I managed. I charged across the top of the hill and headed for the trail that led to the street and the safety of the streetlights. I was flying, my feet barely touching the ground, my arms and legs pumping, white breath pouring out of my nose and mouth.

Who was I kidding? There was no way Tommy Lee would pull something like this no matter how mad at me he was. Deep down inside, I knew who was after me. Any idiot could figure that one out. It was Mr. McDonald.

Had to be.

He must have followed me to the dance the way he followed me over to Central, and now he had his chance to catch me alone.

I had been so stupid. I had gotten all caught up in dancing with Sandra and Tommy's Big Weirds and turned down Connie's dad's offer of a ride. Stupid, stupid Archie. Walk home alone in the dark? What was I thinking? I ran even harder.

I was deep in the dog's business. Mr. McDonald was a GI who had seen combat in two wars. The army had taught him how to see in the dark and how to circle through the woods and cut off the enemy, ambush him, and cut him to ribbons. Army guys knew that kind of stuff and they never forgot. They were trained killers.

I ran even harder.

That was how he would get me. He would circle ahead, hide behind a tree, and when I ran past the tree he would jump out and grab me with a choke hold or a jujitsu move and slit my throat with a jagged knife he took from some Nazi or Chinese Red he had killed in a war. He could be lurking behind any tree up ahead.

I had to outsmart him.

I left the path at a dead run and charged straight into the woods. The low branches slapped me in the face and I stumbled over some roots but I kept going, running and scrambling, ducking under thick branches, zigzagging back and forth. Nobody could figure out where I was going. Including me.

I tripped over a root and went sprawling, but I bounced up and kept charging through the dark woods. I ripped my pants on a low branch but I didn't care. If I could just get out of the woods and get to the houses on the edge of the neighborhood I'd be safe. I could do it. I knew the woods a lot better than Mr. McDonald did. He might know all that army stuff and killer stuff but these were my woods and he wasn't going to catch me. No matter what.

If I could get to the creek, I'd be okay. There were houses on the far side of the bank. Lights. People. Safety.

The water glistened in the moonlight. Normally, I'd step on a couple of rocks in the stream to get across, but not tonight. Tonight I hit the bank at a full gallop and took off like a broad jumper.

I missed the opposite bank by inches. My foot landed in the creek and I lost my balance and slid into the freezing, knee deep water.

I scrambled up the bank, sliding and slipping in the mud. Behind me I heard a noise that sounded like a giant wolf growling.

Once I got to my feet, I might as well have been in a track meet. Archie in the hundred-yard dash. My wet pants made running hard. No problem when you're scared outta your gourd. I covered the distance from the creek to the houses in record time.

I flew past the houses and dashed down the middle of Maplewood. My shoes made a squishing, clopping sound.

I turned up Cherrywood, my legs pumping like pistons. When I reached the Clarks' house, I raced up the driveway and galloped through their backyard until I came out on Pinewood.

I could see the lights in our house.

My chest ached and burned and my legs told me they didn't have much left.

I made it to our driveway and with one last surge of energy reached the door in our carport. I threw open the door and went hurdling into our den, slamming the door behind me.

My father sat on the sofa, still dressed in his tie and suit pants from work, watching *Have Gun—Will Travel* on the TV set.

"Archie, what in the world . . ." My mom sat in the easy chair, reading a book, covered up with a red-and-black afghan.

I spun around and locked the dead bolt on the door behind me.

"Honey, what happened? Your clothes are all torn and you're all wet." My mother tucked a bookmark in her book and put it on the table beside her.

"The dance . . . over . . . walking home . . . Mr. McDonald . . . tried to kill me . . ." My breath came out in rasping heaves.

"Calm down, Arch." My dad glanced back at Richard Boone who had the drop on the bad guys. "We'll get to the bottom of this. Are you hurt?"

"No. I'm okay. I ran . . . fast as I could . . . had to get away . . . Mr. McDonald . . . waiting for me . . . chased me through the woods."

My mother shook her head. "Now, Ted Williams, think about what you're saying. I don't think one of our neighbors chased you. Calm down and let's find out what really happened."

"Was Tommy Lee with you?" My dad asked. "Did he see any of this?"

"He . . . left early . . . got mad . . . just me in the woods. Me and . . . Mr. McDonald. He's gonna . . . gonna . . . kill me."

"Come on now, Archie. That's pretty far-fetched," Mom said. "Clearly, something took place on the way home and we need to find out the truth. Not what your imagination dreamed up."

The room started to spin. I leaned my back against the door. I wanted to cry. I looked at the paintings of hunting scenes on the wall and the magazines on the coffee table. Everything seemed normal. Except me.

Nobody would believe me.

My mom and dad both thought my overactive imagination had gone into overdrive and I knew what that meant.

My overactive imagination was a big deal to my mom and dad. Truth be told there was this thing that had happened summer before last. Looking back on it I guess I had gotten a little carried away. Okay, maybe more than a little. Actually it had been a pretty bad fumble.

We were down in Destin, Florida where my dad took us to the beach for the first vacation of his whole life. The early part of the trip was fun. We stayed in this little beach house, and I got to sleep out on the screened-in porch where I could hear the waves of the Gulf of Mexico every night as I fell asleep.

During the day we took a couple of boat rides way out in the ocean and my dad and I went deep-sea fishing. He loved it. I had never seen my dad that happy. He reeled in a couple of really big fish and had the boat captain take his picture with the fish. Dad was nothing but grins for a couple of days—and, of course, so were Mom and I. My mom and I played miniature golf on this great course that had these wild sea monsters guarding the holes. We didn't even keep score. We just laughed a lot.

The three of us swam in the gulf every day and ate seafood every night.

Things couldn't have been better.

Until we went to the post office.

How could things go so wrong just going to the post office? For me, it was pretty easy.

While my dad mailed a package of souvenirs back to his family in south Arkansas, I wandered around the little post office. By far the most interesting things in the place were these wanted posters.

They had about half a dozen of them, with photos

of scary looking guys facing left and right and staring straight at the camera. Mug shots. There was one guy who looked like a refugee from your worst nightmare. His name was Willie Hockersmith. He had thinning, slick-backed hair and a big nose. His narrow eyes promised death and destruction. The FBI wanted him for bank robbery and assault and a couple of other things. He was last seen in Miami. The poster said to call the FBI if you had any information regarding the whereabouts of Willie Hockersmith. There was a phone number on the bottom of the poster.

Dad mailed his packages and we headed back to the beach house, with me staying as close to Dad as I could.

The next day Mom and Dad wanted to go to this movie, but they thought it would have too much kissing in it for me so my father bought me seven packs of baseball cards to keep me busy while they went to the show. Mom told me to stay in the beach house until they came back. Then we were all gonna go for ice cream.

The baseball cards were great—Wally Moon and Don Blasingame of the Cardinals and Andy Carey of the Yankees and Richie Ashburn of the Phillies—some of my favorites. I played with the cards for a long time. Then I went out on the porch and read a chunk of this Hardy Boys book I had brought with me to Destin.

Then I got bored. It seemed like my folks had been gone a long time, even though I knew they weren't due back for a while. Staring out the window, I had this terrific idea. There was a little town center about a half a mile from the beach house. I had seen a drugstore there and thought they might have some comics. My dad had given me two dollars for the trip, so I tucked the money in the pocket of my khaki shorts, put on a clean white T-shirt and my sneakers and took off for the town center.

Bad idea.

The drugstore had comics. I bought a Dick Tracy and a Batman. I also bought a spiral notebook and pen. I was into drawing that summer. After I paid for the stuff, I wandered out onto the main street of the town. It was a neat little place—a grocery store, a café, a bank, and a shop that sold swimming gear and suntan lotion.

It was awfully hot and humid for late afternoon, and the people on the street moved slowly like they needed a nap.

And that's when I saw him.

Willie Hockersmith! From the wanted poster.

He was standing under the awning in front of the café, smoking a cigarette while he watched the bank across the street. He was casing the joint. I swear.

I stopped in front of the grocery and looked closely. It was him. No doubt about it. Same slicked-back hair. Same big nose. He had on sunglasses but they didn't fool me. It was Willie Hockersmith. The bank robber.

I had to do something.

So I did. A lot of somethings. A lot of stupid somethings as things turned out.

I ducked into a phone booth and called the FBI. *If you have any knowledge of the whereabouts of Willie Hockersmith contact the FBI immediately.* I remembered the phone number because it was a combination of my number on the Edison basketball team plus Tommy Lee's number minus one plus the number of Hardy Boy books in the series. My mind always remembered weird stuff like that.

I told the woman who answered what I what I had seen and she connected me to a real FBI agent. I described the guy looking at the bank and explained how I had seen the poster and how it was the same guy. The FBI agent asked me for my name and where my family was staying in Destin. Then he hung up.

I slid out of the phone booth and crouched down behind some apple crates in front of the grocery store. I peered over the top and watched Willie Hockersmith casing the bank. He kept smoking cigarettes and pacing back and forth while he looked at the bank. The robbery was gonna go down any minute.

But not if I could stop it.

It would take the FBI a few minutes to get there and I couldn't just walk into the bank and tell them what was going on. I was eleven years old. A big eleven years old. But still. So I came up with another plan.

I whipped out my new spiral notebook and pen and wrote a note. "The bank is about to be robbed." I tore the page out of my notebook and folded it up. Then I strolled across the street like I didn't have a care in the world, making sure not to look at Willie Hockersmith.

Inside the bank the air conditioning slapped me in the face. The place was like a meat locker. There was only one teller and three customers in a line. I spotted a fat security guard sitting on a stool in the corner. He had a big ketchup stain on the front of his uniform. He also had a gun in his holster.

"Hi," I said, walking up to the guard. "Nice and cool in here."

The guard nodded.

"A guy gave me a quarter and told me to give this to you." I handed the note to the guard. He looked half asleep. He took the note and mumbled "thanks." After he read the note he didn't look half asleep anymore.

After that an avalanche of bad stuff fell on my head.

Cops came to the bank. They talked to me. One of them went across the street and talked to Willie Hockersmith. Phone calls were made, including one to the FBI.

The guy casing the bank turned out to be the owner of a Destin men's clothing store. He had been waiting for his wife to finish her business in the bank. More phone calls were made.

Finally, two uniformed cops drove me back to the beach house. I sat in the back of the police car. One of the cops was nice. He admitted that the men's clothing store guy sorta looked like Willie Hockersmith on the wanted poster. Except the poster said Hockersmith was 6'3". I hadn't read that part. They said the men's clothing store guy was about 5'7".

My parents met us as we pulled in the driveway of the beach house. The FBI had called them. The nice cop talked to them. They looked relieved. Then they looked mad. The cops left. Mom and Dad hit the ceiling. They reminded me that I wasn't supposed to have left the beach house. And wanted to know what I could have been thinking, calling the FBI. Our last two days in Destin were miserable for me. Not only because my parents were so mad, but everywhere we went I was sure that Willie Hockersmith had heard I had ratted him out and was after me. Even after we got back to Little

Rock, I was sure a man like Willie could find me there and I kept looking out for him whenever I went anywhere. And the nights were horrible. Every sound I heard I was sure it was big bad Willie Hockersmith breaking into the house. Night after night I couldn't sleep.

My parents became really worried about me. The dark circles under my eyes made me look like an old man. Finally, my parents had enough and they took me to a child psychiatrist who made me take all these tests. And then I met with him to talk. I went to see him once a month for a while. Then I quit going. I had nothing more to say to this man who always mumbled "uh huh" anytime I did say something. He gave my mother an order for these yellow pills that he said would help me sleep and calm me down. I have to give him that—I was able to sleep with those pills. I guess he told her as far as he could tell I was a victim of an overactive imagination. Boy, did I hear that phrase again and again every time I said something my parents thought was odd.

Probably the worst thing that happened as a result of the "Willie Hockersmith Incident", as my mother referred to it, was that I had to hear the story of the little boy who cried wolf about a gazillion times. Every chance she got, my mom told me the story. I got it the first time.

School finally had started again and things had slowly gotten back to normal. Sorta. But you know what? I bet the men's clothing store guy in Destin was secretly Willie Hockersmith's twin brother.

That was the last time I was the little boy who cried wolf.

Until Mr. McDonald. Which was totally different. I mean you're not the little boy who cried wolf if the place is crawling with wolves? Right?

Wrong.

The kid shrink thought Mr. McDonald and Willie Hockersmith were the same thing.

When my mom hauled me back to see him after Mr. McDonald chased me through the woods he said my imagination had gone into overdrive again. Can you believe that?

When we had gotten back from Florida and my mom had said she wanted to take me to a child psychiatrist, I had thought she meant some little kid who was so smart he was a psychiatrist. Stupid Archie. She had meant this old fart, who was supposed to know what made kids tick.

Believe me, he didn't have a clue. At least not about Mr. McDonald. The kid shrink had a little office in a building downtown, where we sat opposite each other in these fakey leather chairs. Every time I'd say something he would scribble on this yellow legal pad. And besides that, he smoked a pipe that smelled like burning rabbit turds.

He sat there in this stupid blue bow tie, nodding his head, and sucking on his pipe stem. He had a silly little moustache that was slightly lopsided and brown hair that was going gray at the temples. I told him about what happened after the community hall dance. He just kept scribbling. I didn't tell him about what happened on Halloween.

When I finished my story he wrote some more on his pad, looked up, and smiled. He said I didn't have anything to worry about. Showed how much he knew.

According to Dr. Know-It-All, some kids have such great imaginations that sometimes they can't tell the difference from what's in their mind and what's actually happening.

That sounded a lot like crazy to me.

The shrink told me to think about Willie Hockersmith. And then think about Saturday night after the dance. Were there some similarities in the two situations? After the dance I had slipped through the woods before Mr. McDonald caught me, sprinted up Pinewood, and burst into our house with my suit all torn up and my face scratched and bleeding. I was hollering my head off about Mr. McDonald chasing me through the woods, trying to kill me and everything.

But, as my mom and the kid shrink reminded me over and over, I never actually *saw* Mr. McDonald. I heard a lot of sounds. I got scared, which anybody would, running all alone through the woods in the dark. So my mom and the kid shrink figured that my overactive imagination got the best of me again. Case closed.

I just wished they'd been there.

The kid shrink leaned back and asked me about school. Did I like it? Did I do my homework? What were my favorite subjects? That kind of stuff. I told him about the Quack and the Race of Life and how it wasn't much fun to be dead last in the Race of Life.

He chuckled and wrote some more on his legal pad.

When we finished, Dr. Know-It-All told me he'd see me again in a week and then he took my mom back into his office while I sat in the waiting room and read old copies of *Reader's Digest*. When Mom and I left the shrink's office we stopped by old Mr. Swanson's drugstore and got a prescription filled. We got a whole bottle of the little yellow pills that cured my overactive imagination last time.

My mom made me take one when we got home. I washed the pill down with a root beer and an hour later my head felt like it was in a fish tank. Everything around me swam by real slow, and I fell sound asleep on the living room sofa.

I dreamed I was waltzing with Sandra in this giant crystal ballroom. She wore her emerald green dress and held me so close I could smell her soapy scent. There wasn't anyone else in the whole place. Just me and Sandra, waltzing around the ballroom.

Until I noticed this balcony at the far end of the ballroom. Way back in the shadows of the balcony there was someone watching me and Sandra. I couldn't see who it was, but I could take a good guess.

CHAPTER TWENTY-FOUR

Thanksgiving Day, 1957.

The sun was shining but the air felt cool and crisp. From my bedroom window I could see a few rebel trees up on the ridge that were stubbornly clinging to their red and orange and gold autumn colors. All of the trees and grass in Kingwood had already turned the bleak brown of winter.

In the middle of the morning my dad's family from Crawfordsville pulled up in front of our house in Grandpa Lane's old black Studebaker. Grandpa Lane parked the car in front of the house and shuffled up our driveway. He was a wiry old guy with tufts of white hair on his head and blue veins around his nose. His face looked tough and leathery. Since it was a holiday he wore his white shirt and a wide red tie from the forties and blue suspenders underneath his dirty old red-and-black plaid jacket.

Grandma Lane was a boney woman who clomped around in big old fashion shoes. She always wore her hair in this really tight bun and rarely talked.

Uncle Clyde was my dad's oldest brother. He worked in the sawmills with Grandpa Lane and was a definite roundbelly. He didn't talk much either.

After they all poured through the front door and hugged and kissed and wished everybody a happy

Thanksgiving and everybody told me how much I had grown, me and Uncle Clyde and Grandpa Lane and dad flopped down in the living room while Mom and Grandma Lane worked on the Thanksgiving dinner in the kitchen.

Dad picked imaginary lint off his trousers and asked about people he had grown up with in Crawfordsville. He didn't seem too interested in the people. I think he was just being polite, just making conversation. All the people were doing fine. Everyone nodded and agreed it was good they were all doing fine. Everybody was fine. Everything was good. It was a pretty boring conversation.

After a while, Grandma Vickers came over from North Little Rock. She was a chubby little woman who looked like Mrs. Santa Claus. She laughed a lot and told stories about the high school football team Grandpa Vickers had coached before he died. She was always teasing me about my imagination, telling me I lived on Planet Archie. Grandma Vickers thought that was really funny. She brought a covered dish and joined the other women in the kitchen.

Finally we all sat down at the table, which Mom covered with a white tablecloth. Our best china and silverware were neatly arranged at everyone's place. My dad said grace.

Mom hadn't cooked the turkey long enough, and it would have been easier to eat a catcher's mitt. Grandma Vickers was a worse cook than her daughter, and the yams were all runny and the pumpkin pie tasted faintly like bug spray.

Conversation lagged. Grandpa Lane made an effort to talk about the weather, which everyone agreed was fine. Several times.

After the meal, all the men, including me went back into the living room while the women cleaned up. Grandpa Lane fell asleep in his chair and Uncle Clyde smoked his annual Thanksgiving cigar. My dad yawned a lot. There was a football game on TV, but my dad's family didn't like football.

I excused myself and retreated to my room, where I took off my slacks and dress shirt and put on jeans and a gray sweatshirt. I played around with my baseball cards for a while until I realized I was lonesome.

I thought about what to do for a minute, but I never really had any doubt. Even though we'd been having a lot of trouble lately, I did what I always did when I was lonesome. I called Tommy Lee.

"So how 'ya doin'?" I wasn't gonna mention the Community Hall dance or any of the bad stuff that had been going on between us. I figured that no matter what happened, Tommy Lee and I would be best friends forever.

"Okay," he said. "My folks are taking a nap. The trip down to Arkadelphia to see my mom's people made everybody sleepy."

"I know what you mean."

"You want to do something?" Tommy Lee sounded like his old self and I felt a big grin creep across my face.

"Sure," I said, trying not to sound too excited." You wanna ride bikes?"

"Nah," Tommy Lee said. "Let's shoot hoops. Up at the schoolyard."

Because of the way Tommy Lee had been acting lately I had been afraid to suggest going up to the schoolyard. "You think they might be there?" I asked.

"They might," Tommy Lee said. "If their Thanksgiving is as boring as ours. Besides, I still think we can beat 'em. You and me."

"You're on. Let's do it."

All the craziness at Central and up in the Heights and at the Community Hall dance vanished. Tommy Lee and I were right back where we'd left off. Best Buddies.

I had a lot to be thankful for that Thanksgiving, and I promised myself I'd never let anything mess up our friendship ever again.

We wandered down the familiar streets of Kingwood, dribbling and passing the ball, laughing and joking. We were on our way to play some serious hoops and that felt great. Tommy Lee had on a hooded blue sweatshirt, which made him look like a dwarfish medieval monk, and I felt really lucky to have such a great guy for a best friend.

The day was calm and cloudless. Perfect weather for hoops. But then, weren't they all? We jumped the Creek at its lowest point and when we came out of the woods at the schoolyard Jerome and the Phantom were shooting imaginary hoops on the asphalt court. They didn't have a ball.

Their faces exploded into big grins when Tommy Lee and I walked out of the woods. Swallowed up by a raggedy red sweater, the Phantom looked about ten years old. Jerome wore a worn white T-shirt. They both had on patched corduroy pants with the cuffs rolled up.

They didn't ask where we had been for the last couple of weeks or anything. "Ya'll want to play a game?" Jerome said in this real quiet voice.

Tommy Lee arched a long set shot that swished. "Yeah. I guess so. Might as well."

What happened next was the best game ever from the very first shot—a swisher from the corner by the Phantom. A couple of minutes in and we were playing one of those rare games when all the players are totally absorbed in every play. One of those super games, when the tough shots drop and nobody walks with the ball or throws it out of bounds or argues about the score.

Even the misses rebounded just right so you could grab the ball with both hands and fan your elbows. The game that day was all sharp passes, great shots, fast breaks, and tough rebounds. After a while the four of us were lost on our own planet, which had to be the best planet in the whole galaxy.

At twenty–twenty Tommy Lee stole a pass and raced down the court. I trailed him down the right side. We had the Phantom between us in a two on one fast break. Tommy Lee threw the ball to me and I took three dribbles. The Phantom picked me up, cutting me off from the basket. Then I flipped the ball behind my back to Tommy Lee for the lay-up.

I swear. Behind my back.

I had never thrown a pass behind my back. I had seen Bob Cousy do it on TV once, but I had never been able to do it. Until now.

"Nice play!" Tommy Lee laughed as we headed back down court. Even Jerome grinned and clapped his hands. I lowered my head and tried to look like the pass was something I did all the time.

Jerome answered with a jumper from the top of the key. The chain nets went "clink", which sounded almost as good as "swish." Tommy Lee drilled a set shot. Clink. Back and forth—thirty-two–thirty-two. Up and down the court—forty-four–forty-four. A sweeping hook shot, a steal, another jumper, a big rebound— fifty-six–fifty-six.

Even though the shadows of the trees had reached the middle of the court and the breeze felt frosty, I felt like somebody had left me in the oven too long. My gray sweatshirt had turned a shade darker than when we started, soaked in sweat. I called a quick time-out, pulled off the damp sweatshirt and tossed it behind one of the goals and went back to the court in my T-shirt.

The game went on—sixty-eight–sixty-six. Then seventy-two–seventy-two. Back and forth, up and down the court. I hit another hook shot and Tommy Lee stole the ball for an easy lay-up. We surged ahead seventy-eight–seventy-four. The biggest lead of the game.

Jerome signaled for a time out. "Let me wear yo' shirt, man," he said to me. "I'm freezing my butt off." He rubbed his bare arms with his hands.

"It's kinda wet," I said.

"Don't matter." Jerome massaged his arms harder. "It's better'n what I got."

"Sure, go ahead." I shrugged. I was anxious to get back to the game. While Jerome slipped on the sweatshirt, Tommy Lee and I trotted back to the other end of the court to set up our defense.

"You'll have to bury that sweatshirt now," Tommy Lee said in a low voice. "Either that or burn it."

"What?"

"It'll smell like jigaboo now. Sweaty jigaboo. You'll never get the smell out."

I stared at Tommy Lee. I couldn't believe he

thought about stupid stuff like that. There we were in the middle of the most fun basketball game ever and he was still thinking about all the hateful things that had been creeping into his mind since they let the colored kids go to Central. I felt sorry for him.

"I guess that's my problem," I said.

Tommy Lee held his nose for a second before he moved out to the top of the key to guard the Phantom, who was dribbling the ball down court.

Everybody, even stupid Tommy Lee, upped their game after the time-out. We had never beaten Jerome and the Phantom and we both sensed this was our chance. But they weren't going to give the game to us. No way.

Jerome, encased in my sweatshirt, spun around me for a neat reverse lay-up. Tommy Lee answered with a set shot. I blocked a running jumper by the Phantom. Back and forth—eighty-four–eighty-two. I connected on a pair of jumpers and a scoop shot and we pulled ahead ninety–eighty-four.

Tommy Lee's hair was plastered to his head with sweat, and we were both panting like dogs. I answered with a hook shot. Ninety-eight–ninety-two. Us.

Tommy Lee looked pooped. The Phantom drove around him and fed Jerome. Clink. Ninety-eight–ninety-four.

One more shot and we had our first win ever over Jerome and Phantom, the two best basketball players I'd ever been on the court with.

We set up on offense. Tommy Lee dribbled around, waiting for me to get open but the Phantom stole the ball off the dribble and made an easy lay-up. Ninety-eight–ninety-six.

We still needed one more basket.

I came back to midcourt and Tommy Lee tossed me the ball. One more basket. One on one. Me against Jerome. I dribbled the ball down low to set up my favorite turn around bank shot. I backed Jerome into the lane.

As I started to make my move the Phantom left Tommy Lee and tried to double-team me. I spun around and spotted Tommy Lee wide open under the basket. I jumped but instead of shooting the ball I fed it to my best friend. He was all alone. Piece of cake.

Tommy Lee banked the ball too hard off the backboard.

Jerome grabbed the rebound. Tommy Lee scrambled back on defense, his head down. He was tired and cold and had choked on the winning shot.

Down at the other end of the court, Jerome missed a hook, but I knocked the ball out of bounds. Jerome threw it in, and the Phantom launched a jumper from the top of the circle. It was dead on the money. Clink. Ninety-eight–ninety-eight.

One more shot and we could still win. My exhaustion fell away. I wanted to win more than anything so I set up on the low post and signaled for the ball.

Tommy Lee rifled a nice bounce pass to me on the baseline. The pass left me a little far out, but I had the ball and the game in my hands.

CHAPTER TWENTY-FIVE

"This ain't no jungle bunny playground."

I stopped my dribble and whirled around. Bobby Sanderson and Calvin Mashburn and Ricky Thorne were standing at the top of the key in the middle of the court. They had come out of the woods and we had all been so into the game we hadn't noticed them.

Bobby stood in front of his buddies. He had on jeans and a blue-and-black plaid flannel overshirt. His thumbs were hooked in the empty belt loops of his jeans. Calvin and Ricky had on their winter coats, their hands jammed deep in their pockets.

The Phantom's eyes were pools of fear. He took a couple of quick steps backward.

"Tommy Lee Rush, you little turd, what in the world are you doin' out here playin' with a bunch of jigaboos?" Bobby was furious.

Tommy Lee swallowed hard and shook his head, indicating he didn't know.

"We gotta go," Jerome said.

"You ain't goin' nowhere." Bobby growled.

"Come on, Bobby, they're not hurting anybody." I had never hated anyone as much as I hated Bobby Sanderson at that moment.

"Shut up, Dipstick. These coons ain't supposed to be in our neighborhood. They ain't welcome."

"Ah, come on, Bobby. We were just playing ball."
I looked Bobby up and down. When you got right down
to it, he looked fat and slow and I wasn't scared of him.
I hoped the look on my face told him I wasn't going to
back down. Because I wasn't.

"Get out of my way," Bobby sneered. "We got to
take care of business."

"We goin' home." Jerome jerked off my sweatshirt
and handed it to me. "Thanks," he whispered.

Jerome had a lot of muscles, and when Bobby got a
good look at them he didn't like what he saw. So he
changed strategies and focused all his anger on me.

"You let a coon wear your shirt?"

"Yeah. What about it?"

"You gonna put that shirt on? After it's been on a
colored boy?" Ricky and Calvin giggled.

I stuck my arms in the sleeves of the sweatshirt and
pulled the wet shirt over my head and down my front.
Then I glared at Bobby.

Ricky and Calvin looked stunned.

"What are you gonna do about it?" I was steamed.

"Cool off, Archie," Tommy Lee said in a trembling
voice.

"Whose side are you on?" Bobby pointed at
Tommy Lee. "Which side? You little turd."

Calvin and Ricky surrounded Tommy Lee. "Our
side or the coons'?"

"I'm on your side!" Tommy Lee yelled. "You guys
know me. I'm with you. You know that."

The Phantom turned and looked at Tommy Lee
with so much hurt in his eyes I had to look away.

"How 'bout you, Lane? Which side are you on?"
Bobby clinched his fists.

"Any side but the one you're on. Leave us alone, Bobby. Go mind your own business."

"Let's take care of the coons first," Calvin said. "Teach 'em a lesson. Show 'em they ain't welcome in our neighborhood."

"Show 'em what'll happen to them if they try to go to our schools." Ricky clinched his fists.

The Phantom started backing away. "We didn't mean no harm. We jess wanted to play a little ball. That's all."

"Leave him 'lone." Jerome positioned himself between the Phantom and the Little Klan.

"Shut your coon hole," Bobby sucked in his gut and joined his friends in a line facing Jerome. "Your little buddy's a chicken. He ain't gonna fight. That makes it three against one, jig. You like them odds?"

"Make that three against two." I moved next to Jerome.

"My God, Lane. You just ruined yourself in this neighborhood," Bobby said. "Siding with the coons against your own kind. You're a traitor to your race, buddy-boy. That's serious business."

I shrugged.

Calvin started toward me, but Jerome cut him off. Calvin's eyes told me he didn't want to tangle with Jerome, and I'd bet Ricky didn't either.

"Take your little coon friend and get outta here." Ricky tried to sound tough but it didn't work.

Jerome charged and Calvin and Ricky spun around and took off for the woods. Jerome kept after them. The Phantom trotted along behind Jerome.

Out of the corner of my eye I saw Tommy Lee as he vanished behind the school building.

Right after Ricky and Calvin disappeared into the woods, Jerome and the Phantom spun around and sprinted across the playground in the opposite direction and hurdled into the woods on the other side of the schoolyard.

That left me and Bobby Sanderson.

Bobby took a wild swing at me but the blow landed on my shoulder. I connected with a shot to Bobby's left ear that rocked his head back. His mouth locked in a snarl. "You're gonna pay for that, Lane. You can take that to the bank."

Bobby stepped in front of me until our noses were inches apart. Then he shoved me in the chest with both hands. I stumbled backwards and brought my fists up into boxing position the way the fighters on TV did. My heart started racing and my mouth was so dry I couldn't even lick my lips. I just hoped I could lick Bobby Sanderson.

He circled me with his fists up. Bobby started mouthing off, but I didn't hear what he said because when I glanced over his shoulder toward the edge of the woods I went into some kind of walking coma.

Mr. McDonald was standing under a tree, watching us. He looked like he was waiting for a bus, standing there in his gray slacks and tan windbreaker, working on his wad of gum.

My teeth started chattering even though I wasn't cold. Bobby Sanderson didn't scare me. He might be tough, but I figured I was as tough as he was. Mr. McDonald was another story. He had followed me, and this time I knew he had come to kill me. If Bobby Sanderson didn't kill me first.

I didn't have much time to think about Mr.

McDonald because Bobby charged, swinging a big roundhouse right. I ducked and moved away.

Bobby was even slower than he looked. I had time to step back in and land a solid punch to Bobby's jaw. He let out a sharp cry of pain.

A right cross caught me on the neck. I jabbed Bobby square in the nose with my right fist and the blow made this awful squishy noise. I danced away. Bobby's nose started gushing blood in rivers.

"Bobby, come on, man. Let's stop this right now. There's no reason for us to be doing this."

"You made my nose bleed! Now you're really gonna pay!" Stupid Bobby rushed me, but he stumbled and I deflected his punch with my forearm. He snuck in a second blow that landed squarely over my left eye, snapping my head back.

Bobby tried to hit me again, but I grabbed him around the neck and we did this awkward dance under the basketball goal, each one of us trying to slug the other one. But we were too close together to do any damage. The whole thing was stupid.

As we spun around and around I saw Mr. McDonald still standing by the edge of the woods, watching us. I thought he might race across the playground and help Bobby kill me. Maybe he figured Bobby didn't need any help.

Bobby broke free from my headlock, which had smeared blood in his hair and all over his face. A thick, steady red trickle flowed from his nose.

He tried another charge but this time I ducked and tackled him. He made a wheezing sound as all the air rushed out of his body. His knees buckled and he sank to the ground, where I collapsed on top of him. I pinned his arms with my knees and sat on his chest. He kept wiggling and struggling but it was no use. I had him.

I raised my fist, ready to smash his ugly, stupid, fat face. Bobby looked really petrified. He couldn't get his arms loose to protect his nose, and he knew that if I slugged him in the nose again his whole face would explode and splatter all over the playground.

He started bawling. "Please don't." His voice came out in a little weenie whisper. "Please don't hit me."

"Say Uncle." I spit the words out in the meanest growl I could manage. "Say Uncle, now!"

He sucked blood and snot back up into his nose. He didn't have a choice. "Uncle! Uncle!" Big tears rolled down his cheeks, mixing with the blood and dirt on his pimply face.

I got off Bobby's chest. I was puffing and panting and I felt sick to my stomach. I touched the swollen lump over my eye. The thing hurt like crazy.

Bobby staggered to his feet and stumbled off towards the woods, sniffing and sobbing and trying to make his stupid nose stop bleeding with his shirttail. In a minute he disappeared into the trees.

I sat down and leaned my back against the pole that held up the basketball goal and looked around the playground and the woods on the far side. Mr. McDonald had vanished.

My mind started racing. How did Bobby and the little Klan know we'd be playing ball with Jerome and the Phantom on Thanksgiving afternoon? I could only come up with one answer. Tommy Lee had told Bobby we'd be there. That had to be it. But that meant that my best friend had . . . I couldn't think about it anymore.

The sun dropped behind the ridge and the shadows

of the trees covered the basketball court. It would be dark in less than an hour. A cold breeze made me shiver. I hoped Jerome and the Phantom got home safe and sound.

Geez, ninety-eight–ninety-eight. And I had the ball for the winning shot. What might have been?

I pressed my back against the goal support and looked at the Thanksgiving sunset and let my breath get back to normal.

I felt like the most alone person in the whole universe.

Just me and my overactive imagination. All alone on Planet Archie.

CHAPTER TWENTY-SIX

On Monday morning I didn't wait for Tommy Lee to walk to school. I walked by myself and by the time I reached Edison I had made a decision that I knew was going to change my whole life.

When I got to the Quack's class several of the kids looked at the giant blue-and-yellow bruise on the side of my face but nobody said anything. They were too excited.

This was the day our class was scheduled to visit the Little Rock Zoo. The teachers thought it was good for us to see wild animals. The WPA built the zoo back during the Great Depression, and the workers made the whole thing out of sandy-colored stones from central Arkansas. They spread the grounds out over a gazillion acres so the bigger animals would have plenty of room to roam around. A trip to the zoo was always fun.

A couple of years ago one of the baboons had a little baby baboon, and every year we all clustered around the monkey cages to see how much the baby had grown. I don't know what the baby's real name was, but we started calling him "Mickey" after Mickey Mantle, the star player of the New York Yankees. I couldn't wait to see how much Mickey had grown over the past year.

On the bus ride to the zoo, I sat in the back with

Harry Foster. Harry's not much of a talker, which was fine with me. Tommy Lee wound up in the front with Fat Jerry. Every few blocks my best friend would turn around and look at me with this puzzled look on his face. I looked out the window.

I wanted everyone, including Tommy Lee, to leave me alone. I had to sort out everything that had happened at the school ground the day before.

I knew Calvin and Ricky wouldn't tell anyone that Tommy Lee and I had been playing basketball with Jerome and the Phantom because then they'd have to tell how me and Jerome backed them down and how I whipped Bobby Sanderson. After a thrashing like that, Bobby sure wasn't going to say anything to anybody. But the more I thought about it the more I didn't care if anybody knew I played ball with a couple of colored guys or not. It was none of their business.

But I had other stuff to think about.

The bus let us out in front of the zoo, and we marched through the entrance and up the little hill that led to the elephant pen. The animal smells hit us as soon as we started up the graveled path. An unseasonable sun pounded us and a light sweat broke out under my windbreaker.

"My brother says you guys have a real shot at winning the Christmas Tournament," Ann Koch said as she fell in step with me.

"Maybe," I said, trying not to grin too much.

"He says you're the best scorer to come along in years."

"Nah. There are lots of guys who can shoot the rock."

"Not many like you." Ann had on a pretty blue and

green print dress that was so starched it made a crinkling sound when she walked.

I wanted to tell her about Jerome, who could score with anybody, including me, but I let it go.

"I can't wait for the tournament," Ann said. "It's like a big party that marks the start of the Christmas holidays."

Up ahead, Tommy Lee, who was walking with Lewis Goodman, turned around and gave me a palms-up gesture. I turned and looked at Ann. "Yeah. I'm excited," I said.

At the elephant pen the class stopped to say hi to Ruth, the elephant that's lived in the Little Rock zoo since before I was born. She was gray and had tough looking elephant skin and was the size of a small house. She never paid any attention to us, which was a hoot. She just went on munching hay or drinking water or strolling around her pen. Ruth was one of the few things in life you could always count on.

After we checked in with Ruth we moved on to the reptile house and looked at the snakes. Most of them were asleep. I guess there's not much to do if you're a snake locked up in a glass cage.

As we were filing out of the reptile house I heard a voice behind me.

"Don't be sore at me, Arch."

I paused at the exit and turned around. Tommy Lee hung back in the shadows. Ann went past me on her way to catch up with her girlfriends. She shot me a smile that was like the first beam of the morning sun. I smiled back.

A couple of other kids filed out and Tommy Lee and I were alone. Outside I could hear the Quack's voice, promising our class that as soon as we saw the hippos we'd head over to the monkey house and check on Mickey.

"I'm somewhere way past sore," I said, finding it hard to look at Tommy Lee. "You told Bobby and Calvin and Ricky about our games with Jerome and the Phantom. That's the only way they could have known."

"No way. It wasn't me." Tommy Lee's hair stuck up and his eyes were red and puffy. There were grass stains all over his jeans and his shirt strained at the buttons.

"You never could lie very well."

Tommy Lee ran his tongue over his lips. His eyes darted around the glass cages of snakes. "Okay. I told. But I had to. I didn't have any choice."

"You always have a choice," I said.

"Not this time." Tommy Lee bit down on his lower lip. "I hate myself for playing ball with the jigs. It was all your idea. I couldn't stand the thought of what might happen if everybody found out. We wouldn't have any friends left. Junior high would be hell next year. We'd be the Jig Lovers. We'd have to fight our way in and out of the school."

"You liked the games as much as I did."

"No. I just did it because you made me." Tommy Lee's words came rushing out like a racehorse that had been held in the starting gate too long and then released. "I was mad at you for making me do it. Look, you know it and I know it. You're gonna make the seventh grade team next year. Maybe even the varsity. I don't have a prayer. I'll get cut the first day. Then where will I be?"

"I don't see what that has to do with—"

"Bobby and those guys like me. I could be a part of their crowd next year. But not if they knew I liked playing ball with jigs. But if I told them the jigs were going to be in our neighborhood they'd trust me. They'd know I was one of them. I'd be set for next year. See, Arch. I didn't have a choice."

"So you sold me out to Bobby and the Little Klan!" My anger roared out like an exploding volcano.

"No. It wasn't like that."

"You little jerk. Jerome and the Phantom aren't any different than you and I. They're good players. Nice guys. They love the game. They risk everything to come over to Edison so we could have the best games you and I have every played in. And you sicced that oaf Bobby Sanderson on them."

"If you had stayed out of it, Bobby would have left you alone. But you had to side with the jigs. How could you do that?"

"Because it was the right thing to do."

"God, you've been so weird lately. Hanging around with that gimp. Dancing the dirty bop with Sandra. What's wrong with you?"

One of the snakes woke up and slithered up on a branch in his cage. He cocked his head and looked at us, flicking his long tongue in and out of his mouth.

"Shut up, Tommy Lee! I don't want to hear any more and I don't want to have anything to do with haters like you and Bobby Sanderson."

"Come on, man. We're best friends. We've always been best friends."

I sucked in a deep breath and let it out slowly. "Not anymore." My voice came out low and even. "You and I aren't best friends anymore. You got it?"

Tommy Lee nodded, his mouth hanging open wide in disbelief.

I whirled around and stomped out of the reptile house, leaving Tommy Lee behind with the other snakes.

I hustled by the hippo pit and caught up with the class at the monkey house. I was shaking all over as the realization hit me. I didn't have a best friend anymore, and now I was speeding down my own highway with no idea where it would take me.

My classmates were clustered around the baboon cage, laughing and pointing. I stood on my tiptoes and looked over their heads. Inside the enclosure, Mickey, the baby baboon, was all grown up.

CHAPTER TWENTY-SEVEN

I had never been without a best friend and I didn't know what to do. So I moped around the house for a few days. The anger I felt toward Tommy Lee shadowed me the whole time. Not only had he sold me out but now Jerome and the Phantom would never come back to the schoolyard and we'd never find out if we could beat them.

Plus the image of Mr. McDonald watching the fight with Bobby Sanderson at the schoolyard still haunted me. If the big creep wanted to scare me so bad I wouldn't tell anyone what I saw on Halloween night he was doing a terrific job. But more than ever I wanted justice for Roy. But how? That was the big question.

I wanted to tell my mom about Mr. McDonald trying to scare me, but I knew she had closed the door on the subject. My father was never home. But I knew somebody I could tell. Somebody I could trust. Somebody that could help me figure out what to do.

I dialed Sandra's number.

And got a busy signal.

Didn't matter. I didn't have much time to talk anyway. It was time for my regular visit with the kid shrink. We sat in his office and he asked me how I got the mouse on my head. I said I was in a fight, and he laughed and asked me how the other guy looked.

Grown-ups sure seem to think that's a funny line. I didn't tell him about Mr. McDonald and he mumbled some more about my vivid imagination and gave my mom another prescription for some more pills.

Friday night the big City Christmas Tournament tipped off and it was the first thing I honestly wanted to do since the fight with Bobby Sanderson. The Tournament really was a huge deal. They held it every year downtown at the Boys Club on Cumberland Street, and kids had been looking forward to playing in the tournament each holiday since way before the war.

The games started at five o'clock in the afternoon and ran all evening. By the time my mom and I got there for our game at seven the Boys Club was packed. As usual, my dad had to work.

The Boys Club was an ancient red brick building. Inside it smelled like stale popcorn and old kneepads and jock socks and boy sweat and years of basketball games and boxing matches. I inhaled it like perfume.

Parents and players from all the schools in the city packed the lobby. The guys were all decked out in their basketball uniforms. At the concession stand a pair of high school girls sold candy bars and cokes and Dreamsicles and popcorn as fast as they could to a long line of people. The yelling of little kids in the concession area mixed with the chatter of the parents and the sound of the popcorn machine made the lobby feel like a carnival.

The gym was on the second floor and to get there you had to walk up this wide, winding staircase with black banisters and stairs. The top of the banister was slick and shiny from all the people who had run their hands over the polished wood on their way to the gym year after year.

At the top of the stairs, a narrow hallway opened into the gym. There was a game going on and everybody in the bleachers was chanting and cheering. The buzzer would sound, signaling a substitution or a time-out and the crowd would yell even louder. The cheerleaders chanted, "Go! Fight! Win!" while they clapped their hands and stomped their feet.

I paused at the top of the stairs and something magical happened. All the horrible garbage that had been going on—Roy's death, Mr. McDonald, the split with Tommy Lee, the fight with Bobby Sanderson—all vanished. I knew all of it would be there waiting for me when the game ended, but when I walked into the gym and heard the buzzer and listened to the cheerleaders and the crowd, I forgot about all the bad stuff. Playing in a basketball game felt better than Christmas Day, my birthday, and summer vacation all at once.

The game that was going on when I walked in was between Garland and Centennial, a couple of downtown schools. We played Kramer from the east side next and the winner of our game would play the Garland-Centennial winner. The little electric scoreboard high up in the corner of the gym was covered with wire mesh and said that Centennial was winning twenty-nine–nineteen deep in the fourth quarter.

Underneath the scoreboard, Mr. Sewell and his pregnant wife and some of my teammates were huddled away from the action on the court. My mom squeezed my shoulder and wished me luck and I trotted around the stands to join my team.

The Edison Red Ravens had on jeans and sweatshirts over their basketball uniforms. Tommy Lee had on his druid sweatshirt and I nodded to him as I joined the huddle. I didn't want what happened at the schoolyard with the hoods to mess up our chances of beating Kramer. Tommy Lee nodded back. He understood.

While Mr. Sewell talked to us about how our zone should shift and how we should work the ball around on offense, Mrs. Sewell waddled around the huddle, patting guys on the back, wishing them luck, accidentally bumping them with her swollen belly. She loved basketball as much as any of us. You could see it in her face.

We peeled off our jeans and coats and sweatshirts and dropped them in little piles at the end of the gym and waited for the Centennial-Garland game to end. The Red Ravens had new uniforms for the year—red satin pants with a buckle in the front and a white jersey with red numbers. I was number 50.

My teammates and I couldn't stand still. We hopped around like we were standing on top of a hot stove. It was the biggest game any of us had ever played in.

Centennial beat Garland, thirty-six–twenty-five and we rushed onto the court, formed two lines and started shooting lay-ups and feeding the next guy in line. All the colors in the gym seemed brighter than usual. The satiny red of our new uniforms and the light blue and rich gold of the Kramer uniforms, the polished wood of the court, everything just seemed to shine.

There was no place in the whole universe I'd rather have been at that moment than on the basketball court in the upstairs gym of the Boys Club on a cold December night, waiting to play in the City Christmas

Tournament.

The Red Ravens creamed Kramer, forty-one–twenty-eight. It was a close game until right after the half when the guy guarding me fouled out. I scored ten straight points on his sub. Tommy Lee hit a couple of nice outside shots and Harry and Lewis played well. When the game ended Mr. Sewell beamed and said we had played a great opening game. He and Mrs. Sewell hugged everybody.

The next night we hammered Centennial, forty-four—thirty-two. Their guards gave Tommy Lee and Harry some trouble, but I got loose inside a lot and scored twenty-five points. After the game, some dads came up to me and shook my hand and said I was the best player in the league in years.

My dad had left that morning to go to Shreveport on laundry business.

Four teams in the whole city were left in the tournament.

Next Friday night we would play Woodruff in the semifinals. I was beyond excited. We were a good team and had a real shot at winning the trophy. It was all I planned to think about the next week.

Unfortunately life had other plans.

On Sunday afternoon Sandra called me. At first I assumed she wanted to congratulate us on making the semifinals of the Christmas Tournament, but she didn't mention basketball at all. Her voice on the phone sounded like she had taken some cold medicine. I figured her dad had been on a rampage. Sandra put up with a lot from her dad.

Sandra told me to meet her at the Playhouse, so I slipped on a pair of jeans and my sweatshirt and headed out.

There were so many heavy clouds it may as well have been midnight for all the light that broke through. Cold and wind attacked Kingwood. I sprinted across the neighborhood backyards to the Playhouse, my hands jammed tight in the pockets of my jeans trying to keep warm.

Sandra hovered in the doorway of her Playhouse. She wore her fuzzy pink sweater and a pair of black wool pants. She had pulled her hair back in a tight ponytail that looked dull and stringy instead of shiny and bouncy like it usually did. Her face was locked in a strange frown I had never seen before.

"Hi," I said, hopping up on the Playhouse stairs. "What's going on?"

"I'm scared outta my gourd. That's what's going on."

"Scared of what?"

"Come here." Sandra motioned for me to follow her inside. "Take my hand."

I reached out, took her hand, and we walked into the Playhouse together.

It looked like a bomb or a tornado had destroyed the inside of Sandra's hideaway. Everything was in shambles. The bulletin board had been ripped off the wall, and all of Sandra's stuff that had been tacked to the board had been shredded into little pieces.

Somebody had smashed the hi-fi and little wires stuck out of a jagged hole in the machine. The turntable had been ripped out and dropped on the floor. All of Sandra's 45 records had been broken in two. The sofa had been slashed and tiny tufts of the white stuffing inside peeked out like frightened little animals.

Dark red marks zigzagged all over the white walls in random patterns.

"What happened?"

"Someone broke in this morning while my parents and I were at church. My mom said they had to have done it while we were gone because otherwise we would have heard them."

"Did they go in your house?"

"No. Just the playhouse."

"Geez. I'm sorry. What a mess."

Sandra cleared her throat. "Archie, look behind you. This is the worst."

I turned around and my heart stopped beating for a second.

The vandal had drawn a huge tombstone on the wall with the red stuff. Across the top of the tombstone they had printed RIP, and, in the middle of the tombstone, they had scrawled the name ARCHIE.

"Is that red stuff blood?" I didn't want to know the answer.

"Lipstick."

"Oh."

Sandra squeezed my hand. "I leave some lipstick out here in case I want to experiment with my makeup."

I nodded. A tombstone with my name on it in lipstick in the middle of the wrecked playhouse. Great. Just great. At least it wasn't written in blood.

"Archie, who in the world do you think did this awful thing?"

My first reaction was Tommy Lee. He was hurt and mad because we weren't best friends anymore. He blamed Sandra and he'd been weird enough lately to do something stupid like trash her playhouse.

But it wasn't Tommy Lee.

The vandal had struck on Sunday morning while the Harrison's were at church. Tommy Lee's parents went to the Pentecostal church out on the highway every Sunday morning no matter what. Rain, snow, sleet, hail. Tommy Lee, Mike, and their parents spent every Sunday morning in church. You could take that to the bank.

So there was only one answer. Mr. McDonald. Had to be. Since he had been following me around he had to know I hung out in Sandra's playhouse. He must have figured out I planned to tell Sandra about Halloween night, and he wanted to scare me so bad I'd never tell anybody ever.

I started pacing the room like a caged lion looking for a way out of the zoo. "I've got to do something," I said, more to myself than to Sandra. "I can't let this go on and on. It has to stop."

"What are you talking about?"

My heart was pounding so hard I thought it might burst out of my chest. "I gotta do something. I gotta make him stop."

"Archie, calm down. What are you talking about? You can tell me."

"I have to make him stop. I just have to. If I don't make him stop, I'll go crazy."

Sandra took a step backwards. Her eyes had a look that seemed to say she thought I was already crazy.

CHAPTER TWENTY-EIGHT

Weird times followed. A week of getting up every morning, going to school, going to basketball practice, doing homework, watching TV, going to bed, tossing, turning, and staring at the ceiling. Just like any other kid who lives next door to a homicidal maniac who planned to murder him.

I made one last effort to tell my mom what was happening, but I should have saved my breath.

I told her about Sandra's playhouse and the drawing of the tombstone with my name on it. I told her how Mr. McDonald wanted to scare me and how he planned to kill me the first chance he got.

Mom laughed.

Then, just like I knew she would, she said something about the little boy who cried wolf. Some things never change.

"Come on Archie," Mom said. "You're getting a little paranoid. That's a big word that means I'm imagining that people are out to get me. "A couple of kids were probably just playing a prank on Sandra. Maybe a couple of girls from her school. Don't worry, everything always works out for the best."

How do grownups know that?

After that flop I decided to keep quiet.

On Wednesday afternoon, right after school, my

mom and I picked out our Christmas tree at the Optimist lot over by the baseball field. We always buy our tree from the Optimist Club. Mom says the Optimists are a group of business guys who eat lunch together and believe that no matter how crummy everything in the world gets they will still make money. But they do sell a lot of Christmas trees and give the dough to poor orphans or needy families so we always buy our tree from them.

Mom and I selected a short fat one with full branches and stuffed it in the back of the car and drove home extra carefully so the tree wouldn't fall out of the open trunk. It was almost dark by the time we got back to Kingwood.

We stuck the tree in the metal stand by the corner window in the living room and put the little white cover over the stand so it would look like it had snowed in our living room. Then we hauled all of the decorations— red and green balls and tiny angels and Santas and elves and reindeers—down from the attic and arranged all the stuff out on the coffee table, ready to be hung on the tree. We had everything set for the annual decorating of the Lane's Christmas tree. All we needed was my dad.

Then we waited and waited. And waited.

My father didn't get home from work until almost 9:00. "Ho-ho-ho!" he called as he let himself in the back door. "Merry Christmas!"

It didn't work.

"Where the heck have you been?" My mother didn't move from her seat on the living room sofa, where she had been sitting and staring at the lonesome, undecorated tree for the last couple of hours. "Damn it, Warren. We agreed you'd come home early tonight to decorate the Christmas tree." She had smoked a bunch of cigarettes and a smoky haze hung over the living room.

"Couldn't help it, Hon. The Imperial Inn folks from Houston were in town. These people are important clients. You know how it is. One thing led to another."

"Jesus, Warren. All you ever think about is—"

"No use crying over spilled milk. Now, let's get to that tree. What d'ya say? Hi, Arch. How's tricks? You guys gonna be ready for the big game Friday night? You gonna whip those Wilson boys?"

"Woodruff," I said.

"Yeah, that's what I meant. Ya'll give 'em your best shot, okay?" My father pulled off his suit coat and tossed it on a chair and we started hanging decorations on the tree. I was willing to bet my dad was the only man in the universe who hung Christmas tree decorations with a tie on.

"Seems like the Christmas season comes earlier and earlier each year." My dad had a case of the motor mouth. I didn't mind. Listening to him jabber was better than obsessing over my impending doom. "Before too long they'll be trying to get us to do our Christmas shopping before Thanksgiving. Wouldn't that be something?"

He plugged in the electric tree lights and the living room glowed red and green as the tiny bubbles started their endless journey around and around the little glass tubes.

"The American people will never buy it though," my father droned on. "After all, Christmas is only one day. You can't just spend and spend for one day. No day can deliver that much joy if there's too much anticipation. If they start advertising before Thanksgiving it'll drive everyone to the poorhouse. Don't you agree, Hon?"

My mother had been hanging the same little Santa Claus ornament on the tree for five minutes. Actually, she had hung the decoration and then let her hands stay on it while she stared into the colored light, humming "Cherry Pink and Apple Blossom White."

"What?" She realized my dad had been talking to her. "Right. I think that's absolutely right." She said it in that way she did when she had no idea what someone was saying. Then she went back to hanging her Santa and humming her tune and drifting around on her own planet.

By the time I went to bed our living room glowed from all the lights and tinsel and icicles and colorful decorations on the Christmas tree.

'Tis the season to be jolly.

*   *   *   *

But the next day I didn't feel so jolly. Tree or no tree. Not speaking to Tommy Lee was getting me down. We had been best friends since the day my family moved to Kingwood. Tommy Lee and I had always done everything together. It didn't feel so hot to be on my own.

When I got home after school, I didn't know what to do since calling Tommy Lee was no longer an option. I hung around in my room for a while then I called Sandra, but she had to go Christmas shopping with her mom. Finally, I peeked out of my bedroom window and made sure Mr. McDonald's T-bird was gone and I dug out my old basketball from the closet and drifted out to the backyard to shoot some hoops.

The sky was an ugly slate gray but the air felt warm and I just wore my maroon sweater and a pair of jeans.

I shot around for a long time, pretending to be Bob Pettit of the St. Louis Hawks or Terry Day of the Razorbacks until I got winded, and I plopped down in the seat of the swing set in our backyard. The ground beneath the seat was all worn away from me dragging my feet on the grass when I was a little kid. I was a swinging maniac way back then.

Nobody ever used the swing anymore. That made me sad. It was such a great swing set and I had a ton of fun on it when I was little, but now the swing set just sat sad and lonely off in the corner of the yard, hoping somebody would come along and swing on it again.

I sat down in my old swing and scraped my feet over the bare ground and let my mind wander.

"Hey, kid. How's it going?"

My heart jumped up in my throat, and I lost my balance and almost fell out of the swing. Katherine McDonald was standing behind the swing set. I whirled around, trying to regain my balance. Katherine had on a navy pea jacket with the collar flipped up over a pair of black petal pushers. Her face looked pasty and her black hair hung in limp strings around her shoulders. She had a glass of her special orange juice in one hand.

"Oh, hi." I balanced myself back in the swing and kicked at the worn out place in the grass. I hadn't seen Katherine since Roy's funeral, and I wasn't sure what to say.

"I saw you through my kitchen window."

Katherine walked around to the front of the swing. She seemed to have trouble keeping her balance. "I was lonesome. Joseph's gone back to Boston on business and the house gets awfully quiet. You know what I mean?"

Mr. McDonald was out of town. I immediately felt a gazillion times better. "Yeah, sure," I said. "I know what you mean."

"The Christmastime blues, I guess." Katherine took a sip from her glass.

"Yeah. The Christmas blues."

"I've been so lonesome since Roy passed away." Katherine wasn't talking to me. She wasn't really talking to anyone. She was just talking. "Roy had been the focus of my life for so long. I had to do so much for him every day. Some days I hated his little clicking sound. It meant I had to go and do more chores for him. Now I'd give anything to hear that little sound just one more time. You know what I mean?"

"I'm sorry Roy died." I really was sorry—for a lot of different reasons.

"We knew it would happen sooner or later," Katherine said. 'Poor Roy had so many health problems. His lungs and kidneys never did work right after he got polio. I felt so sorry for him."

I was more than happy to let Katherine do the talking.

"I read all about these juvenile delinquents in the newspaper and I can't help but wonder why God didn't strike one of them with polio. I mean why strike a nice kid like Roy? He would never have been a juvenile delinquent. He would have been something wonderful like a teacher or a scientist. I know he would."

"Yeah," I said. There was something about Katherine that was making me nervous, but I couldn't put my finger on it. "Roy was a neat guy. I know I only met him a couple of times but I liked him. I think we would have been friends. He liked baseball and rock 'n' roll. Just like me."

"Rock 'n' roll. All you kids love that music. Roy couldn't get enough of your records. I even liked 'em myself." Katherine giggled into her glass. "Imagine someone my age liking that noise." She took a long swig from her glass.

I wrapped my arms around the chains that held up the swing.

"Speaking of records." Katherine wiped her mouth on the sleeve of her peacoat. "I still have your record from that day. 'The Great Pretender.' It was Roy's favorite. Why don't you come over to the house and get it?"

Panic seized me. "I . . . don't know. Maybe some other time."

"Oh, come on. You don't look too busy. I'll give you some eggnog. Without booze. The kind you buy in the market, all thick and sugary. You like that stuff?"

"Yeah. I guess."

"Come on over and we can have a nice talk."

From somewhere deep in my brain came a tiny but powerful voice. *Big Mistake, Archie. Do not go over to the McDonald's house. Big, big mistake.*

But Katherine seemed so lonely. What was I supposed to do? Her son had died. "I'd like that." I pulled the plug on the voice in my head. "It's getting kinda dark and cold out here anyway." I hopped off the swing and we walked across the yard together and then

Katherine let us in the front door of her house.

And I knew right away that I had made a big mistake.

There must have been a gazillion lighted candles in the McDonald's house. They were all over the place. Long candles, short candles, fat candles, red candles, blue candles, green candles—all lit and casting flickering shadows off the walls. There were no other lights on in the house.

Back in the den, Roy's iron lung was gone and the room looked like a candle garden. Glowing, flickering candles everywhere—on the coffee table, in the bookshelves, on the TV, on the kitchen counter. The light danced off the statues of Jesus and made his eyes seem to move like he was alive and watching me.

Katherine went over to the hi-fi, moved a big red candle, and put on a Christmas album. Bing Crosby or Perry Como or one of those old crooners singing "Jingle Bells."

I sat down on one of the swivel bar stools at the counter that separated the den and the kitchen while Katherine fixed the eggnog. She poured mine out of the carton into a blue plastic glass and set the drink on the counter in front of me.

She poured more OJ in her glass and then splashed in some vodka.

"Well, here we are," Katherine said. "Just you and me." She sat down at the other counter stool and took a sip from her drink. "Archie, do you believe in Heaven, where all the good children go when they die?"

"Yes, ma'am," I lied. I hadn't made up my mind about that one.

"Well, if there is a heaven I know my Roy is there.

There never was a finer boy than that one. He was far better than I deserved." She took a giant gulp of orange juice.

"It's sad. What happened to him," I said, wondering how much Katherine knew about what really happened to Roy on Halloween night. She had been asleep on the couch the whole time. But maybe she had rolled over and had seen something. It would only take a second. Or maybe she had heard Roy's clicking sound right before he died. I had heard it all the way out in the backyard.

On the other hand, the first day I had visited the McDonald's house, Katherine had said something about Roy not being with us next spring. What did she mean by that? Did she know what was going to happen?

"Joseph blames the doctor," Katherine said, reading my mind. "Because the old fart didn't get us the new iron lung soon enough. But I don't know. Roy could have choked even in a new machine. I think God decided Roy had suffered enough." Katherine drained the contents of her glass and wiped her mouth with the back of her hand.

I sipped my eggnog and let Katherine keep talking.

"That's what life is all about Archie. It's all about suffering." Katherine's face sagged. She looked like she was getting older by the minute. "You ought to enjoy being a kid. It's your time of innocence. After that— Pow! Right in the kisser."

Katherine abandoned the counter and wandered back into the kitchen, where she refilled her glass with vodka. Then she splashed in some more OJ from the carton and stirred the drink with her finger. "For my sinuses," she said as she returned to the counter.

"I'm sorry." That had become my favorite all-purpose response to everybody.

Katherine rested her chin in her palm. "We're all sorry, Archie. Every one of us. But it doesn't help. Because you always know somewhere deep inside of you that if you've been bad in this world, God will punish you in the next world. So no matter how much you suffer in this life, it's going to be worse in the next life."

I gnawed on my lower lip. "I don't think Baptists believe that." What Katherine said somehow just didn't sound right. Sure, sometimes things weren't so hot but they always got better. Didn't they? That's what my mom was always telling me.

"And believe me, kid. We've all done bad things." She took another long drink. The OJ made her face turn a deep red like she had a fever or something. "Even Saint Joseph. Yeah. Even the great football star, the war hero, the long suffering husband, the palsy-walsy of the high and mighty Lancasters." Katherine's voice kept rising until she was almost shouting.

"Mrs. McDonald, maybe I should take off now."

Katherine wandered back into the kitchen and started pacing.

"It's getting late and my dad will be home any minute and I—"

"If they only knew! If the world only knew the real Joseph McDonald."

I was way out in deep water with no floatees.

"Saint Joseph thinks he can do anything he wants. He thinks the rules don't apply to him." Katherine paced faster, taking giant gulps from her glass, talking to someone who wasn't there. "Let me tell you, some things are never excused. No matter what. You know what I'm saying?" She stopped in the middle of the kitchen floor and glared at me like everything was my fault.

What things? What was she talking about? Katherine was telling me something but I wasn't sure what it was.

"I don't care who he is, he can't get away with it! Nobody does that and gets away with it! Nobody!"

Then it hit me. Katherine knew.

She knew what happened on Halloween night. Maybe she woke up at the last minute and saw the same thing I saw. However it happened, Katherine knew her husband had killed Roy. That had to be it. What else could it be?

"Big football star. Big war hero. Big deal. He knew what he was doing was wrong. But the Great Joseph McDonald did it anyway. Saint Joseph does whatever he wants."

Katherine was coming unglued right in the middle of her suburban kitchen, right in front of me and everything in her brain was tumbling out of her mouth.

"He behaves that way, but I'm the one God keeps punishing." She burst into tears and threw the glass against the wall of the kitchen. Hard. Like a Robin Roberts fastball. The glass shattered and rained crystal shards and orange juice all over everything. The sound that came out of Katherine's throat was way past awful.

"I have to go now," I said.

Katherine jerked open a drawer and utensils flew all over the floor. The clanking of eggbeaters and bottle openers and sieves hitting the tile made me jump.

"Ahhhhhh!" She found what she wanted and

whirled around, facing me, her cheeks all puffy and red, her face contorted into one huge, angry snarl. She had an ice pick in her hand.

Katherine raised the ice pick above her head like she intended to stab somebody. Then she looked straight at me. "He won't get away with it! Do you hear me?"

I'm pretty sure the neighbors down the block could hear her.

"He won't get away with it!" Crying and screaming, Katherine rushed toward the counter, drawing the ice pick back into stabbing position. She was ready to send me to join Roy.

I scrambled off the bar stool but I stumbled and fell on the floor. Archie Lane, quick and agile in the clutch.

Katherine sprinted past me and raced into the den, where she attacked one of the photographs on the wall. She grabbed the one of the soldiers huddled together in the snow and stabbed the picture over and over with the ice pick. She sobbed and moaned and made all these horrible sounds from deep inside her throat.

She stabbed a photograph of a soldier standing near a jeep without even taking the picture off the wall. She jabbed the picture over and over, the ice pick going deeper and deeper into the wall each time.

I crawled to my feet, unable to stop looking at Katherine.

"He can't do this to me! I won't let him!" She left the ice pick sticking in the wall and started thrashing around in the den in this awful dance, her arms flailing about, knocking stuff off of the coffee table.

I ran to the sliding glass door and pulled on the handle.

Katherine's wailing and screaming got louder. She shoved over one of the Jesus statues and kicked it. I pushed the door open and wiggled out through the narrow opening. I had to get out of the McDonald's house. I had to get away and find help. Katherine McDonald had gone nuts.

CHAPTER TWENTY-NINE

My dad called the police.

Right after I charged into our house, yelling and hollering my head off about Katherine going crazy and ripping the photographs off the wall and stabbing them with the ice pick, my father took one look at my face and picked up the phone.

Then my dad, who had just gotten home from work and was still in his overcoat, did the bravest thing I'd ever seen him do. He rushed out the back door and ran across the side yard, ducked under the clothes on the clothesline, and went into the McDonald's house.

Dad told me later that by the time he got into the house, Katherine had used up all of her energy and was crumbled up on the floor in the corner of the living room, crying and staring at this big statue of Jesus. Dad said no matter how hard she tried, Katherine couldn't stop crying.

While my dad was in the McDonald's house my mom stood behind me in front of my bedroom window with her arms around my shoulders. We watched the police car pull into the McDonald's driveway. The officers didn't use their siren or the red light on the top of the car, and Mom said if they did that it might frighten all the people in the suburbs and make them think they weren't safe.

Two policemen went into the McDonald's house through the carport door. My dad let them in and in a little while the policemen came out with Katherine, who had an old army blanket wrapped around her shoulders Indian style. She could barely walk and, like Dad said, she couldn't stop crying. Not even for a second.

One of the policemen kept patting Katherine on the back. I watched his lips and knew he was telling her everything would be all right. I don't think Katherine believed him. I sure didn't.

When my dad came back to our house he kept his overcoat on and sat down in the breakfast nook, mumbling about all the candles and statues of Jesus in the McDonald's house. He kept shaking his head and saying that the McDonald's were a cursed family. Mom gave him a cup of coffee.

Dad said the policemen would take Katherine to the state hospital over on Markham Street, which is the hospital for crazy people in Arkansas. Mom said the doctors would look after Katherine until Mr. McDonald could get home and even then she might have to stay in the hospital for a long time. She used the words "nervous breakdown" a bunch.

After a while, Dad went to change clothes and Mom gave me two of the yellow pills the kid shrink prescribed for me to cure my imagination. The doc had told me to just take one but Mom said I was too upset and two were needed to calm me down.

Mom left and I sat on the end of the bed, waiting for the pills to kick in. A couple of minutes later, my dad slipped into my room and closed the door behind him. He ruffled my hair then sat down on the bed beside me. We didn't say anything for a while.

"I'm sorry you had to see that," Dad finally said. "I'm sure it was awful."

"It was."

Dad nodded. "Seeing awful things is a part of growing up. It gets you ready to be an adult."

"I can hardly wait."

"I think it's necessary," Dad said. "One time your Uncle Clyde and I were hunting out by the Spring Hill bayou. We found the remains of Clarrisa, your grandfather's milk cow. She had wondered off and a pack of coyotes got her. Tore the poor thing to shreds. Clyde found her head on the far side of the clearing. I cried like a baby."

"I'm sorry."

"It was terrible alright. But I learned something that day. Life just can't be nice and safe all the time. Things just don't work that way."

I let out a deep breath. "I think I'm learning that same lesson these days."

"Seems like it."

We sat in silence for a while. I could hear the wind outside rustling the leaves in our yard. I stared at this drawing of a pirate ship I had done a couple of years ago. My mom put a frame around it and hung it over my drawing board.

"Maybe you and me could go fishing some time," Dad said. "Take off a Saturday. Go down to Crawfordsville. I still know some good streams down there."

"I'd like that."

"Me too. It's been . . . too long since I felt a pole in my hand. Felt that tug on the end of the line. It's a good feeling."

"I bet."

"Maybe this spring."

"Sounds good to me."

My dad stood up and ruffled my hair again. "Hang in there," he mumbled. Then he slipped out of my room.

The pills knocked me out cold like some stumblebum who wandered into the ring with Rocky Marciano. I lay down on top of the bedspread and drifted into the faraway land of nothing.

When I woke up around noon my dad was sitting on the edge of my bed. He had dark, sleepless raccoon eyes. He handed me a glass of milk. It felt strange to see my dad home in the daytime, but he told me he was about to leave on a Chamber of Commerce trip to Kansas City. Every year a bunch of local businessmen got selected to go to Kansas City on the train to get more business for Little Rock. He said getting selected was like making the varsity.

Dad said he hated to go because of what had happened yesterday at the McDonald's house and because of the City Christmas Tournament semifinals against Woodruff that night. He said he thought I would understand since I played on a team. He couldn't let his teammates down. They were counting on him.

I told him I understood. He didn't mention going fishing.

*   *   *   *

There was no school because of Christmas break and that night the Red Ravens slipped past Woodruff thirty-four–thirty in the City Tournament. I might as well have stayed home in bed. I missed my first four shots, and the guy I was supposed to guard had a field day, scoring pretty much whenever he wanted. I played a lot of matador defense, just waving at him as he blew by me. My brain and body couldn't seem to get on the same page. The image of Katherine coming at me with the ice pick raised over her head just wouldn't go away.

Fortunately for the Red Ravens Lewis and Harry and Tommy Lee got hot and we broke away from a twenty-six–twenty-six tie late in the fourth quarter to win the game.

Driving home my mom said not to worry about playing so lousy. She confessed she shouldn't have given me two of the yellow pills because they made me sleepy and stupid acting. I guessed even moms mess up every once in a while.

Mom swore the pills would wear off by the time we played Jefferson School for the tournament championship Saturday night. She sounded really excited when she talked about the game. All I could think about was sleep.

Saturday night was wild. Jefferson had upset Forrest Park the night before and a huge crowd gathered in the upstairs gym of the Boys Club—parents, brothers, sisters, grandparents, and even guys from the other teams in the tournament—and everybody was yelling and cheering and stomping their feet on the wooden bleachers.

The trophy for winning the championship sat on a table in the corner of the gym, and all the Red Ravens went over and looked at it before the game. The trophy was gold and had this basketball player on the top and places for the names of the guys on the winning team at the bottom. If we beat Jefferson we got to take the trophy back to Edison and put it in the glass case in the school's lobby, where it would stay forever and ever.

Someday my grandchildren could go over to the school and look at the trophy and say, "Wow. There's old granddad's name. He played on this great team that won the Christmas Tournament Championship. There's his name right there." I thought that was pretty cool.

When we started to warm up I knew I was back to my old self. The pills had worn off and the magic of the crowd and the gym was working just like always. I watched our guys jumping like frogs on the their lay-ups, and I saw the look of determination on their faces and knew we were going to rip Jefferson apart.

Then the Jefferson Eagles came out to warm up. They had on blue jerseys with white numbers and satiny blue shorts. They wore matching blue kneepads and white T-shirts under their uniforms. They looked sharp. Not to mention big. If I hadn't known better I would have thought they were all a couple of years older than us.

They had this one super tall guy. He was pudgy and had pale skin and a funny blond curl that flopped around on his forehead when he ran. I watched him shoot during warm ups and noticed that he didn't move very well but he never missed a shot, including a nice looking hook shot. He also passed the ball like a pro.

While Jefferson warmed up the Red Ravens drifted over to our bench and waited for Mr. Sewell. We waited and waited, shooting imaginary jump shots, watching the Jefferson guys shoot around. Everybody had one eye on the door to the gym. Still no coach. The referees came out with the game ball. Game time had arrived. We all looked at the door. Nothing.

Finally one of the refs went over to the stands where our parents were sitting and talked to Harry's dad and to my mom. After a while my mom walked across the gym floor and told us to go back and form two lines and shoot more lay-ups. She said she would try to find out what had happened to Mr. Sewell.

After we got tired of our lay-up drill we just shot around some until my mom came back. She stopped in front of the stands and talked to the Fosters and Lewis' mom and Mr. Rush, Tommy Lee's dad. They all looked real serious and nodded a lot. Mom walked back across the gym floor and signaled us over to our bench, where we all crowded around her.

"Okay guys, here's the story." My mom had a big grin on her face. "Mrs. Sewell went into labor late this afternoon. Coach rushed her to the hospital and about thirty minutes ago she had a baby boy. Mother and child are doing well."

We all clapped and cheered.

"Uh, Mrs. Lane, uh . . . what are we gonna do about the game?" Harry said what all the guys on the team were thinking. "The refs are ready to start. When is Mr. Sewell gonna get here?"

Mom cleared her throat. "Coach can't make it tonight," she said. "He needs to stay at the hospital. Mrs. Sewell and Coach's new son need him. I talked to the other parents and they decided that, if it's all right with you guys, I'll act as your coach tonight. My father was a coach and I know a little something about basketball."

Nobody knew what to say. Including me. Everyone

shifted their weight around and looked at the gym floor or the scoreboard or the Jefferson team over in their huddle.

"What about Harry's dad?" Lewis asked. Lewis's dad died when he was a little kid and he lived with his mom and four sisters. Dads were a big deal to Lewis.

Harry shook his head. "He doesn't like basketball," he said. "In fact he hates it. The only basketball games he's ever seen are the ones I've played in. And he's only seen a couple of those."

"But the Jefferson guys will laugh at us," Rusty Whisenhut said. "We can't have a mom coach. It looks stupid. People will think we're a bunch of sissies. What about your dad, Tommy Lee? He's over there in the stands."

"My dad only likes football," Tommy Lee said. "He doesn't know squat about basketball." He shot Rusty a hard look. "But I'll tell you this, Dipstick. I know Mrs. Lane and she knows her hoops. She'll be okay."

Tommy Lee was right. Mom did know a lot about basketball, probably more than any of the other parents, which was weird. Still, I felt less than thrilled with having my mother coach our team in the finals of the City Christmas Tournament. The whole thing didn't seem right.

"Thanks, Tommy Lee." Mom turned and nodded to the ref and then got back in the huddle. The ref looked puzzled and shrugged. "Okay, fellows." My mom sounded like a real coach. "Let's go with the usual starting lineup. Two-one-two zone on defense, double post offense."

The buzzer sounded.

As we started out on the court for the center jump I patted Tommy Lee on the butt. "Thanks," I said.

Tommy Lee nodded. Now I was ready to play. We were going to tear Jefferson apart and win the Christmas Tournament Championship and bring the big trophy back to Edison.

I couldn't wait.

CHAPTER THIRTY

The only problem was . . . we got killed.

The tall, pudgy kid with the good hands was a player. When he got the ball down low he could not only shoot, but he could also draw the defense to him and feed off to guys cutting to the basket with all these great passes that went for easy buckets. The guy seemed to have eyes in the back of his head.

The Jefferson guys played good defense—a tight zone that kept me from getting the ball inside. I moved further out and hit a couple of shots until Jefferson switched to a box and one with the odd guy on me man to man. This skinny kid with red hair and Howdy Doody freckles dogged me all over the court.

Harry hit a couple of jumpers and then went cold. Rusty and Lewis were cold all night. I think it really bothered them to have a mom coach the team. Tommy Lee played better than I'd ever seen him, hitting the open shots and feeding me on the post.

Midway through the fourth quarter, Howdy Doody got tired and I started scoring. Turnarounds, hooks. We still had a chance. We pressed full court and Tommy Lee had a couple of steals for easy points and we cut the score to forty-three–forty-two with twenty seconds left.

I fouled the pudgy kid who was trying to dribble

out the clock. Mom called time-out to make him nervous about shooting the game-winning free throws. In our huddle, she set up a good play for when Pudgy missed. She told us not to call a time-out. Just run the play before they could set up on defense. She wanted Harry to take the last shot because Jefferson would be looking for me to take it.

I was disappointed I wouldn't get to take the last shot, but I knew not calling a time-out and having Harry take the last shot was good coaching.

It was a super idea.

Except Pudgy sank both free throws.

The guy was an iceman. After the time-out he walked to the line, pushed the little curl off his forehead, bounced the ball a couple of times, eyed the hoop, and swish.

Twice.

We ran the play Mom had set up during the time out, and Harry scored right before the buzzer sounded.

We lost the City Christmas Tournament forty-five–forty-four.

After the game the Jefferson guys were dancing around and hugging each other. They deserved a celebration. They beat us fair and square.

I felt drained. Losing stunk. Every time.

But I shook hands with the Jefferson players and mumbled "good game" and picked up my sweatshirt and jeans. I didn't even put them on. I just stood in the corner of the gym and stared at the scoreboard wishing if I glared at it hard enough the numbers would magically change.

Didn't happen.

My mom shook hands with all the Jefferson guys

and their coach and with all our guys. When she held out her hand to me, I wasn't sure what to do. I mean who shakes hands with their mom?

"Good game, Archie. You played like a champion." We shook hands.

"We should have killed those guys," I said, as I put on my jeans and sweatshirt and winter coat over my basketball uniform.

"Give the Jefferson guys a little credit," Mom said. "They played a whale of a game. Shake it off. There'll be other games. More than you can imagine." My mom gave me a quick hug. It was better than shaking hands.

The gym had emptied out by the time we started for the door, but the sounds of the crowd and the cheerleaders and the buzzer and the spirit of all the games that had ever been played in the Boys Club gym hung in the air, saying good-bye, and whispering, "See you next time."

Downstairs Mom bought me a Coke in a paper cup with ice and a straw at the concession stand, and I slurped down the drink while we headed for the car.

Winter cold blanketed Little Rock, and my breath came out in wispy little clouds as we walked down the sidewalk beneath the streetlights. The cold drink and the frosty air made me shiver inside even though my body was still warm from the game.

"You were a good coach," I said as we arrived at the car. "It wasn't your fault we lost."

My mom smiled. "Thank you, Archie. I hope Lewis feels the same way. I don't think he was very happy about having a mother calling the shots from the bench."

"If stupid Lewis had hit even one of those four

thousand bricks he threw up we would have won." I was sore at Lewis. "If he says anything about your coaching, I'll knock his block off. Cross my heart."

Mom couldn't hide the grin that forced its way across her face. "Lewis knows he didn't play his best game," she said as we piled into the Chevy. "But this is only the beginning of the season. You guys are still going to have a great year."

I nodded and slurped my drink through the straw.

Mom started the car, but the inside of the windshield was all frosted over and the defroster had more than it could handle. Mom used her gloved hand to clean a place so she could see to drive. She hunched over the steering wheel, straining to see through the tiny opening. Then she eased the car into the light evening traffic.

I cleared a place on my side window with the back of my hand and looked at the Boys Club as we drove past the stately brick building.

Mom slowed down to avoid the parents and players who were still drifting out of the club. I saw Pudgy standing next to a Plymouth with his mom and dad. They looked like nice people, all smiling and laughing. His dad was smoking a cigarette and his mom wore thick glasses.

As we crept past the Plymouth I looked right at Pudgy. He glanced up and our eyes locked. He smiled, gave me a two-fingered military salute, and mouthed the words "good game." I grinned and pointed at him through the window—back at ya.

Mom drove on, picking up speed as we cleared the Boys Club crowd. And then about a block away I saw it. Mr. McDonald's black Thunderbird parked right there on the street. And right then, Pudgy and the Jefferson game and the annual Christmas Tournament turned into ancient history.

I couldn't believe it. The car had to be his. How many great black T-birds with porthole windows are there in Little Rock anyway?

As we drove by, the whole thing got worse.

Inside the Thunderbird, Mr. McDonald sat scrunched down in the driver's seat. I could see his mustache and The Scar through the window. He watched our car go by with mean eyes that promised scary, horrible things.

"Mom! Back there! It's him! It's Mr. McDonald! He's following me! Just like I've been telling you! Mom! Turn around! Look! He's right there in the T-Bird! Back there! Please look! This is not my imagination. It's him. Mom, look!"

My mother's lips were pressed into a tight line and the blood had abandoned her cheeks. She held the steering wheel so tight that her knuckles turned a chalky color. She never turned around.

"Calm down, Archie," Mom whispered. "I saw him." She sped up, turned down Ninth Street, and headed west, driving fast.

I whirled round and tried to look out of the back window to see if the T-bird was following us, but I couldn't see anything because of the frost on the glass.

Mom focused on the road in front of her. The act of driving the car seemed to take all of her concentration. "This has been a nightmare for you, hasn't it?" The car picked up more speed.

"Yeah," I said. "It has. Nobody would believe me. Mr. McDonald kept showing up wherever I went. I'm really glad you saw him. Now you know it's not my imagination or anything stupid like that. He really is following me."

Mom licked her lips. "I know you're not making it up." Her voice was quiet like she didn't want anyone to overhear her. "This isn't Willie Hockersmith."

"What do you mean you know?" My voice shot up several octaves. "You mean you've known for a long time? You've known Mr. McDonald has been following me around?"

"Lower your voice. It's not what you think it is."

"But you've known and you didn't tell me?" I didn't lower my voice. "Mom. What's going on? Why is Mr. McDonald following me? Please. I need to know the truth. I need to know what's happening."

Mom took a sharp right on Cumberland and sped through downtown Little Rock. She kept her eyes glued to the road. Neither one of us spoke.

Finally, after a long silence my mother said, "I'll put a stop to this. I promise you, Archie. I'll put a stop to it."

Oh sure. Piece of cake. Exactly how did my mom intend to stop Mr. McDonald? She could coach hoops like a pro but stopping a crazed killer from doing whatever he wanted to do didn't strike me as something a mom could just snap her fingers and make happen.

Or was it?

CHAPTER THIRTY-ONE

For the fourth year in a row Santa failed to stop at the Lane house on Pinewood Road in Kingwood on his Christmas Eve journey from the North Pole. Jolly ol' St. Nick didn't come down the chimney, leave me a bunch of neat toys in front of the Christmas tree, and fill the stocking on the mantle with candy and baseball cards and toy trucks and oranges.

That wasn't gonna happen anymore. I outgrew the fun. Christmas was different now and, to be honest, the absence of the merry old fat man changed the whole ball game.

My dad had returned from Kansas City, and he and my mom and I got up around eight in the morning and sat around the living room in our bathrobes drinking coffee and hot chocolate and opening gifts.

Three adults and no Santa. The whole thing didn't feel very Christmassy. Even the presents were dull. My parents gave me a new basketball, which was a good start but then . . . *Santa where are you? A blue sweater? A plaid shirt, three pairs of socks, and five bucks.* I missed electric trains, Erector sets, Lincoln Logs, and Slinkies.

My dad got some new house slippers, pajamas, and a new bathrobe. He said he felt like he was going to the hospital. That was supposed to be a joke but Mom didn't laugh.

Mom got a new watch. There was nothing wrong with her old watch but the new one was nicer. I guess that's why my dad works so hard—so we can all have better and better stuff like watches and shirts and sweaters.

My dad is always saying that making money is everything. Nothing is in second place. He says that's how people judge you—by how much dough you bring home. He says people will say they care if you're honest or work hard or go to church or stuff like that—but if you make a ton of money they don't care about all that other junk. My dad says money is how they know you've got what it takes. He says that a lot.

He cried the day we moved into the house in Kingwood. It was the only time I ever saw my dad cry. He was so happy he ran around the house, touching the walls and flushing the toilets. His own house. He hugged my mother and he kept saying, "See! See! I told you! Someday! Our own house! Our very own house!"

On Christmas morning, I gave both my folks fancy bookmarks made out of Popsicle sticks that we made at school. The bookmarks were all painted with cool designs and decorated with stars and glitter. I thought they were pretty neat. I'd saved up my allowance and bought my mom a paperback book called *Something of Value* that I heard her say she wanted, and I bought my dad a fancy box for his desk that held paper clips and pens and stuff.

After we opened the gifts, Mom fixed pancakes that tasted like sawdust and we ate breakfast. Then we sat around the living room, Christmas wrapping paper scattered all over the floor, our presents stacked on the coffee table, and the lights on the tree blinking on and off.

We might as well have been three strangers waiting at a bus stop. We were all being so polite it was like we had all just met.

"Weatherman on the radio said there's a big front moving in from Alaska," my father said, blowing on his coffee. "Should be here by New Year's. We may get snow. Wouldn't that be something? A snowy New Year's in Arkansas."

"I don't imagine the snow will reach Houston," my mother said, obsidian sharp. "So you'll be warm, Warren."

"Oh, come on, Hon. Give me a break. It's Christmas morning." Dad set his coffee cup on the table, where it made a wet ring. Mom scowled but I knew the scowl had nothing to do with the ring on the table.

"I can't help it if the Houston people want to meet right after Christmas," Dad said. "But I'll be back on the second. I promise. I have to go. These people are opening up six motels right here in Central Arkansas. The laundry contract would be a real feather in my cap. I have to go."

"You always have to go." Mom stared into the lights on the Christmas tree. "I'm used to you worshipping at the Great Shrine of Business. But I'll tell you one thing. I'll be damned if I'm going to sit home alone on New Year's Eve. I'm going to the Hamilton's New Year's Eve party with or without you. I'll give everybody your regrets."

My father grimaced.

The conversation made me nervous, so I jumped up

and dribbled my new basketball across the living room rug. The ball needed air.

"Stop that, Archie. Not in the house." My dad didn't sound mad or anything. In fact I think he was glad for the diversion. "We'll talk about New Year's Eve later," he said to my mom.

"Of course, Warren. The proverbial later. I can't wait."

"Just drop it, okay?"

Sometimes I wished my parents would let go and yell and scream at each other. Get mad. Go on and tell each other off. Sometimes politeness can be worse than hollering.

A lot of nights my dad and I would watch a couple of hours of TV together—*I Love Lucy* or *Your Hit Parade* or *Robin Hood*, and my mom would sit back in her chair in the bedroom and read her Book of the Month Club book the whole time. So everything seemed peaceful.

My favorite show was *The Millionaire*, where this guy gave all these strangers a million dollars just to see what they'd do. I hoped he'd come and give the million bucks to my dad someday. Then people would know my dad's a winner, and he wouldn't have to try so hard to prove it all the time.

I gathered up my Christmas loot and retreated to my room. That used to always be one of the best parts of Christmas Day. You hauled all your new stuff back to your room and played with everything the rest of the afternoon. I couldn't kill ten minutes playing with shirts and socks and sweaters.

So I flopped down on my bed and tossed my tennis ball in the air and caught it. Again and again. Once you took Santa out of the equation, Christmas Day was not that big a deal.

As usual, I thought about me and Mr. McDonald. Mom promised she would do something about the big creep following me around, and she told me not to mention Mr. McDonald to Dad because my father was so busy with his business and everything.

But I suspected Mom might be out of her league on this one. Katherine was still out at the state hospital, and Mom said she might be there for a few weeks. So right at the moment I suspected Mr. McDonald was sitting around next door at his kitchen table, drinking coffee and thinking up new ways to kill me, and there wasn't anything my mom could do to stop him.

If anybody was going to stop Mr. McDonald, it was going to have to be me. And if anybody was going to find justice for Roy, it would definitely have to be me.

I could go to the police and tell them what I saw on Halloween. That made a lot of sense. In fact last year this super nice guy named Officer Jones came to our school on career day and told us all about being a policeman. I liked him. He was tall and had thick blond hair and smiled a lot. I could tell he liked being a policeman.

I could take the bus downtown and go to the police station and find Officer Jones and tell him the whole story. Everything—what happened on Halloween, what happened at Central, the fight with Bobby Sanderson, Sandra's trashed playhouse, how Mr. McDonald shadowed me the night of the Christmas Tournament finals, and how he was waiting outside to kill me when the game was over.

After I told Officer Jones the whole story he could come to Kingwood and kick in Mr. McDonald's front door and rush into the creepy house with his gun drawn and arrest Mr. McDonald for killing Roy and following me. Would that be great or what?

The plan had a lot of merit except Officer Jones probably wouldn't believe me, and my mom would have a cat if I told the police. I promised her and crossed my heart I would never tell anybody what I saw.

But the truth was I'd already planned to break my promise to my mom and tell someone. I just hoped they'd believe me.

If they did, I had a better plan than going to find Officer Jones. I needed evidence that proved what happened on Halloween night, and I had a way to get that evidence.

My plan would take a heap of guts and a mountain of courage. Not to mention some help from my new ally. I just hoped I had it in me.

Believe me, Christmas was a lot more fun when Santa came.

CHAPTER THIRTY-TWO

The Arkansas River was a forty-five-minute bike ride from my house, but Sandra and I made it in just over thirty. There are no businesses or houses down by the river, and I imagine the tiny clearing where we stopped looked pretty much like it did when the French explorer, Bernard de la Harpe, floated down the river looking for gold in the eighteenth century and named the little clump of stones just up from where we were "The Little Rock."

Surrounded by a grove of thick magnolia trees on three sides, the clearing provided us with an open view of the river on the fourth side. The spot was quiet like only winter can be, the grass brown and dead.

Across the river we could see the lights of North Little Rock twinkling through a late afternoon mist that hung heavy over the water.

Sandra had on her black pedal pushers and a white jacket with a white furry collar. Her cheeks were red from the bike ride. With her long blonde hair she looked like the snow princess in the fairy tales.

"Do you think you could swim across the river?" I said, stalling.

"Maybe. I'm on the swim team over at Holy Souls. I'm a good swimmer."

"Yeah. I know. That's why I asked you. You're not afraid of the currents or the snakes or the river monsters?"

"Not in the least. And I don't think there are any river monsters. I think that's something the older kids over at Edison tell the younger kids. Like the ghosts that guard the Lancaster Property."

I laughed.

Sandra tossed her hair in a cute, saucy way.

I had on my gray sweatshirt, dungarees, and Chuck T shoes, but as the wind off the river played tag with us, I wished I'd worn a jacket like Sandra.

The air reeked with the smell of the dead leaves that crunched under our tires as we pushed our bikes into the clearing.

"I've been thinking about Roy," I said, hoping to sneak up on the subject of Mr. McDonald. "He never had a chance to swim the river or play on the football team or play the guitar like Buddy Holly. He missed so much."

Sandra wrapped a little curl of blonde hair around her finger and twirled it. "I can't believe he's dead," she said. "I liked him a lot. I think we would have all been good friends. If . . . you know."

"I know."

"What's going on, Archie?" Sandra said as we parked our bikes under one of the magnolia trees. Sandra rode a spiffy new red English racing bike. I still jockeyed the battered old blue Schwinn I'd had for years. "What's all the mystery you wanted to talk about? I'm all ears."

I had phoned Sandra earlier and asked her to take a bike ride with me. I told her I needed to talk to her about something important. I guess I had sounded mysterious.

We found a couple of flat rocks to sit on. They were facing the river and we watched the murky brown water slowly churn its way toward its ultimate rendezvous with the mighty Mississippi. I pegged a couple of baseball-sized rocks into the river. Down by the Broadway Bridge, a barge leisurely drifted with the current.

"I'm in trouble," I said in a low voice.

"You're always in trouble." Sandra laughed.

"This is different. This is Big Trouble."

Sandra stopped laughing. "You want to tell me about it?"

"I didn't," I said. "But now I do. You're the only person I can trust."

Sandra nodded.

"Somebody wants to kill me," I said.

"You mean Bobby Sanderson? I heard about the bad blood between you two."

"No. Not Bobby. This is bigger. It's . . . well . . . It's . . ."

"Why don't you just tell me from the beginning?"

And I did.

The whole story came pouring out of me—the wreck in the pickup, cutting through the McDonald's backyard, how the curtains blew back in the breeze, how Mr. McDonald kept the iron lung door open, waiting for Roy to die, how Mr. McDonald had been following me all over town, sending me a silent warning not to tell anyone or he'd kill me.

When I finished Sandra's eyes were wide. "Wow, Archie," she said softly. "No wonder you've been in Weirdsville the last few weeks."

"I tried to tell my mom what I saw on Halloween,

but she says I have an overactive imagination. My dad agrees." I didn't mention my shrink who also thought I had an overactive imagination. "Nobody believes me. There's no point in telling Tommy Lee. He wouldn't believe me either. We're not even friends anymore."

"I've heard. You guys have been drifting apart for a while.

I pegged a couple more rocks at the river.

Sandra watched the stones skim across the water. "I believe you," she said.

"I knew I could trust you."

"You always could."

We watched a flock of geese glide over the bridge in the distance, on their way south for the winter.

"It feels pretty lonely without a best friend," I said.

"You gotta be your own man, Archie," Sandra said. "You're too good a guy to get down in the gutter with Tommy Lee and Bobby Sanderson and the Little Klan. I'm proud of you. I know it's not easy to be out there all by yourself."

"I'll be okay," I said with more confidence than I felt.

"What are you going to do about Mr. McDonald?"

I pursed my lips. "I kinda have a plan," I said. "That's why I wanted you to come down here with me. I need your help. It'll take both of us."

"Is it going to be dangerous? Like when we went over to Central?"

"It might be."

"Good. I don't want to be in on some wimpy scheme."

I grinned.

"Tell me what we're gonna do. I can't wait."

I filled my cheeks with air and exhaled a big raspberry. "Okay. Here's the way I see it. I've got to turn the tables on Mr. McDonald. I've got to let the world know what he did. I can't let him get away with killing Roy. But nobody's going to believe me. Everybody will just say the wreck rattled me or Halloween always plays tricks with kids' imaginations."

"So you need some kind of proof. Something other than just your word."

"Right."

"How in the world are you going to find something like that?"

"There's only one possibility," I said. "And that's where my plan comes in."

Sandra left her rock and sat down beside me. Her perfume smelled faintly like honeysuckle. She hooked her arm though mine. "Just tell me what I need to do," she said.

I turned my head and looked into her eyes. "You're the best, Sandra."

"So are you, Archie Lane. The very best."

Our faces were inches apart, and the thought crashed into my mind that I should kiss Sandra. On the lips. Like in the movies. Talk about a scary thought. Maybe I should tell her my plan first but that seemed dumb. I could tell her after I kissed her. If she wanted me to kiss her. How do you know when a girl wants you to kiss her?

Maybe you just give it a shot and see what happens.

So I did.

And boy was I glad.

CHAPTER THIRTY-THREE

"This is big time scary," Sandra said.

"I know. I wish I knew another way to find out what happened that night," I said. "But this is all I can come up with."

We sat in the front of a nearly empty city bus, rumbling down Hayes Street. Just Sandra and me and an old woman with a brown scarf tied over her head and a thin young man in a rumpled gray suit.

"It's a good plan," Sandra said. "Only I've never been to . . . one of those places."

"Me either. We'll just have to make it up as we go along."

"Sounds like a plan." School had let out a half an hour ago and Sandra still had on her school uniform—a blue and green checked skirt, a white blouse with a little tie, and a blue sweater. I hoped we wouldn't have to run any. Her black Patton shoes weren't made for sprinting.

I looked out the window at Forest Heights, where I'd be going to junior high next year. The school sat on top of a wooded hill, a big campus with covered outdoor walkways. The sight of the school made me a little nervous every time I saw it.

When we reached the new shopping center on Markham Street, we took a left past a full parking lot at the shopping center, which struck me as funny since my dad called the thing a waste of time and money. According to my father people would always rather do their shopping downtown and not way out here in the suburbs.

We stopped at St. Vincent's hospital to take on passengers—a couple of nurses, a pair of well-dressed colored women, who dutifully made their way past rows of empty seats to the back of the bus.

The bus passed the municipal golf course and the football stadium where the Razorbacks played a couple of games every year. My dad says he and I will go to a game one of these days. I'm not holding my breath.

And then we were there—the Arkansas State Psychiatric Hospital. I stood up and pulled the cord, signaling the driver to stop at the next corner. Sandra gave my arm a big squeeze as we got off the bus.

The hospital was located behind the fire station and a couple of other buildings, and when I saw it I fought back a strong urge to turn around and get back on the bus. Sandra and I paused on the sidewalk and stared at the complex of blonde brick buildings. Some of them were single story, some multistoried. All woven together in a maze connected by a network of concrete sidewalks.

"I thought it would be one building," I said. "Like a real hospital."

"This thing covers acres," Sandra said. "I never dreamed there were this many crazy people in Arkansas."

"I guess we better get started. Let's start with the first building and start asking around."

"Lead on MacDuff." Sandra gave my arm another

squeeze.

In the first building we found a big desk in the lobby. A gray-haired nurse sat behind the desk.

"Hi," I said, shooting the woman my best smile. "We've come to visit a friend of ours."

The nurse didn't smile back. "You look awfully young to come here by yourself."

"My mom dropped us off. She's coming in in a minute. After she parks the car." Sometimes lying is so easy.

"I see," the nurse said. "What's your friend's name?"

"Mrs. McDonald. Katherine McDonald."

"Let me see what I can find." She started thumbing through some pieces of paper on a clipboard.

I shifted my weight and looked around the lobby. There wasn't much to see.

"Okay," the nurse said. "Here it is. Katherine McDonald." She skimmed the page. "She's in the North Wing. Building 5A. You'll have to check with the wing supervisor."

Sandra and I looked puzzled.

"That would be Dr. Schaffer. He's in charge of the North Wing. You'd have to talk to him."

"Thanks for your help," I said. "Which way is the North Wing?"

"Why don't we wait for your mother," the nurse said. "Let me talk to her. Why don't you kids wait here until she gets the car parked? There are some magazines on the table over there."

"That's a good idea," Sandra said. "We'll wait for his mom. Thanks." Sandra might look like Marilyn Monroe but her acting left a lot to be desired.

"You're welcome," the nurse said in a frosty voice.

Sandra and I drifted over to the table. We sat down in a couple of red vinyl chairs and started thumbing through old issues of *Life* and the *Saturday Evening Post*. When the nurse reached for the console behind her to answer a ringing phone, we scrambled out the door.

"My mom is parking the car?" Sandra said with a grin.

"Best I could think of," I laughed.

"Okay, what now?"

"We find the North Wing. Building 5A."

We wandered around the grounds for the better part of half an hour. I thought we might see crazy people dressed up like Napoleon or wrapped up in straightjackets running around all over the place. But we didn't see anybody. The place seemed deserted.

Finally, we followed the walkway to a single story building that was isolated from the rest of the complex. Shrubs lined the front, which gave the building a homey appearance. We spotted a small sign on the door that read: North Wing. Building 5A.

As a stalling tactic we walked around to the side of the building. All the windows had bars on them.

"There's no way they're gonna let us in there to see Katherine," Sandra said. "Besides, the place is probably full of really scary crazy people. No telling what they might do."

"Yeah. This is a little tougher than I thought it would be."

"Do you think we should give up?"

"Nope. This is my only shot at finding some evidence to prove what happened to Roy. It's my only chance to find some justice for him."

"I think you're a little crazy, but at least you're not a quitter." Sandra said.

"Does that mean you're still with me?"

"To the end." She gave my arm a playful punch. "What's the plan?"

"I'm not sure. Let's go sit over there and think about it."

We walked over to a grassy knoll across the walkway and sat down in the grass and stared at Building 5A.

"We could say we are Katherine's children," I said even though I knew it sounded stupid.

"What if they said Katherine has no kids?" Sandra said.

"Maybe we could sneak in and talk to Katherine before anybody figured out we were there."

"That might work, but how are we going to sneak into a mental hospital?"

"Details, details. Don't sweat the small stuff. We'll think of something."

Not much came to mind.

Rain clouds gathered off to the west.

After a while the roar of an engine shattered the stillness of the hospital grounds. We looked behind us and saw an old-fashioned motorbike weaving its way over the walkways that connected the hospital buildings. The bike took a sharp left and sped toward Building 5A.

A mammoth young guy with fiery red hair and a neatly trimmed red beard drove the cycle. He had on a black leather jacket over a starched white work shirt with his name over the pocket and white work pants.

He stopped the bike in a grove of trees across the walkway from where Sandra and I were sitting. He cut the engine and looked at his watch.

"I bet that's an orderly," Sandra said.

"Looks like."

The orderly dropped the kickstand, jumped off the bike, and sprinted toward a side door. When he got to the door, he fumbled in his jacket pocket for a set of keys.

He searched through the ring, found the one he wanted and let himself into Building 5A.

We sat in silence for a couple of minutes.

"I saw this movie on TV," Sandra said. "These soldiers wanted to blow up this bridge. But all these Nazis were guarding the bridge. So the soldiers blew up a truck down the road and all the Nazis ran down the road to see what happened and the soldiers snuck in and set the charges on the bridge while the Nazis were gone. Robert Mitchum starred in the movie. He thought of blowing up the truck."

"A diversion," I said. "That might work."

We watched the building for a few more minutes.

"What about the motorcycle?" Sandra said, pulling her sweater around her shoulders.

"You want to blow up the motorcycle?"

"No silly. I don't want to blow it up. But I did notice the orderly left the keys in the ignition."

"Which will help us how?"

Sandra stretched her arms over her head. "Do you know how to kick-start the bike?"

"Kinda. Tommy Lee's brother used to have a Harley. I started it once. Are you thinking of stealing the bike? I really don't think that's going to help us find

Katherine."

"We're not going to steal it but what if you started the motorcycle, revved it up really loud, and when the orderly came out the door to check on his bike, we ducked through the door behind him?"

"A diversion," I grinned.

"Why not?"

The first raindrops hit the sidewalk.

Sandra's idea seemed funny sitting on the knoll. Not so funny perched on the big orderly's motorcycle. If the guy remembered he had left the key in the bike and came back and found me fooling around on his motorbike I would be in some serious dooty.

Sandra positioned herself behind the place where the building jutted out to form the archway of the side door. She motioned for me to start the engine.

I had come too far to chicken out so I switched on the key, brought all my weight down on the kickstarter, and turned the handlebar to give the engine some gas.

Only nothing happened.

Sandra looked puzzled. I gave her the palms up sign and shrugged. She motioned for me to try it again. So I did.

This time the engine roared to life. Rum-rum-rum. I gave it a lot of gas. Rum-rum-rum. The bike needed some muffler work. I gave it full throttle. Rum-rum-rum. Mickey the baby baboon could probably hear the bike ten blocks away at the zoo. Rum-rum.

I killed the engine, hopped off the bike, and sprinted over to Sandra. We hovered behind the archway extension and pressed our backs against the side of the building.

Suddenly the side door flew open and the red-bearded orderly came flying out. He ran across the walkway to the grove where he had parked his motorcycle.

While he looked up and down the walkway and the grounds, Sandra and I slipped into the building through the open side door.

And ran right into the largest woman on the planet.

She loomed directly in front of us, her hands planted on her broad hips. "Where are you going?" She didn't sound angry. Just curious.

"I . . . uh . . . uh . . . well . . . we were . . . uh . . . . ." Archie Lane, the boy with the Silver Tongue.

"I'm looking for my sister's room," the woman said. "But I'm lost. This place is so big. You could fit my whole little town in here. I'm Flo Wyatt from Marmaduke." She wore a blue- and-white flowered dress that seemed to go on forever. She was so tall I had to crane my neck to see her face.

"I'm Connie and this is Tommy Lee." Sandra was a fast thinker.

Flo's rear end was the size of Rhode Island and she wore a big floppy-billed hat that left her face in shadows.

"We're suppose to meet his mom," Sandra said, indicating me. But we got lost too."

"Humm." Flo looked us up and down. "Why don't you have a visitor's badge? Like mine." She pointed to an official looking card that was pinned to the front of her dress.

"His mom has it," Sandra was on her game.

"Well, no mind," Flo said. "You can tag along with me and we'll look together. I'm looking for room number 115. That's where they put my sister, Julie Ann. She was over in the South Building last time. That's where they put the real nut cases. Being over here makes me think Julie Ann's getting better. Who are you here to see?"

"My aunt." My voice returned.

"That's nice. Well, come along now. Maybe we'll run into your mother on the way." Flo whirled around and stalked down the hallway. Sandra and I followed like tugboats in the wake of a battleship.

"There's room 105," Flo said. "It seems to me room 115 should be 10 down. But it's not. I tried that corridor a minute ago. The numbers start with 125. No wonder everybody's crazy around here. Makes no sense."

"None at all," I said.

We proceeded down the hallway and took a right that led us down another corridor. Flo kept up a barrage of constant chatter. "See. Now the rooms all have single digits. This is so confusing. This is the women's wing. The men are housed next door. Hard to believe there are this many crazy women in Arkansas."

A nurse passed us in the hallway. She looked at Sandra and I and frowned but when she saw Flo's visitor's badge she smiled and nodded.

"Excuse me," Flo spoke to the nurse. "I'm trying to find room 115." Her voice went up like it was a question. Sandra and I crowded behind her and tried to look like we belonged. "It's my sister's room. We're from Marmaduke and she's always running around town in her nightgown. I hope ya'll can fix her."

The nurse shook her head. "Go back and turn right at the next hallway. The room's in the middle of the corridor."

"Thank you so much."

The nurse didn't even look at Sandra and me. She seemed in a hurry and scurried off before Flo could ask her about finding my "mother." Talk about a break.

Once we turned the corner, I noticed that the rooms all had removable name tags beside the door as well as numbers. None of them said "McDonald."

But one more turn and there it was. A door had a tag beside it that said "K. McDonald."

I pointed to the door and Sandra said, "Bingo."

We stayed behind Flo until we reached the end of the hallway. "There's my sister's room," she said. Room 215. Of all things. I think I walked right past it a few minutes ago. I guess I'm getting crazier than Julie Ann. Well, maybe not that crazy. Say, you want me to help you find your mother. I'd be glad to."

"No thanks," I said. "We'll just go back and ask that nurse. She seemed really helpful."

"Suit yourself." Flo pounded on the door to room 115. "Open up, Julie Ann. It's Flo. Your sister."

Sandra and I waited until Flo disappeared into room 115 and then did a run-walk back down the hallway to the room with "K. McDonald" on the name tag.

The corridor was deserted and seemed strangely quiet without Flo and her chatter. We stopped in front of Katherine's room and I took a deep breath.

"Okay," I said. "We're in business." I knocked on the door. I waited a minute, and when I didn't hear anyone moving inside I knocked again.

Katherine opened the door. She looked small and frail, her eyes encased in dark circles. She wore a blue hospital gown and her hair was a mess of tangles. Her skin looked wrinkly and dirty. Her eyes were narrow slits.

"Yes?"

"Katherine. It's us. We came to visit. We really need to talk to you."

Katherine blinked and pursed her lips. Then she shook her head. "Who on Earth are you?"

CHAPTER THIRTY-FOUR

Katherine stared at us like we were monkeys in the zoo. "You've made a mistake," she said, closing the door.

Then she stopped. "Wait. I do know you. You're Archie. The boy who brought the records to Roy."

"Right," I smiled.

"And your pretty little friend . . ."

"Sandra."

"Yes, yes. I remember. You came to visit Roy. He couldn't stop talking about you. Of course. Please come in." She ran her hand through her unruly hair.

Katherine's room was tiny and cramped. There was a single bed, a wooden dresser, and an uncomfortable looking chair. That was it.

After she let us in, she shuffled over to the chair and sank down on the threadbare cushion.

I closed the door and Sandra and I perched side by side on the bed, facing Katherine. Outside, the rain made a pinging sound against the barred window. The clouds had gotten thicker, leaving the room in semidarkness. Katherine didn't bother to turn on a light.

We sat like that for a couple of minutes. Katherine tried to smile but it seemed to take too much effort. An alarm clock on the dresser made a loud ticking sound. The room was full of high-tension silence.

"We just stopped by to say hi," Sandra said. "See

how you are doing."

Katherine let the question sink in. "I'm better," she said in a slurred voice. They give me a lot of pills. The pills make it hard to remember. Hard to think. But the pills take away some of the hurt."

"That's good." I didn't know what else to say.

"We have group therapy in the dayroom. Everybody talks. It helps. And I see Dr. Schaffer. He wants me to understand what happened. He wants me to reframe everything. See it in a different light. He's very nice."

"That sounds lovely," Sandra said. "I'm sure you're getting excellent care here. My father says this is a topflight facility."

My father called it the Nut House.

Katherine folded her hands in her lap. "It's hard sometimes," she said in a dreamy voice.

"I'm sure it is." Sandra shifted her weight on the bed. She smelled like soap. "You experienced a terrible thing," she said. "You need time to get over it."

Katherine nodded. Then we lost her for a couple of minutes. She just stared at the wall. Panic rose inside of me. Katherine wasn't going to be of any help. The pills had turned her brains to oatmeal. She probably couldn't remember what she had for breakfast let alone what happened on Halloween night.

"Sometimes Dr. Schaffer makes me talk about it," Katherine said, snapping out of her reverie. "He says I need to face it head-on. I can't hide in the booze. I can't run away from it." Her voice never went up or down. She spoke every word in the same monotone.

"You mean what happened to Roy," Sandra said.

Katherine nodded.

I decided to make my move. "Mrs. McDonald, what exactly did happen that night?"

"My Roy died and went to heaven."

"I know," I said. "But I mean how did it happen? The last time I visited at your house you said what Mr. McDonald did was wrong. You said you wouldn't let him get away with it."

Katherine looked at me and cocked her head. "I remember your visit. I was in my cups, but I think I did say that. Yes, that's what I said."

I drew in a deep breath. "You said some things are never excused no matter what."

"That's true," Katherine said, looking puzzled. "But . . . but . . . what does that have to do with the night Roy died?"

"Didn't Mr. McDonald . . . you know . . . do something with Roy's iron lung that night?"

Katherine thought for a minute. "That wasn't what I was talking about."

Now I was the one that was confused.

Sandra came to my rescue. "Mrs. McDonald, could you tell us what happened that night? If it wouldn't be too painful."

"Okay. Dr. Schaffer says I need to talk about it. No more hiding."

Sandra smiled.

I didn't have a clue what was going on.

"It was my fault," Katherine droned on in her monotone. "I drank too much that night. Way, way too much. I didn't close Roy's machine tight like I should have."

Sandra and I both leaned forward on the bed. This wasn't what we'd expected to hear.

"Roy couldn't breathe. I was on the sofa and couldn't get up. Everything sounded so far away. I couldn't move. I felt so tired. I needed to sleep."

"Where was your husband?" I said.

"Back in his darkroom, developing film. He ran into the den as soon as he heard Roy," Katherine said. "But it was too late."

"Roy was already dead?" I whispered.

"Almost. He couldn't breathe. He lived with so much pain. The doctor said he would die in a matter of days anyway. Roy had been so much worse the last few weeks. Joe did the merciful thing. He just didn't act quickly. He called it a mercy killing. Even the doctor said that under the circumstances Joe did the humane thing. Roy was so far gone before it happened the doctor didn't even file charges against me. But, you see, it was all my fault."

Sandra worked her arm alongside mine so I could take her hand. Her head came close to mine until her hair brushed my cheek.

I hadn't seen a murder on Halloween night. I had witnessed something else.

"But what about all that stuff you said?" I was still confused. "He can't get away with it. He can't do this to me. What did all of that mean if you weren't talking about what Mr. McDonald did to Roy that night?"

Katherine's eyes narrowed. For an instant she looked more like her old self. "You're very young, Archie," she said. "When you're young, things are not always what they seem. Do you remember the song Roy loved? He thought it was 'The Great Green Teddy Bear' because he heard it from all the way over in your house next door."

Sandra looked puzzled.

"But the song was really called 'The Great Pretender,'" I said. "It wasn't what he thought it was."

"Exactly," Katherine said. "It wasn't what Roy thought. You think you're hearing a song from next door, and it's not what you think it is."

"Mrs. McDonald, I'm not sure I understand what you're saying," Sandra said.

Katherine slumped down in her chair. Suddenly she looked exhausted. "You will," she said. "When the time comes . . . you will."

Katherine cast doubt on my version of what happened to Roy on Halloween night. I wasn't sure how I felt about that. But now we had another mystery to solve.

"I'm tired." Katherine barely got the words out. "My pills are kicking in. I need to lie down now."

"I'm sorry," Sandra said. "I hope we haven't stayed too long."

"No, dear. You're fine. But when I think about my Roy and what I did my head hurts and I get tired. You'll have to go now. The nurse will be here in a minute. They check up on me all the time. You can't be here."

Sandra and I helped Katherine out of her chair and onto the bed. "Remember the Great Green Teddy Bear," she said as her head rested on the pillow. She closed her eyes.

And then she laughed.

CHAPTER THIRTY-FIVE

New Year's Day, 1958

I climbed out of bed and put on my blue robe that was decorated with cartoon cowboys and Indians. The sleeves stopped short of my wrists and the bottom barely came to my knees. But it was the only robe I had and I still liked the way it felt, all soft and warm and worn.

There was something really exciting about the first day of a new year, a year that comes only once in everybody's lifetime. I mean 1958 will never happen again. There won't be any do-overs or second chances. You only get one 1958.

I went to the window and saw a thick blanket of snow covering all the yards around the circle. The street had completely disappeared under the soft white covering. Even the trees were bending over with the weight of the heavy white powder. It looked like the universe had sent the snow to cover up all the ugly stuff from the last year, and now the New Year would start with everything clean and fresh and white.

The sun reflected off the snow, making a glare that forced me to look away. Despite the sun, I could feel the icy cold through the windowpane.

While I stood at the window, the furnace kicked on and filled the house with warm air and that neat burning furnacy smell. I walked out in the hall and stood on the grate, letting the heated air blow up my pajama legs.

The door to Mom's bedroom was closed, so I knew she was still asleep. The wall clock in the kitchen read 9:30.

In the living room, I found these great looking cardboard hats on the sofa. Mom had brought them home from the Hamilton's New Year's Eve party. She and Dad did that every year. Some years they'd bring me noisemakers or fancy paper cups. This year it was hats. One of the hats was a green top hat covered with all this glittery stuff. The hat had a loose rubber band around the bottom. . The other hat looked like a sparkly red dunce cap.

Happy New Year.

I put on the green top hat and walked around the living room. I imagined all the people at the party dancing in their New Year's Eve hats and toasting the arrival of 1958, and I was sorry my dad was in Houston and my mom had to go to the party by herself.

I wandered into the kitchen and fixed a bowl of Sugar Pops and ate breakfast in front of the TV in the living room. I watched this big parade with all these neat floats and marching bands and cowboys on horses. The parade had something to do with the Rose Bowl football game out in California. The people on the floats smiled and waved, having a terrific time in the sunshine.

In the middle of the parade, this guy in a flattop and thick glasses cut in on the program with a local weather report. He looked real serious and said that all the roads and streets in Little Rock were closed because of the snow and ice. He said everybody should stay home and not go out unless they had an emergency because cars were slipping and sliding and wrecking all over town. The New Year had arrived like an angry polar bear.

I watched some more of the parade before I went back into my room. In a little while I planned to call Sandra and see if she wanted to get out her sled and go over to the ridge. I knew she would. We both loved sledding down the back slope of the ridge. What a great way to start 1958.

While I was hanging around in my room, thinking about sledding and parades and stuff I heard the back door slam over at the McDonald's house. Curiosity got the best of me and I got on my knees and crawled across the rug to the frosty window and peeked out.

Mr. McDonald stood in the carport next to the T-bird. He had on a heavy tan overcoat with a fleece collar and a dark blue navy pea cap. I drew in a quick breath and held it. My heart started pounding like crazy. I scrunched down in the corner of the window and peeped out again.

Slapping his gloved hands together, he shuffled down the driveway to the street, where he tested the ice on the road with his foot. The snow on the street and driveway was thick and must have been icy because Mr. McDonald slipped and went down on one knee on the way back to the carport. He caught himself with his hand, climbed back to his feet and then made his way carefully up the slippery driveway. The weather guy on TV had been right on the money. Little Rock was snowed in.

Despite his fall, Mr. McDonald wore this goofy grin. Being from Boston maybe he missed the snow.

Now he had all the snow he could handle. After walking around the carport a couple of times he checked his watch, shrugged, and circled around the side of his house. He opened the gate and went into the backyard. In a minute I saw him vault over the wall on the far side and disappear beyond the ditch that ran around the back of his property. It was a great vault. Especially for a guy his age.

Mr. McDonald must have decided it was too icy to take the T-bird out on the streets and decided to walk wherever he was going.

Then, all of a sudden, in a flash of Stupid Lightening, I had an idea. It just grabbed me in a big ol' bear hug and wouldn't let go. I mean this idea was probably the Most Super Colossal Horrible Idea of all time. As Ed Sullivan might say, this was a Reallllly Big Mistake.

But I didn't care.

Here was the chance I had been waiting for. Since Halloween night Mr. McDonald had been following me around, trying to scare me, or worse. What if I turned the tables and followed him? Katherine had explained that Mr. McDonald hadn't murdered Roy, but I still didn't know why he had been following me. I couldn't figure it out and not knowing was driving me nuts.

Katherine had said there was something else I didn't know about. Something big. Something I didn't understand. Like when Roy thought the song was called 'The Great Green Teddy Bear' and it wasn't.

Now I had my chance to find out what she meant.

The more I thought about it, the madder I got. The big creep had been tailing me all over town. Showing up when I least expected it. Scaring the bejesus out of me. I was sick and tired of being afraid. Now I had a chance to follow him. Yeah! It wasn't a stupid idea. It was a great idea. Let's see how *he* liked it. Yeah!

I could track Mr. McDonald through the snow the way this guy tracked a panther in this neat story I read in *Boys' Life* magazine. Mr. McDonald would never see me. Then I would know where he went and what he was up to.

Seized with this incredible inspiration, I jumped into my jeans, put on my heavy plaid shirt and slipped into my boots. Then I went into the kitchen and wrote a note on Mom's memo pad. "Gone over to Harry Foster's to play. Happy New Year. Love, A."

I found my new winter jacket and my hat with the floppy fleece lined ears in the hall closet, put them on and crept out the back door and launched my big adventure.

Outside, the sunlight ricocheted off the frozen snow, creating a glare that made me squint. The cold air stung my lungs. My boots crunched over the lightly packed snow and I sank down a little in the white mush, which made walking slower than a sloth.

The whole world was quiet. There were no birds, no cars, nothing. It felt like everyone and everything in the neighborhood had been sucked up into a giant spaceship and whisked off to Mars, leaving me all alone. The only sound was the steady crunch-crunch of my boots in the crusty snow.

I vaulted the McDonald's forbidden wall, sprinted across the backyard and hurdled over the wall again at the back of the lawn. Then I picked up Mr. McDonald's tracks on the other side of the ditch. Piece of cake. His boots had thick treads, and I could see his tracks all the way across the ditch and into the next backyard.

It helped that they were the only tracks in the whole snow-blanketed neighborhood. You didn't have to be Sergeant Preston of the Yukon to follow them.

I took my time and shadowed the tracks up Elmwood Road, the street that ran next to the woods surrounding Edison. The only sign of life in the houses on the street was an occasional puff of smoke from one of the chimneys. The Great Tracker, Archie of the North, was all alone, and I marched right down the center of the street, stalking my prey.

At the corner of Elmwood and McKnight Streets, the tracks turned right and I followed them past the front of Edison and the deep woods across the street that made up the Lancaster Property. The tracks cut left down McCloud Road on the far side of the Lancaster block. There were houses on the right side of the street and the fenced-off woods of the Lancaster Property on the left side.

I slowed down and crossed over to the sidewalk, where I moved behind the cars parked at the curb. If Mr. McDonald slowed down or stopped somewhere up ahead I didn't want him to see me. So I stayed crouched down on the sidewalk, where I could still see the tracks in the middle of the street as I inched my way from car to car. It was an old tracker's trick. I guess.

Then the weirdness started.

Mr. McDonald's tracks disappeared.

Vanished.

When I peeked out from behind this little Nash Rambler there were no footprints in the middle of the street. They just marched up to this one place and poof—they were gone. Nothing but smooth white snow the rest of the block. Weird, huh?

I raced back to the Rambler and crouched down behind the right front tire. I listened hard. There was still no sound on the street. Then I inched out from behind the Nash, checked in both directions, and crept back out into the middle of the street. To get a look-see as us trackers say.

That's when I realized what had happened. The reason the footprints didn't continue past the Rambler was that Mr. McDonald had taken a sharp left into a little gate in the middle of the block that led into the Lancaster Property.

I looked up and down the street before I moved across the snow-covered road. The tracks indicated Mr. McDonald had walked up to the gate, shuffled his feet in the snow, opened the gate, walked right in, closed the gate behind him, and hiked on down this little path that disappeared into the forbidden Lancaster woods.

I waited a couple of minutes and then pushed on the gate.

It was locked.

Mr. McDonald must have had a key to the gate.

So much for the adventures of Archie, the King of the Snow Trackers.

All I had found out was that Mr. McDonald probably went to visit Cantrell Lancaster and his crazy son on New Year's Day. Big woo.

I was disappointed. I wanted more. I wanted to know what he was doing in there. I wanted to tail him the way he'd been tailing me. I wanted to turn the tables. But did I want to follow him all the way into the Lancaster Property?

Do you think I'm nuts? Forget it.

I hiked back to McKnight Street, my boots crunching on the fresh snow, whiffs of fog coming out of my mouth and nose like I was puffing on a Chesterfield. When I got to the front of Edison, I stopped in the middle of the street.

The whole world was nothing but snow and silence.

Even the fence that surrounded the Lancaster Property had snow piles on top of it. The thick snow covered up the strip of barbed wire that circled the top of the fence.

I could go into the Lancaster Property if I wanted to. If I wasn't chicken. If I wasn't the biggest chicken-baby in Little Rock I could go right in there.

I could get in like this old dog Tommy Lee and I saw one time. I could dig through the snow and the soft earth until I could wiggle under the fence the same way the dog did it. Of course, we never saw the dog come out. But I didn't want to think about that.

I could get into the Lancaster Property and turn the tables on Mr. McDonald if I wasn't such a yellowbelly. I could do it if I was crazy. Or mad. And boy, was I mad. The big jerk had been following me all over everywhere. And now it was my turn.

I could go into the Lancaster Property if I was willing to do something no kid had ever done before. Sure, no kid had ever had the nerve to go in there and see the house or the killer guard dogs or the ghosts or the land mines or any of it. If a kid went into the Lancaster Property he would never come out alive.

It was something to think about.

But I wasn't just any kid. I was Archie Lane, the boy with the overactive imagination, and I could go into the Lancaster Property if I wanted to.

And I wanted to.

I wanted to show Mr. McDonald that I wasn't afraid of him or anybody else. I wasn't afraid of the scariest man in the world inside the scariest woods on the planet.

"Yeah!" I shook my fist in the air and ran across the street, slipping and sliding on the ice. Then I found a place close to where Tommy Lee and I saw the dog burrow under the fence and got down on my knees and started scooping away snow with my hands. Piece of cake. In a couple of minutes I reached dirt. The dirt was frozen but after I chopped at it with a stick I discovered that only the top part was hard. Right below the surface I found nothing but soft, squishy mud.

I dug and scratched and clawed out a hole big enough to roll under and then I scrunched up my body into a little ball, burrowed into the hole and slipped under the fence. When I came out on the other side my clothes were all wet from the snow and muddy from the dirt in the hole but snow and mud didn't bother Archie, the King of the Snow Trackers.

I was inside the Lancaster Property. Me, Archie Lane. I was the first kid to ever get inside the fence, to go the one place where every adult said absolutely, positively no kid could go. I was the bravest kid in the history of the Edison School.

Either that or I was the dumbest.

CHAPTER 36

Right off the bat, the Great Tracker got lost.

The woods inside the Lancaster Property were really thick and the snow was deep and I kept a look out for wild attack dogs and ghosts and land mines or whatever else might be guarding the scary, dark forest. So I got lost.

I trudged from tree to tree, crunching through the ankle high snow. Everyone said there was a house in the center of the property, but after about a half an hour of creeping through the woods, I came out on the Hayes Street side of the woods. That meant I had hiked through the entire five blocks of thick forest.

If there was a house, I had missed the place completely. I couldn't believe it. Me. The Great Tracker. I couldn't even find a house. I leaned against a pine tree and tried to figure out what I had done wrong.

I finally concluded that I must have zigzagged across the northern border of the woods, somehow missing the center where the house was supposed to be located.

I was disappointed but determined. Feeling more confident since I hadn't been attacked by Rottweilers or phantoms on my first go round, I angled in toward the middle of the block. I moved slowly from tree to tree, always on the lookout for danger. The Great Tracker was back on the trail.

Then all of a sudden, I stumbled out from behind this thick grove of pines and there it was, right in front of me. Rich old Cantrell Lancaster's house, right smack dab in the middle of the woods just like everybody said.

I was the first kid who had ever seen the place, and I hoped I would be the first kid to live to tell the tale.

I hunkered down behind this enormous oak tree and peeked out to check out the place. A dirt trail, barely big enough for one car lead up to the front door and made a circle. I figured that had to be the same path Mr. McDonald had used to hike in from the McCloud Street gate.

The house was fantastic. Not a mansion or a castle or anything like that. Just neat. The structure was made out of dark wood and big rocks and looked like these pictures of modern houses I once saw in a magazine in the kid shrink's office. They were supposed to blend into the environment and Cantrell Lancaster's house certainly did that.

Half of the house was two stories and half was one story, and since the house was made out of wood and stone the whole thing blended into the surrounding forest like it had been a part of the woods forever.

The house didn't have a carport or a garage, and there were no cars in the driveway or on the trail. That wasn't such a big deal except I noticed smoke coming out of the chimney. You didn't have to be Joe Hardy or Johnny Dollar or Dick Tracy to figure out someone was in the house.

I was so thrilled with finding the place and so full of myself at being the first kid to ever go inside the Lancaster Property that I wandered out from my hiding place behind the tree. That's when I heard the noise. I froze and waited to be ripped apart by blood thirsty Dobermans or furious demons.

A stupid squirrel ran across the path and leaped into the tree next to me. The tree branch groaned and a bunch of snow fell off and thudded to the ground.

I jumped back behind my tree. Maybe killer squirrels guarded the Lancaster property instead of German Shepherds or landmines.

Once my heart rate returned to normal, I moved out from behind the tree, ran toward the house, and ducked behind a clump of bushes next to the driveway. Peering over the top of the shrubbery I located Mr. McDonald's footprints on the path leading to the house. I had been following those tracks all morning and the tread marks of his boots were unmistakable. The tracks came right down the middle of the trail and marched right up to the front door.

But there was also a second set of footprints that came down the path. That seemed really strange. The Great Tracker surveyed the situation. The person who had made the second set of prints had smaller feet than Mr. McDonald and stayed more on the outside of the path until they reached the house. That told me that the two people had come down the trail at separate times rather than together. The second person must have arrived while I wandered around the northern border of the woods.

The quiet made me nervous. I wished a bird would sing or an airplane would fly over or the stupid killer squirrel would come back.

I watched the house from my hiding place and kept trying to figure out what was going on inside. I knew

Mr. McDonald was in there. But what was he doing? Then it hit me. If you want to know what's going on inside the house you have to look *in* the house not hang around in the stupid bushes outside. Action was what was called for and Action was my middle name.

So Archie Action Lane, the Great Tracker, made his move. I dashed across the dirt driveway and when I reached the side of the house I pressed my back against the building and listened, waiting to see if something would happen.

Nothing did.

Getting down on all fours, I crawled underneath this big window in the front of the house and slowly raised my head so I could look inside at the living room. A big curved couch occupied one corner of the room, thick carpet covered the entire floor, and a fireplace surrounded by built-in bookshelves fronted the sofa.

There were lots of photographs on the walls. The weird thing was they were photographs of army guys in Korea, and I realized some of them were the exact same pictures as the ones hanging in the McDonald's den.

There was no one in the room and no fire in the fireplace. That seemed strange since smoke had been pouring out of the chimney ever since I got there. There had to be another fireplace in the house.

It's hard to fool the Great Tracker.

I circled around the building and peeked in the kitchen window. Still no people.

Mr. McDonald had to be upstairs. But that posed a tough question. How could I find out what he was up to if he stayed upstairs?

As my eyes drifted up to the window, I saw my

chance.

All I had to do was climb up this white trellis that was nailed to the side of the house. The trellis ran next to an upstairs window and if I climbed the thing I could lean over a bit and look into the window. Well, maybe a little more than a bit.

I'd bet that in the spring, the trellis would be covered with beautiful blossoms but on a snowy New Year's Day it only hosted a handful of dead, brown vines. I took a deep breath and climbed the first couple of rungs. The trellis wobbled like crazy and felt like it was made out of Popsicle sticks, and I had to admit that scaling the thing may not have been the greatest idea of my life. But I didn't want to be a weenie.

So I climbed the rest of the trellis. Slowly and carefully. When I got to the window on the second floor, I paused and pressed my cheek hard against the wall of the house, catching my breath. The stone wall felt colder than ice, and I was afraid that if I left my cheek on the surface my face would freeze to the side of Cantrell Lancaster's house forever.

Then I looked down and got a jolt when I realized just how high up I had climbed. Looking at the ground down below made me dizzy and I gripped the trellis hard and vowed not to look down again.

The moment of truth had arrived. It was time to find out what Mr. McDonald was up to. So I balanced my weight on my left foot, leaned way, way over and peeked into the upstairs window.

That let me look into a big bedroom with a fireplace on the far wall. Can you believe that? A bedroom with a fireplace?

A fire smoldered in the fireplace. Not much of one

but enough to crackle and pop and put out a little heat on a snowy New Year's Day. A four-poster bed with gnarly wooden posts sat off to one side of the fireplace. Whoever had been sleeping in the bed hadn't bothered to make it up. A small blue sofa faced the fireplace.

Mr. McDonald sat on the sofa with his legs stretched out on the coffee table in front of him. His slicked back hair glistened like he had just gotten out of the shower. His scar had turned a ruddy purple and he was wearing a maroon bathrobe with the initials CL in white cursive above the left pocket.

Empty coffee cups and newspapers littered the table. A bottle of champagne and a stemmed glass rested on the table. I knew it was champagne because I saw this movie last summer with Cary Grant and he sipped champagne all through the movie in a glass that he kept refilling from a bottle like the one on the table.

Suddenly someone said something to Mr. McDonald from somewhere over by the bed. Whoa. There was somebody else in the bedroom. I leaned out as far as I could go, balancing on the trellis on one foot, but I still couldn't see the other person across the room. Mr. McDonald smiled and said something back. Then his face broke into this goofy grin. He stood up and laughed and faced the other person with his arms out.

The next five minutes of my life felt like all the fireworks in the whole city had exploded at once. Bottle rockets, firecrackers, roman candles, black cats, the whole works blowing up at one time. Bam-Bam-Bam.

My mother walked across the room with a champagne glass in her hand.

She was barefooted and wore tan slacks and a black sweater. She had on lots of makeup and her hair was all combed out. She looked like the pictures of these Greek goddesses I saw in this library book once. Terri the Goddess of Kingwood.

Mr. McDonald held out his arms, and my mother skipped across the room and they hugged. Right there in front of me. Then they kissed each other. On the mouth like in the movies. It was the barfiest thing I had ever seen in my whole life.

I didn't want to see any more, but I couldn't help myself. I leaned way over and stared through the glass, balancing on my toes on the trellis, gripping the windowsill with both hands.

I must have made a noise because my mom turned around for a second—and saw me looking at her through the window.

Our eyes locked and then something really bad happened. My foot slipped off the trellis and I lost my grip on the windowsill. Suddenly I was like the coyote in the Roadrunner cartoons when he runs off the cliff, jogging on air with nothing to hold on to and no place to put his feet.

Unlike the cartoons, that didn't last long. Before I could blink, the snow-covered ground rushed up at me like a giant white-mouthed monster that wanted to devour Archie, the King of the Trackers.

CHAPTER 37

When I hit the ground all the air whooshed out of my lungs and I couldn't get my breath. All I could do was lie in the snow, which sucked me down like freezing quicksand. It was not a fun experience. I landed on my right arm and this horrible pain shot all the way from my wrist to my shoulder. Fortunately, I crashed in some pretty thick snow, which broke my fall. At least a little.

My mom ran out of the house and covered me up with a couple of scratchy old blankets and propped up my head so I could breathe and in a few minutes an ambulance with its red lights and siren blaring came crunching down the trail on thick tire chains and stopped in front of Cantrell Lancaster's house.

Mr. McDonald never came outside.

I was a mess. Seeing my mother with Mr. McDonald was my own personal Hiroshima, and I knew from that moment on nothing would ever be the same and nothing would ever turn out for the best. No matter what the stupid grownups told me.

The ambulance guys were a pair of idiots. Sid Martin from my school grown up. Both of them were flabby and had pimples and stringy hair. They kept arguing and telling each other how to load me on the stretcher without breaking my back. I tried to tell them it was my arm that was hurt, not my back, but they were too dumb to listen. They got me up on the stretcher and into the vehicle without breaking my back, but the moron banged my hurt arm on the door while they were loading me into the ambulance. Fresh pain shot all the way up to my shoulder.

The tire chains crunched through the snow and ice as we made our way out of the Lancaster Property and headed for the hospital.

Mom sat with me in the ambulance while we crunched across town. We didn't speak to each other the whole trip. We didn't even look at each other.

At St. Vincent's Hospital, a nurse x-rayed me and a doctor looked in my eyes and ears and thumped my knees and told me I was a lucky kid to not be hurt any worse than I was. The fall had broken my arm in two places and the doc put a cast on my whole arm and asked me how the other guy looked. I knew he would ask that. They all sure do love that line.

One of the nurses gave me a Tootsie Pop and wished me a Happy New Year. Somehow I didn't really think all the Tootsie Pops in the universe would make the pain go away. The real pain—not the pain in my arm.

Mom and I took a taxi home. It was the first cab I had ever ridden in and the experience left me a little disappointed. I always thought taxis were a big deal, but the whole thing was just like riding in a regular car. Big woo.

All the way from the hospital to our house my mom and I just looked out our windows at the snow and acted like a pair of total strangers.

We passed a basketball goal in a driveway and I thought about Jerome and the Phantom. They wouldn't be coming to the school ground on Sunday afternoons anymore. Thanks to Tommy Lee and Bobby Sanderson and those other morons. Our games to a hundred were over for good.

I'd miss those games. I'd learned a lot from Jerome and the Phantom. I used Jerome's hook shot all the time now. Same with the Phantom's hesitation dribble. More than anything I'd miss the fun we had. All those good shots and rebounds and close games. I'd miss those hours where basketball was all that mattered. Not race or hate or any of that other junk.

I wondered what would happen to Jerome and the Phantom. My guess would be they'd both make the varsity over at Dunbar Junior High, the Negro school. Then I bet they'd both go on to play for Horace Mann, the Negro high school. And they would go up north and play college ball at one of the schools that didn't care if colored guys and white guys played together.

Maybe, just maybe one day I'd be playing for the Razorbacks and the team would play one of those northern schools in a tournament in Chicago or New York and Jerome or the Phantom would be on the other team. I loved the dream and I wished both of them the best wherever they might wind up.

When we pulled into Kingwood, I saw a bunch of little kids dressed in red-and-blue snowsuits building this great snowman in somebody's front yard. The snowman stood tall and thick and had a carrot nose and a big cowboy hat on his head. His name had to be Tex Snowman.

The kids' faces glowed pink from the cold. Their noses were running and their lips were chapped and cracked, but they were all having a super time, laughing and packing more snow around Tex's middle and throwing snow on each other. They were really having fun and I wished I could have been out there with them. Just me and Tex and the little kids and the snow.

When the taxi got to our house, my dad met us at the front door. He had gotten home early from his business trip, and his bags were still piled in the hallway. He still had on his coat and tie like a soldier who never takes off his uniform. He looked at my arm in the cast and got real upset and demanded to know what had happened.

Mom said she would tell him later. I was too shook up to say much of anything. The pain pills I took at the hospital kicked in and made me even sleepier than my yellow kill-your-imagination pills the kid shrink gave me. I ate a peanut butter and banana sandwich and then went to my room, where my dad helped me take off my clothes and put on my blue pajamas.

Even though it was almost dinnertime, he tucked me into bed. Then he patted me on the head and whispered, "I'm sorry," and then tiptoed out of my room and closed the door behind him.

My arm ached and throbbed and I had a tough time going to sleep with the cast on. I wanted to cry but that seemed to take more effort than it was worth.

Way off in the distance, I heard my mother and father yelling at each other. The angry sounds grew further and further away like my parents were on a boat and I was on the dock and the boat was drifting out to sea.

Then I was all alone except for Tex Snowman who had somehow talked me into going outside to play in the snow. So there me and old Tex were, standing in the snow and laughing and throwing snowballs and having fun.

When I woke up my head felt worse than my arm, which hurt a lot, and my whole body felt stiff like after the first day of basketball practice. My mother slipped into my room and announced that it was dinnertime. I had slept almost twenty-four hours.

I had already missed a whole day of 1958. But if the rest of the days of 1958 were all going to be like the first one I didn't think sleeping through a bunch of them was such a bad idea. Mom gave me another pain pill and another peanut butter and banana sandwich and a big glass of milk. She said my dad had gone to work.

My mom's face looked red and puffy and I knew she had been crying. She tried to pretend everything was okay and a regular day was starting but you could feel the weirdness hanging in the air like moss on a magnolia tree.

I told her how stiff I felt and she said I needed to walk around some to loosen up my muscles and get my blood circulating. She said she'd go outside with me if I wanted to walk up to the ridge or somewhere.

Mom fixed up my busted arm in this cloth sling they gave us at the hospital, and she and I bundled up in our coats and hats and marched out the front door. Outside the sun was on its last leg for the day and night was coming on like gangbusters.

We hiked across the circle and down Pinewood, our breath pouring out of our noses and mouths in foggy wisps. My arm nestled in the sling underneath my coat, so the right sleeve of my jacket flopped around with each step I took.

The day's sunlight had melted a lot of the snow

and what remained on the sidewalk had become a slushy mush that looked like dirty oatmeal. Mom kept her hands stuffed in her coat pockets. Her red scarf covered the lower part of her face and, with her white hat with the red fluff ball on top, she looked like a patriotic Santa's elf.

"Oregon State," Mom said after a while.

I wasn't much in the mood for the nickname game. "Beavers."

"CCNY?"

"Also Beavers. Nice try." It came out grumpy.

Mom got the message. "Okay, here goes," she said gnawing on her lower lip. "As I'm sure you already know, there's a lot of grown up stuff going on here, Mickey Mantle."

"Then call me Archie," I said. "That's my name."

I could see the hurt in Mom's eyes. "All right . . . Archie. If that's what you want."

"What I want is to know what's going on, okay?" We sidestepped a pile of slush and turned up Luckywood, passing beneath the streetlight. I felt mad and sad and a bunch of stuff in between and I wanted to scream and yell and punch somebody in the face. Broken arm or not.

Mom scrunched up her nose. "I understand. I can imagine how terribly upsetting all this is to you, and I don't blame you for being hurt and angry. You're entitled to know the whole story." She thrust her hands deeper into the pockets of her coat and started walking faster. "But I want to try to explain my side of all this."

"So explain. Nobody is stopping you."

Mom exhaled a long breath. "Mr. McDonald and I are in love with each other."

Her words hit me harder than Bobby Sanderson's fists and hurt a lot worse.

"You're in love with that scary, creepy weirdo?" I almost shouted. I couldn't help it. "Since when?"

"Since early last summer," my mother said. "I didn't mean for it to happen. Neither of us did. I ran into him at the Piggly Wiggly a couple of times. We were next-door neighbors. We said hello. We talked. He was friendly, but he was always very sad. He lived with a burden more terrible than anything I could ever imagine, but he was so brave about the whole thing." The words came whooshing out of my mother like they had been trapped inside of her for a long time.

"He invited me for coffee, and one day he invited me to his studio up in the Heights to see his photographs. He was so proud of those pictures. He let me see some of his work before anyone else. Oh, Archie, his photographs were terrific. Believe me, I didn't plan to fall in love. It just happened. Joe touched something magical in me. You'll understand when you're older. Being in love is the best feeling of all. Nothing else compares."

My head was reeling and I didn't want to believe what my mother was telling me. "Does this mean you don't love Dad anymore?"

Mom slowed down. "I need to be honest with you, Archie," my mother said. "You're right. I don't love your father the way I used to and I'm sorry about that." She pulled her hands out of her pockets and wrapped her arms around her middle, hugging herself tight. Her eyes were all wet.

I kicked at some clumps of snow in the middle of the sidewalk, but I missed and almost fell down. It was hard to keep my balance with my arm in the sling. "Are you and Mr. McDonald gonna get married? You know . . . to each other?"

My mother slowed down. "We don't know yet. We're just not sure what we're going to do. It's a big step and it depends on a lot of things."

"Like what?"

"Like how soon his wife gets out of the hospital, and he can tell her he wants a divorce."

"That'll help her get well."

"Archie, listen to me," Mom said. "One of the important lessons you'll learn as you get older is that things in the adult world are not always black and white, right or wrong, win or lose. Adult life is full of shades of gray. Grown up life is full of 'sort ofs' and 'maybes' and 'kind ofs.'" My mother made "Adult Life" sound like the *Twilight Zone*.

We walked along for a while, circling through the little shopping area on Durwood Road where the barbershop and the drugstore were located, and then we trudged up the hill to the ridge. Darkness descended on the third day of 1958. Only 362 more to go.

"Joe and I thought we'd be safe at the Lancaster house," Mom said to no one in particular. "It seemed like the safest place in the whole world. Cantrell Lancaster and his son were in Florida for the holidays and the house was isolated in the woods. Your father had gone to Houston and you were playing over at Harry's. At least that's what I thought." She paused and let out a long sigh. "I guess no place in the universe is ever truly safe."

"I guess not." I tried to sound sarcastic, but I wasn't very good at it.

But it didn't really matter. Mom wasn't paying attention anyway. "Cantrell Lancaster thinks Joe is a saint because he helped Lancaster's son survive a bad time during the Korean War. Mr. Lancaster would do anything for Joe. He even gave him a key to his house, so Joe could use it when Mr. Lancaster was out of town. Joe gave me a duplicate key to the gate and the house. The house became our romantic hideaway. Our special place to go to get away from the ugliness of the world."

"Like me and dad?" My sarcasm got better. Mom still didn't say anything. I shuffled through the mushy snow for a block or so. There was a lot of stuff going on that I didn't understand and probably a lot of junk I never would understand. But I had to know about one thing for sure.

So I stopped dead in the middle of the sidewalk, faced my mother, and asked the $64,000 question. "What about Halloween night?"

CHAPTER 38

"You're right, Archie," my mother said in a sad voice. "You have a right to know about that night. But I have to warn you. Halloween was not my finest hour."

"You know what happened that night, don't you?" I said. "You know about Katherine and the iron lung and the mercy killing. You've known all along, haven't you?"

My mother sighed. "I should have told you," Mom said. "But then you'd wonder how I knew, and it might give away my secret life with Joe. Archie, what happened Halloween night is one of those gray areas of grown up life. God should have taken Roy a long time ago."

My mother fumbled in her coat pocket and pulled out a crumbled pack of Kents and a book of matches. Her hands shook as she got a cigarette out of the package. "The boy suffered horribly," she said, stopping and cupping her hands around the cigarette to shield it from the wind.

She lit her smoke on the third match. "But sometimes God doesn't act quickly enough." She blew smoke out her nose and into her mouth or maybe it's the other way around. Sandra says it's called "French inhaling." Whatever it is, it looks gross.

"The poor child had been deprived of oxygen for

God knows how long. It was a blessing he died. I know that sounds cruel but it's true." My mother sounded like she wanted to convince herself as much as convince me.

"Your imagination went into overdrive that night." Smoke bellowed out of my mother's mouth. "Joe called me right after it happened. We only talked for a minute. He got so choked up he couldn't talk anymore. That was why I was so upset when you came home that night. I had already heard you had been in some kind of car wreck, and a few minutes later Joe called and told me about Roy."

"You could have just told me. Told me I had it wrong."

"I thought you'd give up that obsession about murder in a day or two. I didn't want you to know I'd been talking to Joe."

"Thanks a lot."

"Oh, Archie. Joe didn't even see you that night. He was too upset about Roy."

I started walking again, my head down, dragging my feet through the slushy snow. "Okay," I said breathing angrily through my nose. "So if Mr. McDonald didn't see me, why did he start following me around? I thought it was because he wanted to scare me so I wouldn't tell anyone what I saw on Halloween night. If he didn't even know I was there that night why did he follow me?" I asked, doing my best Perry Mason imitation.

My mother shook her head. "He shouldn't have followed you. But it had nothing to do with what you think you saw on Halloween. When Joe and I were together I talked about you all the time. I told him what a wonderful child you are and what a great basketball player you are. I talked about how much I loved you."

"Thanks for nothing."

Mom ignored my sarcasm. "After Roy died Joe realized how much he wanted a normal son. A son like you. You were mine and he loved me. We thought we'd be together some day. So he tried to make you the normal son he never had, and he sort of tried to borrow you for a while. At least until his hurt healed some. Honest, Arch. He wanted to look after you. Something your father is always too busy to do. That's the whole story."

This wrinkle to Mom's story was hard to take. Besides, I hated the way she kept calling Mr. McDonald "Joe." That was really annoying.

"Joe followed you over to Central," Mom said, "because he knew you were up to something when he saw you and Tommy Lee and Sandra skipping school that day. He would have protected you if something bad had happened with the mob. Joe said you have a wonderful spirit of adventure. If not always an abundance of common sense."

"You knew we went to Central?"

"Yes, but I couldn't say anything. Joe was the only one who saw you there. I didn't want anyone to know I'd been talking to him. It would have been too hard to explain."

"What about Thanksgiving? When Bobby Sanderson and I had the big fight at the school ground?"

Mom smiled. "Joe said you didn't need any help that day. He was proud of the way you defended yourself against that bully. He said you were a heck of a tough kid and with a little coaching you could be a good boxer someday."

I didn't see any point in holding anything back, so I faced my mother eye to eye. Man to man. Or boy to woman. Or whatever. "If you knew Mr. McDonald was following me and you knew he was scaring me half to death, why didn't you tell him to stop?"

"Archie, I tried. Believe me." Mom dropped her cigarette butt on the sidewalk and crunched it out with the heel of her boot. The embers made a hissing noise in the slush. "But Joe was so depressed about Roy I think being involved with the life of another boy, even in such a strange way, made him feel better. That's why he came to the finals of the Christmas tournament. So he could stand in the doorway and watch you play. I had told him all about the tournament and how exciting it was. He loves sports and watching you made him feel a part of something he had missed."

"Oh great, Mom. That's just great. Protect old Joe's feelings by letting him scare your own son half to death. Thanks a bunch."

"For God's sake, Archie. His child died. His wife is a crazy alcoholic. He's all alone. Show some mercy."

Bad choice of words.

I made one last try. "Why did Mr. McDonald have to trash Sandra's playhouse? Draw a tombstone with my name on it. Why did he have to do that?"

"Joe didn't do that," My mother snapped. She was running out of patience. "Sandra's mother told me about that. You might want to check on how Tommy Lee spent that Sunday morning. His mother and father were both in bed with the flu and missed church."

I opened my mouth but nothing came out.

Everything in my mind was all jumbled up. Day was night. Up was down. Black was white. Everything I knew was wrong. Could I have been that mistaken about what I saw on Halloween night? That misguided about why Mr. McDonald was following me?

CHAPTER 39

We started hiking up the last leg of the hill, heading toward the ridge. The energy of our conversation made our strides long and fast. When we reached the crest of the ridge we were both panting like crazy.

My mother draped her arm around my shoulder. Lights appeared in all the houses, and I could see the glow of the TV screen in everyone's living room.

"Archie, listen," Mom said. "I was scared. Really scared. Everything was about to blow up. And I didn't want to hurt you and your dad. I took you back to the doctor hoping he could get you to stop obsessing about Joe. Maybe give you more pills to calm you down. I thought if I took you back to the shrink he'd make you believe what was going on was like what happened in Florida. You'd think it was all in your imagination."

"He'd convince me the wolves weren't really there."

"Something like that."

"Only I didn't buy it."

"No you didn't. And I'm so sorry. I shouldn't have done that. I was wrong. I know this is hard for you to understand right now," Mom said. "There's a lot of grown up stuff here. Falling in love at my age is a funny thing to do, and I know all of this has ended up hurting you and your father. And I'm sorry about that.

But I can't help myself and I just can't live without Joe. I hope you'll forgive me someday."

We walked the loop at the top of the ridge and started back down the hill. The streetlights and the glow from all the houses lit the way through the snowy neighborhood. Our feet crunched on the snow all the way home.

"Does Dad know about all this?"

A deep breath, held too long. "Yes. Katherine figured out what was going on. Women are good at that sort of thing. The night she went off her rocker and your father went over there to help her—she told him about Joe and me."

"Geez. Poor Dad."

"Of course your father didn't believe her at first. When he came back and ask me about Joe I couldn't stand the deception anymore so I told him the truth."

This was Katherine's Great Green Teddy Bear. Things were not what I thought they were. Mom and Mr. McDonald. I never had a clue.

"How could you do this?" I pounded the side of my leg with my fist until my thigh hurt. "How could you mess up our family this way?"

"Honey, it's not like that." She tried to pull me close to her, but I tore away from her grasp and ran down the block. I felt like a tornado was roaring through my body. It was hard to run with my arm in a sling, so I pulled up next to a mailbox. I could hear my mother jogging through the snow behind me.

"I know you're hurting right now," she said as she approached the mailbox. "But the pain will pass. I promise." My mother tried to hug me but since we both had on thick coats and my arm was in a sling, it was the weirdest hug ever.

"Of course your father is upset." Mom dropped the hug. "He can't understand what went wrong." We started walking again and my mother's words poured out of her like a river overflowing its banks. "He keeps saying he did everything he was supposed to. The war, the hard work, the house, everything. He just doesn't understand that sometimes all of that is not enough. There's more to life than buying a house in the suburbs and mowing the grass and washing the car every Saturday. But it wasn't your father's fault, Archie. I don't mean to blame him. It wasn't his fault."

"Whose fault was it?"

"It wasn't anybody's fault. Like the song says, it was just one of those things. Life's not fair or easy to figure out." My mother started crying. Not bawling or wailing. Just crying.

Tears ran down her cheeks, and she began dragging her feet in this weird, tired shuffle. She wanted to say something else, but the words just wouldn't come out.

We hiked down to the bottom of the hill in silence. As we trudged past Sandra's house, I saw the light on in her bedroom. She was probably curled up on her bed reading a book. All cozy and warm. Sandra was like me. Whether it was books or basketball, we liked to escape into our own worlds where all the bad stuff couldn't get to us.

I needed to tell Sandra about everything that had happened—the house in the Lancaster Property, my busted arm, my mom and Mr. McDonald—all of it. And I knew I would. And I knew she'd help me feel better. We'd smoke cigarettes in her playhouse and talk. And talk. I'd tell her everything. And maybe we'd share another kiss. Now that would be great. Yeah. I had a feeling me and Sandra would be together for a long time—at least I hoped so.

My mom and I walked on by the Harrison's house and the Rush's house and made it to our carport, where we stomped the snow off of our boots before we went into the house.

Our car was gone.

Mom didn't seem surprised. "Your father is going to be gone for a while," she said. "This is the worst part. But everything will work out in the long run. It always does. Everything always turns out for the best, Archie. You'll see."

Everybody always said that. But I'm not sure I believe them. Not anymore.

I had a feeling this meant it would be a long time before my dad and I went fishing. But it was gonna be a long time anyway. Dad just couldn't give himself any time off. Even for something he loved.

When I grow up, if I really love something, I hope I can figure out a way to do it. And not just keep saying I'll do it and put it off.

I went into the house through the back door. The furnace kicked on and the heat felt good. I took off my coat and hat in the living room and dropped them on the sofa. Then I sat down in Dad's easy chair and wiggled off my boots by using the toe of one boot against the heel of the other boot. It was the only way to do it with my arm in the sling.

My mother came in the back door. She paused in the doorway like she wanted to say something else but changed her mind. She hung up her stuff in the hall closet and went back to her bedroom and closed the door.

In a couple of minutes she started crying. Louder this time. Terri the Goddess of Kingwood in agony. The sound of her pain echoed all over the house and floated out over the frosty suburban night.

I could see where all of this was going. My mom intended to ditch my dad and me. Then Mr. McDonald planned to dump Katherine when she got out of the hospital. And then Mr. McDonald, the meanest, scariest man on the planet earth, would marry my mom and be my stepfather. That was way too horrible to think about.

It all seemed so neat. Everything had an explanation. Mom and Mr. McDonald fell in love. Katherine got drunk and didn't close Roy's iron lung. A mercy killing went down. Then Mr. McDonald was free to dump Katherine and marry my mother

But what if that wasn't the way it was? What if I wasn't a victim of my overactive imagination? What if Katherine was too drunk to remember what happened that night? What if Mr. McDonald told her she left the iron lung door open and she bought it? What if he told my mom the same thing?

What if I had been right all along . . . ?

I got up and turned on the TV to drown out the sound of Mom's suffering. There was a basketball game on the tube. State or Tech or the Celtics or the Hawks or somebody. It didn't matter. It was hoops. Basketball. The roundball game. The greatest game in the world. I sat in the dark and stared at the screen. I let the game wash over me.

You could count on basketball. Jump shots, fast breaks, zone defenses. They would always be there. No matter what else happened. No matter how bad things got, you could always count on roundball. There would always be another shot, another game, another season. People would come and go in your life. But basketball? That would last forever.

THE END

ABOUT THE AUTHOR

Jim Lester grew up in Little Rock, Arkansas, and now lives in Denver, Colorado, where he hikes the Rockies, walks his cocker spaniel and hangs out with his beautiful wife. He is the author of several books including a YA novel entitled *Fallout*, which *Booklist* called "a fast paced, clever coming of age story . . . Salingeresque in spirit" and a sports history book called *Hoop Crazy: College Basketball in the 1950s*. You can contact Jim at www.JimLesterBooks.com.